Pamela grew up in the East End of London. She left school at 16 years of age and worked in Banking until 2008 when she joined a local charity that specialises in Dementia. Pamela married Kevin Denny in 1976 and they have two daughters, Rachel and Rebecca.

To my parents, John and Alice Surridge, as I know my
dad would have been very proud.

Pamela Denny

A LOAD OF BULLOCKS

AUSTIN MACAULEY
PUBLISHERS LTD.

A CIP catalogue record for this title is available from the British Library.

ISBN 9781786126825 (Paperback)
ISBN 9781786126832 (eBook)
www.austinmacauley.com

First Published (2017)
Austin Macauley Publishers Ltd.
25 Canada Square
Canary Wharf
London
E14 5LQ

All characters in this novel are fictitious and any resemblance to real persons, living or dead, is purely coincidental.

To my darling husband, Kevin, who always supports me.

Prologue

Early 1916

Frank shivered as he clutched on to his rifle, he wasn't sure if it was the sound of cannon fire ringing in his ears or the damp cold of the wet mud seeping through his boots as he lay in the trenches waiting for the commanding officers to give the order to attack the enemy. There had been heavy rainfall in October and the trenches were like a quagmire. The tunnelers had encountered some terrible setbacks and two entire teams had been lost. Frank had watched men shaking and screaming with fear as death stared them in the face as they waited for the orders to advance towards the front line. Some men had been called cowards and labelled as deserters when they had not returned from home leave. They had been hunted down and shot at dawn like animals. It seemed that one way or the other the poor bastards were destined to die. One poor fucker was so full of exhaustion he fell asleep at his post; this, too, was punishable by firing squad. Frank tried to close his mind to the carnage all around him and in his mind's eye he was picturing the roaring fire in the parlour of his mother's house. His mother had a huge smile on her face and she was singing nursery rhymes as she toasted some bread she had placed on the end of a poker. His elder sister Edie and his younger brother Dickie were pushing and shoving one another out of the way both trying to get the first slice of the freshly buttered toasted bread. He swore to God he could almost smell it. His thoughts turned to his wife Sadie and his little girls and he pulled an old photograph from his coat pocket. The photograph had become worn and dog-eared and he could barely make out their faded faces. He pressed it to his lips and placed a loving kiss on each of their faces praying that he would see them again. His thoughts drifted back to when he had first met Sadie, she was almost fifteen years old and she was the most beautiful thing he had ever seen. Her hair was the darkest brown and fell into wonderful long curls around her shoulders. Her eyes were as dark and as velvet as her hair and his heart was lost the moment he clapped eyes on her. Frank and his friends began to hang around the street corner not far from Sadie's house. Sadie and some of her girlfriends would congregate on her front door step hoping to catch their attention. Her parents were not pleased and made their disapproval blatantly obvious. Not only were the boys older than Sadie they were also what her parents referred to as shiksas, which meant non-Jews. Frank had to admit, when his brother Dickie told their own parents of the romance between himself and Sadie they were equally displeased as they were catholic. Frank was annoyed that Dickie had poked his nose in to his business and vowed one day he would pay him back. Once Sadie left school she was allowed even less freedom because she was approaching marriageable age. Her parents insisted that she would be allowed to go out socially only if she promised that she would mix with Jewish boys and girls and no others. She went to the local picture house with her friends and the local café on Saturday afternoons. Sadie's parents were very insistent that while they couldn't be behind her all the time and stop her talking to the local lads they would prefer it if they were kept at arm's length and at all cost she was to keep her virtue intact. Her parents had already been in discussions with a second cousin once removed by marriage about their son and Sadie getting to know each other and an engagement to be announced. Still none of this was going to put a halt to things between Sadie and Frank, it just meant that they began to meet more discreetly. Sadie would tell her parents that she was visiting a friend and her and Frank would sneak off down by the canal and find quiet places which were virtually deserted and hoped that no busy bodies would see them and report back to either set of parents. Both of them were pretty naive about the birds and the bees, they relied on hearsay from other people as their source of information. Sadie was the one who usually had an opinion to share. "Well I was sitting listening to the older girls in our tea break the other day, and they said it was more or less positive that a girl couldn't get pregnant if you DID IT standing up."

"How can you be sure?" asked Frank.

"Well Bella Clarkson," continued Sadie in a very confident tone and feeling pleased with her very reliable information. "Bella said she'd done it this way loads of times and she hadn't got pregnant, so it must be true." Many years later Bella Clarkson, although being married and going at it hammer and tongs to get herself a baby still never managed to conceive and was found to be infertile. Frank was not completely convinced, but his emotions got the better of him and one dark night, when the moon was almost hidden by the clouds, Sadie slipped out of her knickers and they had their first attempt at lovemaking on the banks of the canal. Frank spent all the following week in a panic but when Sadie announced with a huge smile on her face. "It's OK Frank, I got my period yesterday so Bella Clarkson was right after all."

Frank was relieved and so for the following few months they took advantage of 'the one foot on the floor at all times' theory many times. Sadie's parents were almost ready to seal the deal on the engagement with the second cousin once removed. Dowries were about to be exchanged when Sadie dropped the bombshell.

Frank was taken totally unaware the night Sadie's father almost banged their front door down, he was yelling and screaming for all and sundry to hear at how Frank had taken liberties with his Sadie and he was going to kill him. Frank's father squared up to him and they were all but brawling in the parlour. It was thanks to Maud, Frank's mother, who jumped up and stood between them averting a full scale punch up. Maud was always the peace maker and finally managed to calm Sadie's father down into a more reasonable state, and much to Sadie's family's dismay Frank and Sadie were married at the earliest convenience. Sadie quite liked living at the Bullock house. It was a tight squeeze but they all managed to fit in. Frank's sister Edie had to move bedrooms and share with her grandmother Flo in the front room downstairs, Dickie was moved into Edie's little room so that Frank and Sadie could have the larger room, after all they would have to put a cot in their soon enough, so technically there was plenty of room for everyone. Flo wasn't exactly pleased with this arrangement and said she felt like she was being squeezed out of her own home. They all shared the room at the back of the house, which is where they ate and listened to the wireless together, just off of the sitting room, right at the rear of the house was a small kitchen where they cooked and did the laundry. It wasn't a palace but it was clean and comfortable and where they all called home.

Frank jumped as a cannon ball exploded not too far away. It's funny really, he thought, all the Bullock men seem to die young, His grandfather had been killed in an accident at work when he was in his thirties. Flo had brought up three boys on her own and never stopped telling everyone how hard it had been. How she had scrubbed people's front steps and taken in washing. Which incidentally she would add, had to be done on a washboard, no wonder she suffered so badly with arthritis now. Frank's grandfather had been part of a maintenance team repairing the machinery at a local clothing factory. Often when the machines broke down the men would work on them without turning off the power. This particular time his grandfather was unlucky and the machine started up again unexpectedly and caught his arm in the works and ripped it clean off from just below the elbow. He lost a lot of blood, but mainly he died from the shock of the injury to his body. His father had passed away not long after he and Sadie were married. The doctor said it was natural causes, and now it would seem it was his turn to die, it would just be Dickie left with all those women to contend with.

Frank was only nineteen when he and Sadie were married, he couldn't deny he was afraid of becoming a father and all the responsibilities that came with it. Frank's father, who had always been a fit man, had a sudden heart attack and died, this sent Sadie into early labour at six months and their little boy was still born, Frank felt like his heart had been torn out of his chest, he had never experienced pain like this before. His mother was marvellous throughout the whole ordeal. She was a tower of strength. Just a short while before she had buried her husband, then she helped deliver the baby and bury him. Bullock women were by far the stronger sex than the males they had married. Sadie seemed to be true to tradition, she was the one who comforted Frank and within a few months she announced she was expecting again. Although the following few months were an anxious time for them all Frank could not have been prouder when his baby daughter arrived. They had promised his grandmother that the baby would be named George after her late husband but as it was a girl she was promptly christened Georgina and his gran could not have been more pleased. That year was another year of mixed blessings as in the autumn granny Flo got influenza and the grim reaper carried her off. In 1911 and 1912 Sadie suffered two more miscarriages but thankfully she was no more than three months gone. Maud became cross with Frank and said he should stay away from the poor girl and give her chance to recover. Frank always listened to his mother and he did as he was told for a while, but it was a very cold winter and by the new year of 1913 Sadie was in the family way again. Sadie gave birth to a second daughter; they had for some reason expected a boy this time and promised Maud to name him after Frank's father Ronald. Thus daughter number two became Veronica Maud Bullock, just to cushion the blow and please his mother.

The sound of gunfire intensified and the ground shook, Frank still had a smile on his lips as the commanding officer shouted the orders for the troops to move to the top of the trenches and prepare to attack. Frank could hear the sound of grown men crying as they prepared to meet their maker. He clutched his rifle tighter for support and said a quick prayer as he kissed the saint Christopher that his mother had given him to wear the day he left for war. The shout to attack could barely be heard over the raging sound of artillery fire and the soldiers charged towards the enemy firing at will. Men were falling all around him into the cold wet mud.

Frank felt a searing pain rip through his leg and then oblivion.

Chapter 1

1921

Barry sat on the large worn sofa between his two sisters. Georgina the eldest who was ten years old was reading her treasured copy of Beatrix Potter book, Peter Rabbit, to her younger sister Veronica who was six years old and becoming an ardent fan herself, Barry, just sat quietly between the two of them listening to the words of his sister but oblivious to their meaning, and up to now at the ripe old age of two had yet to utter his first word.

"Mum, I think Barry wants his milk," called Georgina, "he's sucking his thumb again."

"Mummy can I have some milk as well?" asked Veronica, "and can we both have a biscuit?" Frank Bullock slammed his newspaper down on the table angrily.

"For God's sake," he yelled, "no wonder that boy doesn't speak, you lot do it for him."

"I'm telling you now Sadie there's something not right with that boy. The girls had half a dozen words under their belts by the time they were his age." Their mother was always quick to defend Barry and would not have a bad word said against him.

"You leave the boy be, Frankie Bullock, he'll talk when he's good and ready and not before." Frank cussed under his breath and stormed off out into the back yard and sat down on an old orange box to light his pipe. He winced with the pain that shot through his leg as he lowered himself on to the old crate. The Thomas Calliper that he wore on his leg helped and he had much to thank, Sir Robert Jones, the great orthopaedic surgeon for. He shouldn't complain he thought, the doctors had told him he was lucky to be alive, the first doctor who examined him when he was taken to the field hospital wanted to amputate his entire leg. If it hadn't been for a young doctor who had wanted to prove himself and try his new skills on saving it, that is exactly what would have happened. Frank wouldn't have thanked him for cutting off his leg, he would rather have died. Maybe it would have been better if he had died at least then Sadie would have received a war widow's pension. Frank's mind was forever clouded about his final hours in the mud-torn battlefield of the Somme. To this day he could not tell anyone who he had to thank for saving his life and for dragging him back to the trench. The two months that followed were lost in an opium-induced state to relieve his pain while his leg healed. He remembered the face of an angel that would come and go as she wiped his brow as he lay in pools of sweat from his endless nightmares. As his leg healed his dosage of opium was reduced and he became more coherent. The angel turned out to be a pretty French nurse who worked in the field hospital in Flanders. Her name was Yvette, she found the old worn photograph in the wounded soldier's pocket and put it safely on his bedside cabinet hoping that looking at his family it would give him the will to get better. As Frank regained his strength she would talk to him of his family and encourage him to talk about them as part of his rehabilitation. After all they were slowly mending his body but his mind was wracked with the horrors that he had seen in battle. He had witnessed men's bodies blown to pieces, some with limbs missing and some with no heads; these images could not be erased and probably never be healed.

Yvette would help Frank write letters to send to Sadie, telling her and the children that he was making good progress and would soon be home. Frank spent six months in the military hospital in Flanders before he was fit enough to be transferred to a rehabilitation hospital in Shepherd's Bush, London. He had been saddened to say goodbye to Yvette, she had become like family to him. Yvette had confided in Frank that she had a liaison with an English soldier. She was very much in love with this man but he had been shipped back to England without any warning. Yvette hung her head down and could not meet Frank's eyes. "I need to find my soldier, Frank, I have to tell him I am carrying his child. Frank agreed she must write to her lover immediately, but Yvette confessed that she did not have his address. She only knew he came from East London. "You could try contacting the war office but I don't hold out much hope that they would pass on his personal details." A smile appeared on his lips as he remembered her. Frank gave Yvette his home address and told her if she came to London and was in need of a friend she was to look him up. Frank wondered if he had been a little hasty as it would have taken some explaining to Sadie and the family. They probably would have thought it was his kid.

The journey across the channel had been arduous, the seas were choppy and he had felt sick all the way across the English Channel. By the time he reached the warmth and safety of his hospital bed he was exhausted and his leg was throbbing.

Sadie came to visit him the following week and her first question was when would he be home. She rambled on about how long it had taken her by tram to get from the east end of London to Shepherd's Bush and how it had cost her 3d. She wouldn't be able to afford to come too often, as it was Maud had bunged her a penny halfpenny towards the fare, and as good as Maud was she couldn't expect her to have the girls too often as she wasn't getting any younger. Well there was Frank's sister Edie to think of as well, she'd never get over losing her Cyril, she vowed she'd never marry now. "What worries me, Frank Bullock, is when you're officially discharged from the Army what will we do for money?"

"How on earth are you going to work with that leg?"

"I don't suppose the Army are going to support us..."

"It's OK when they need you to fight for King and country but when you're no longer any use they discard you like an old wet dishcloth."

Frank laid there listing to Sadie's voice becoming distant. He would never forget how he felt when they told him Cyril had seen him fall and dragged him back to the safety of the trenches, and how some stupid trigger happy prat fired his rifle thinking it was the enemy and blew the top of Cyril's head clean off.

The visiting hour was soon over, Sadie fussed around straightening the bed covers, the truth was she was glad to be going, the strong smell of disinfectant and the groans of men suffering in pain were getting too much for her. She buttoned her coat, kissed Frank goodbye and promised to come again soon if he wasn't home in a couple of days. He knew she hadn't been listening to a word he had said when he told her he had to have at least eight weeks of physiotherapy. He was glad when she had gone as he could feel the noise of cannon fire in his head getting louder and wondered if he would ever be free of his torment.

Sadie drew a deep breath as she stepped out of the main entrance of the hospital, God she could do with a cup of tea before she made tracks for home. Just then the tram she had to catch came round the corner, "Oh well," she thought, "suppose I had better not let this one go, could be ages before another one comes along and the girls will be wanting their tea." Sadie jumped onto the tram and sat down. The ticket collector came down the gangway shouting, "Tickets please," and Sadie pressed her money into the conductor's hand. She stared out of the window and let out a huge sigh, how on earth were they going to manage, there was nothing else for it she would have to get a job herself and there was no point Frank getting on his high horse about it either. With her mind made up she felt a bit better and settled down in the seat for the long journey home.

Twelve weeks later Frank received a wonderful letter from the Ministry of Defence which contained his discharge papers, they thanked him for the devoted service he had given to his country and wished him well for the future. The letter was very polite but reading between the lines it basically said he was no longer any use to them because he was unfit for front line duty. Still the rumour was it would all be over soon. A stern looking nurse appeared at the end of his bed. "It seems you are leaving us tomorrow, Mr Bullock. It's good news on the transport, you and four others are getting a ride back to the east end in the red cross van." Frank's thoughts returned to his discharge letter, how quickly you are dismissed when you are no longer of any use. Still on the bright side it would be grand to see the family again he thought as he laid his head back against the hard hospital pillow.

Sadie popped her head out of the back door. "Frank, love, are you coming in? Your tea is getting cold."

"The children are off to bed now and want to say goodnight." Frank gave Sadie a nod and lifted himself up. The night air was becoming damp and it made the pain in his leg worsen. Maybe he would pop round to his brother Dickie's tomorrow when Sadie came back from her cleaning job. God, he felt guilty about her having to work to support them. His pride was dented and it made him feel humiliated that he could not provide for his own family. The state he had been left in he very much doubted he would ever get work again. Maybe it would have been better if he had have died out there on the battle field, at least Sadie would have got a war widows pension, as things stood they all got jack shit. Men that lost limbs got a pension but all Frank had at the moment was his labour exchange money and a large dent in his pride.

Sadie woke up at the crack of dawn. What she would have given to stay in the warmth of her bed cuddled up next to Frank. She did worry about him and wondered what she could do to help him. Frank would have terrible dreams and night sweats, his body would shake and he would call out, Sadie could not begin to imagine the horrors that he was reliving in his mind. She reached for her dressing gown and slipped off the edge of the bed as quietly as she could, trying not to disturb him. The house was cold and she shivered as she tried to strike the match to light the newspaper in the fire grate. At least the house would have warmed a little by the time she returned to get the girls up for school. She looked at the clock it was five fifteen. She got dressed and put on her shoes and coat; one of her shoes had a hole in it and was still damp from yesterday's wear. She must try and get a piece of cardboard from the hospital before she left today to mend it. There was plenty of packaging around that would be suitable. By five thirty she was quietly closing the front door behind her and making her way get the bus to take her to the hospital where she cleaned for a couple of hours. She knew Frank hated the fact that she was the main breadwinner. She knew he felt undermined as a man and knew how much his pride was hurt. Still, needs must as the devil drives, as her mother would say. Sadie was normally back home by eight thirty and she hoped Frank had got the girls up and had given them some toast and tea ready for school. Sadie didn't like to nag Frank but she did think he could make a little more effort to help her in the house instead of wallowing in self-pity. Sometimes she wished that they still lived at Maud's house then they wouldn't have to find the weekly rent and money for coal. When the girls were born and Frank was working it seemed right that they moved into their own house. While Frank was in the Army their rent was paid by the authorities. They sent her a weekly allowance and she managed to keep their heads above water. But now it was a different story. She felt cross with herself for moaning, many women like her were now widows. Yes, there were others far worse off than they were; at least they had a roof over their heads and food in their bellies.

It was still dark when she arrived at the bus stop, there was a slight drizzle in the air so she pulled up the collar of her coat and tightened her scarf on her head to try and shelter her from the elements. She could feel the wet seeping through the hole in her shoe and made a mental note to pop down the second hand shop to find a pair with no holes in them, just as soon as she had enough money. The bus finally came around the corner and pulled up at the bus stop. Sadie jumped on and sat down, the conductor turned the handle on his ticket machine, she gave the conductor her money and he gave her a ticket, how she wished she had felt up to walking to work, then she would have had something towards that desperately needed pair of shoes. The work at the hospital was hard and she felt weary before she had even begun. Three mornings this week she had been sick and had missed her second period, denial of the situation was not working but she was afraid of telling Frank there might be another mouth to feed. Still she had been down this road twice before in the last year and both times she had miscarried by the fourth month. How on earth would they manage if she had to give up her job? There it was again that awful feeling washing over her, she rang the bell of the bus and it stopped at the next bus stop. She would have to walk the last bit, she inhaled deeply hoping she would not show herself up and vomit in the kerb. She felt rough but with sheer determination and the thought of not getting any wages she made it through to the end of the shift.

Thank God she was finally home she thought as she turned her key in the front door, the smell of toast greeted her nostrils and a smile formed on her lips. He wasn't such a bad old stick, her Frank, he even had the girls ready for school and had made their packed lunch. They grabbed their bags and jam sandwiches and bundled out of the front door trying to out race one and other to be the first one at the school gate. "Blimey, girl," said Frank "you look a bit rough today," and with that Sadie rushed out into the back yard and vomited on the concrete floor.

Frank was none too pleased at Sadie being in the family way again, God only knows why as it was half his fault. "Listen girl," he said, "you go and lie down and I'll take our Barry out with me for a while. We'll go to Mum's for a bit of breakfast and then round to Dickie's, maybe Dot will do us a sandwich for our dinner. That will give you time to tidy up and sort out our tea."

"You're all heart, Frank Bullock," replied Sadie.

Edie had already left for work when Frank arrived at Maud's. Edie had joined the nursing core not long after the tragic death of her Cyril. She had been distraught with grief and only began to console herself when she entered the volunteer nursing sector. Helping others in their hour of need helped ease the pain of her own loss. Once she had decided that there would never be another Cyril in her life she resigned herself to being married to her new vocation. Once the war came to an end her apparent devotion to nursing became abundantly clear she was officially enrolled to become a trainee nurse. Maud supported her daughter and encouraged her, but found it hard to adjust to Edie's erratic shift hours. Maud hated the night shift when every creak and groan of the house would keep her awake.

Maud was always pleased to see her boys, no sooner were they through the front door she had the kettle on to boil and was cracking an egg into the frying pan. She started to cut the large crusty loaf of bread to make toast for a hearty breakfast. She went to the cupboard and found the pot of strawberry jam that she knew Barry loved. Barry sat at the table and devoured his breakfast. Maud glanced up from her slice of toast and looked at Frank over the rim of her old worn specials. "How's Sadie keeping?" she asked.

Frank let out a large sigh. "She's in the family way again."

Maud didn't say anything but gave Frank a look of disapproval, "How far gone is she then?" asked Maud an awkward silence hung in the air.

"About two months I guess," informed Frank.

"Still," said Maud trying to put a strange but positive note on the situation, "you've been down this road before, maybe she'll miscarry again, the last thing you need is another mouth to feed."

Frank didn't feel like one of his mother's lectures right now either. He knew she was right, she usually was and that irritated him as well. "Thanks for the breakfast, mum. Best be going now, I promised Dickie I'd pop round if I had time."

"What do you mean if you've got time? What else have you got to do? You haven't worked since you got back from the bloody war."

Frank winced as he moved too quickly and the pain shot through his leg as a reminder of the past. "In case you hadn't noticed, mother, I nearly got by bloody leg shot off and nobody wants to hire a cripple." Frank scooped Barry up in his arms and headed for the door, Maud chased him up the hallway and just as he was about to make an exit she grabbed his hand and pressed half a crown in to his palm. She looked him square in the face, "It's for the kids," she said, "so don't get all high and mighty on me and refuse it."

He felt a lump in his throat, "Thanks, Mum," he whispered and he knew the moment had passed and they were once more friends.

"Go on then," she said, "you had better be off, and tell that brother of yours I have to look at his picture to remind myself who he is. Wouldn't mind seeing my grand-daughter sometime soon before I go to me grave."

"Yes, Mum," said Frank, "I'll tell him," he said as he waved Maud goodbye.

Frank swung Barry up onto his shoulders and he squealed with delight as they made their way to Dickie's place. Frank wasn't even sure if Dickie would be at home, not since he had started work in the ticket office on the station. Once the war ended he managed to get himself a right cushy little number. Frank didn't mean to make it sound like sour grapes but whatever Dickie had done he always came up smelling of roses. Dickie worked shifts; he would either be on earlies, six to two or lates, two to ten. Dickie liked the late shift because the ticket office stayed open till twelve at the weekend so it meant he would pick up some overtime. As luck would have it Dickie answered the door. "Hello Frank, how goes it?" asked Dickie

"Oh you know, same old, same old," replied Frank. Dickie gave an understanding nod as he lifted Barry down from Frank's shoulders.

"Come on, tiger," he said to Barry. "You run on in to the parlour and see what our Irene has got.

"Who is it Dick?" came a voice from the kitchen, it was Dickie's missus, Dot.

"It's our Frank, get the kettle on girl and make us all a sandwich while you're at it. "I've got to be off soon I'm on the late shift this week," Dickie informed Frank. "I'm actually glad you popped in mate I was coming round to see you just as soon as I had a minute."

"Do you remember old Sid who used to sell the papers outside the station?"

"Yeah," said Frank, "miserable looking bastard if I remember rightly, don't think I ever saw him crack a smile."

"Well," continued Dickie. "A couple of days back he was sitting on that old box like he always did and he just keeled right over and fell off." Frank tried not to laugh as he pictured the scene as he could tell by the expression on Dickie's face this was meant to be a serious statement. "They say he was brown bread before he even hit the floor."

"Is that so?" said Frank. "As sad as it is, Dickie, what the hell has it got to do with you wanting to see me?"

"That's just it, bruv. They need someone to sell the papers, what do you say, are you interested?" Frank didn't answer. "The money's not great but it's more than the big fat nothing that you're getting at the moment." Frank still didn't reply. Dickie became a little irritated, "Well don't get too excited, you might blow a gasket."

"It's not that I'm not grateful, it's just me leg plays me up something rotten, what if I have days when I can't do it?"

"For Christ's sake, Frank just give it a go will you, at least it will help your Sadie out, poor cow looked awful when I saw her a couple of days back." Barry came running down the hallway and grabbed Frank by the hand pulling him towards the parlour. He took Frank over to where his little cousin Irene was sitting on the sofa with a tiny little brown and white puppy nestled on her lap.

"What's all the fuss then?" asked Frank as he looked at the tiny puppy. He certainly was cute and Barry seemed to have taken to him.

"Come on, Barry, you can stroke the puppy but be very gentle," said Dickie. Barry stroked the puppy and giggled.

"Where did you get the mut from then, Dickie?" Frank asked.

"Oh, her next door's dog had nine of them."

"Dog, dog," said Barry.

"Blimey, that's the most he's ever said," admitted Frank.

Dickie smiled. "Why don't you let him have one?"

"I'm sure she would be only too glad to get rid of another one, we can go and get it now."

"Oh I don't know," said Frank. "Sadie might go mad, what with her up the duff again," Frank confessed. Dickie felt sorry for his brother but after all it was his own fault so not much could be said in the way of sympathy.

"It's not doing your Sadie any good the amount of times you get her pregnant, our Irene is a year old and we haven't managed to get caught yet. We still have sex but I whip it out just before, it's not quite as good but it's better than the alternative. We just wait till just before Dot's monthlies are due and make up for it when we know it's safe. It works for us and you and your Sadie should give it a go."

Barry was pulling at Frank's arm again, "Dog, dog," he wailed. Frank felt that the world and his wife were hell bent on lecturing him today. Dickie could see Frank was getting a bit twitchy and hoped he was not going to be responsible for one of his headaches coming. "Come out in the yard for a fag, mate, you'll be able to see them pups running around over the wall." Frank should have known that was a bad move because as they left Dickies place Frank had a little bundle of fur tucked inside his coat, Barry was thrilled but Frank knew he would get it in the neck from Sadie when they got home.

The puppy was an instant success with the girls as well when they came in from school, Ronnie and Georgie played with him until he collapsed exhausted in front of the fire and Barry kept running around shouting dog, dog.

Sadie wasn't as pleased, "For God's sake, Frank, we have enough of a struggle feeding ourselves let alone a bloody dog."

"We'll feed him from the scraps off the table, he won't cost anything," and that is how Scrappy got his name. "Besides," Frank continued trying to take the edge off the situation. He actually felt a little pride creeping in and was pleased to announce, "I got a job today."

Sadie gave Frank a suspicious look, "Oh and who's given you a job then?" she asked.

"Our Dickie put a word in for me to sell the papers outside the station morning and evening."

"Oh and what about the kids then while I'm working at the hospital?"

"They'll be OK for half an hour, our Georgie is quite capable of keeping an eye on the other two, after all she'll be going to work in about eighteen months, she's virtually an adult."

31

Sadie sighed maybe she would be leaving her own job in a few months' time if she didn't lose this baby and she would be there to see the children off to school herself. Sadie felt suddenly weary; it seemed that whatever went on at the Bullock house there would always be more of a burden for her to carry.

Sadie couldn't deny she was glad of the extra money Frank brought home from selling the papers, she tried to put a little away for a rainy day but it was hard. Just when she thought she had a few coppers to spare one of the kids needed something to wear as they had grown another inch or their shoes had become too tight. She worried about her job at the hospital because as the weeks turned into months her belly grew fatter and it was obvious she was going to bring another Bullock into the world. She carried on cleaning until her seventh month and then very reluctantly she had to give it up. Still it was a blessing that Frank had stuck at selling the Newspapers at least there was some money coming in. By the time she got to her eighth month the weather had perked up and she was relieved to be able to hang the wet washing out on the line. She was getting fed up with the horse constantly stuck in front of the fire making the whole house damp. The dog was jumping around her legs and Barry was throwing him a stick and calling to him. She had to admit as much as she hadn't wanted Scrappy he had certainly help bring Barry out of his shell. She pegged the clothes onto the line and rubbed the crook of her back where a dull ache had started to develop. She was just thinking that she might get Barry to have an afternoon nap and lie down with him when Maud's head popped around the back gate.

"It's only me, Sadie, just come to see how you are."

There goes my nap she thought. "Hi, Maud, good to see you. I'll pop the kettle on." How she wished she could shift the pain in her back.

Maud whittled on about Edie and her job. She was working on the men's surgical ward, which in Maud's opinion was a secure and stable position, but no, what did Edie want to do, go off on some foolish crusade. She had become mixed up with some woman who campaigned for women's rights on birth control. "She reckons she was inspired by you on how not to keep getting in the family way, she says women should have a say in how many kids they have, anyway she wants to leave the hospital and go and work over Holloway in some Mothers Clinic. Some do-gooder called Marie Stopes, whose old man has got a bit of money, thinks she can change a woman's lot in life. By all accounts some woman in America called Margaret Sanger has written a book on the subject of birth control but the authorities have banned it saying it's obscene. You mark my words our Edie is going the right way to getting herself in a lot of hot water."

"They might have a point," said Sadie, "pregnancy and birth is not all it's cracked up to be, maybe it's time things changed for women." She rubbed her back again and could feel the dull ache moving into her lower abdomen. Scrappy started to paw away at the back door and Sadie got up slowly from her chair to let him out into the yard for a pee. Suddenly she felt warm wet liquid trickle down her own leg and momentarily thought she had either peed herself or Scrappy had cocked his leg up and relieved himself on her. Before she had reached the back door there was a gush from between her legs and she knew her waters had broken. Maud just sat and looked at her for a moment.

"Blimey, Sadie, you're not full term yet, this Bullock is certainly in a hurry to get out. "I'd better stay here now and sort Frank and the kids' tea out just in case you don't get time to do it."

By the time the girls arrived home from school Sadie's contractions were well under way.

"Hi, Gran, where's Mum?"

"Georgie, will you go up to the station and tell your father the baby is on its way. Tell him not to rush home as I'm here taking care of things, but tell him tea will be on the table at six o'clock and I don't want it spoiling, and on your way back stop off and tell the midwife she's needed."

Gran then turned her attention to Ronnie. "You keep your little brother occupied and don't let him out of your sight." Georgie did as Gran said and went to tell her father the baby was coming and Ronnie played with Barry and Scrappy in the yard. By the time Maud had chucked some vegetables in the oven and made some dumplings Sadie was shouting down the stairs that she had started pushing the baby out and was anyone coming to help her. Maud was getting flustered at the speed things were happening and thought that maybe she was getting too old for all this baby lark, maybe she'd have a quiet word with Edie about contraception for Frank and Sadie when she got home. There was a knock on the front door, "Thank God," she said as she wiped her forehead on the tea towel, "that must be the Calvary."

Sadie's yells could be heard in the back yard. Barry was afraid and covered his ears with his hands and began to cry.

"It's OK," said Georgie who had now joined them. "It's Mum pushing the baby out. It's quite painful having

34

a baby but once its head is out the worst is over," she informed the other two in a very authoritative and knowledgeable voice. This didn't seem to pacify Barry and even Ronnie began to get upset. Their mother gave another piercing yell and then they heard the cry of a baby. Georgie stood up and nodded her head, "It's all over now, the baby's here, Gran will call us in a bit to go and see Mum." She picked Barry up and sat him on her lap and soothed him. "It's OK, little man," she said as she kissed and stroked his head. Barry nestled close to Georgie and fell asleep, he always felt safe when he was with her. Georgie heard the front door bang and guessed that the midwife had left, she felt relieved herself that all the drama was over and made a silent promise to herself that she was never going to put herself through childbirth and would ask auntie Edie if she could become a nurse like her.

By the time Frank had arrived home Maud had the stewed vegetables and dumplings on the table and Sadie and the new baby were upstairs sleeping. The girls were jumping up and down with the excitement and Barry rubbed his eyes sleepily as he opened them wondering what all the commotion was about. Frank took off his boots and rolled up the sleeves of his shirt. He made his way to the kitchen sink to wash his hands before dinner. Maud dished up her stew and dumplings on to the plates and the children eagerly got stuck in. Frank poured the bottle of brown ale that he had brought in with him into the glass. He lifted the glass to his lips and took a large gulp, "Just to wet the baby's head," he said. He was sure Maud had a disapproving look on her face, but he chose to ignore it and exchanged playful banter with the kids instead. "Well then," said Maud feeling a little irritated with Frank for not even asking if the new baby was a boy or a girl. She slammed the salt pot down on the table rather harder than she needed to. This made Frank look up and Maud looked him square in the eye.

"Just in case you're interested, Sadie and the baby are both OK," said Maud. "They are sleeping now." Maud was tired herself, but she couldn't understand Frank's attitude and lack of interest. "Get Dickie to bring round the fishing weights in the morning and we'll see how much this one weighs."

"By my reckoning about ten pound if it's an ounce. What with the size and speed it's a wonder her insides are still intact."

"I wouldn't like to see her go through that again in a hurry. Right kids when you have finished your tea your father will take you upstairs and introduce you to your new sister."

Maud saw the flicker of disappointment run across Frank's face. Frank turned to Barry, "Oh well, champ, maybe you'll get a brother next time."

"If you've any sense there won't be a next time," Maud muttered under her breath, but she knew her comment fell on deaf ears. Maud began to clear away the plates and fill up the sink to start the washing up. She was glad that Sadie and the baby were OK, but it could have been an altogether different story. If anything happened to Sadie who would have to help take care of the kids. It would all fall on her shoulders and she wasn't getting any younger.

Sadie was slow to recover from Geraldine's birth so Maud spent a great deal of time helping with the family. Sadie said Maud shouldn't fuss so much and that she could manage, but if the truth be known the arrangements suited Maud at the moment, as she was a little lonely since Edie had moved over to Holloway to spend as much time as she could at The Mothers' Clinic. Maud didn't like the fact that Edie was living in one room and sharing facilities with other people, but Edie reassured Maud she was rarely there, it was just somewhere to lay her head and she spent sixteen hours a day at the clinic. Maud just mumbled she was working too hard and would make herself ill. The good news was that Edie managed to get hold of a couple of sheaths, she managed to smuggle them out of the clinic and take them home for her brothers. She explained to Frank how they worked, that they were animal insides, intestines, that were to be placed over an erect penis to collect the sperm at the point of ejaculation. They could be washed and repeatedly used. Frank was not at all comfortable about his sister instructing him in such matters. It was private stuff between husband and wife, but on the other hand Dickie and Dot were only too pleased to give Edie's free sample a try.

Chapter 2

1924

In 1924 Britain was buzzing. January 22nd 1924 the first Labour government led by James Ramsey McDonald had come to power and at last the voice of the people was being heard. The 21st March saw the tram strike and by the 28th March the railways had joined them. Ramsey McDonald had the first reading of the London Traffic Bill restricting the amount of bus groups that were allowed to ply for hire and the strike was called off. The excitement mounted as King George V opened The British Empire Exhibition at Wembley on the 23rd of April. Mr McDonald still curried support in the House of Commons as he passed the Protection from Eviction Act to prevent landlords seeking vacant possession or put rents up unfairly. Compensation Act for miners had been passed for the sufferers of silicosis. By the autumn the government fell into disrepute. The Conservatives claimed that because the troops had been ordered not to open fire on the strikers back in March there was a soviet (red) influence, this in turn caused a scandal and the Conservatives called for an enquiry. Mr McDonald said if MPs voted in favour of the enquiry he would resign. The Labour government fell and the Conservatives regained power led by Mr Stanley Baldwin.

Not much changed at the Bullock residence. Georgie had left school and was working in the canteen at Taylor's clothing factory, the money wasn't great, but it was regular work and she was often allowed to bring home the leftovers of the day. In fact the Bullocks had never eaten so well. Ronnie loved to sneak round to granny Maud's and play on the grand piano. Maud said she was a natural and had an ear for music. Ronnie was becoming quite good and Maud would love to lie back in her old chair, close her eyes and listen to the tune coming from the piano carrying her away in her thoughts. Barry would amuse himself in the backyard; he would find a stick and dig out the dirt between the bricks. One of his most favourite pastimes was watching the ants crawling on the concrete and squashing them with his fingers. The only thing that gave him more enjoyment was to find a spider and pull its legs off one by one. Gerry was just a baby and would follow Sadie around the house mimicking her mother dusting and cleaning the furniture while talking to her favourite rag doll.

Gerry still slept in her cot in Frank and Sadie's bedroom as there was nowhere else to put her. Barry still slept in the big double bed between his sisters although now they were all getting bigger it was becoming a tight squeeze. They would lie there in the dark listening to the bed in their parent's room creaking and the moans and groans of their mother. Barry would imagine that his father was inflicting terrible torturous acts on his mother to make her so distressed. He began to hate his father, his sisters didn't seem to be at all bothered, they would just put their hands to their mouths and giggle. Barry couldn't understand this as he thought it was no laughing matter. The noises would finally stop and Barry found it hard to resist the urge to run into his parent's room to check that his mother was alright.

In the morning at breakfast his mother would seem her usual cheerful self but he was sure she was just putting on a brave face for the sake of the children, and his hate of his father just festered and grew.

The day arrived for Barry to start school, he didn't seem to make friends very easily; he spent most of his time alone. He didn't dislike his lessons, quite the contrary; he was like a little sponge that absorbed knowledge. He was popular with all the teachers and was soon known as teacher's pet. Because of this he became the victim of the other boys bullying him. Barry soon learned how to handle himself physically but if a kick and a punch were out of the question he would find another way to win the day. This was the case when Freddie Bird who was six inches taller than Barry, and continuously picked on him, got his comeuppance. Just by chance Barry caught him in the boy's toilets fiddling with his private parts. Freddie never bullied or laid a hand on Barry again, in fact he became Barry's protector until the day that they left school.

By the time Barry reached the junior school he had become someone the other kids did not want to get on the wrong side of. Barry enjoyed the feeling of power. He learned at a very young age that if you could find someone's weak spot you had them in the palm of your hand.

1926

Life at the Bullock house was doing OK thank you very much, Georgie was doing very nicely in the canteen at Taylor's Clothing factory, in fact she practically fed the family these days on the left over's she brought home. Ronnie was working at the same factory as a machinist. She didn't like it much, though, since she was a little girl she had dreamed of becoming a great pianist. From an early age she had played on granny Maud's piano and soon discovered she had an ear for music. Sadie would despair at Ronnie's daydreaming, when would that girl realise she was not born with a silver spoon in her mouth and get a grip on reality.

Barry was moving up to junior school and little Geraldine was about to start infant school. Frank kept on talking to Sadie about getting a job; he said she should make some enquiries about going back to the hospital cleaning. Sadie tried to avoid the subject at the moment, how could she tell Frank she had missed her period. Maybe it was the menopause; some people were quite young when this happened. Maybe she was exceptionally young for this to happen to her, after all she had her first period when she was just eleven years old, maybe she was advanced for her age or maybe she was just kidding herself. Besides she hadn't had any bouts of morning sickness. Sadie continued to ignore the fact that she still hadn't had a period because she felt fairly well. She was a little tired lately but she was getting older and felt that was only to be expected. She had put on a little weight, but who hadn't at her age and had four children; everyone said it was middle age spread. Then one day, right out of the blue, she felt that old familiar flutter in her stomach. There was only one way to be sure. Sadie went to see Edie and confided her fears. Edie examined Sadie, "Well," she said, "there's no two ways about it, I'd say you were about twenty weeks or so."

"But I've had no morning sickness or anything."

"Well," said Edie, "you're lucky then." Right at that moment Sadie didn't feel very lucky.

Frank was furious when he found out the news, it was if it was all Sadie's fault, "How the fuck can you be pregnant?" he asked. "We've been using the fucking contraception, a lot of bloody good that's turned out to be." Sadie couldn't stop crying, as if she wasn't feeling bad enough already she had to listen to Frank's spiteful tongue. There was no way she could have this baby, she would have to find a way to get rid of it as soon as possible

Autumn turned to winter and Sadie was so pleased all the kids were out of the house all day. The girls were working and Barry and Geraldine were at school. Frank would go off to sell the newspapers at the station and she would crawl back to bed. Sadie was growing more tired as the months progressed. Sometimes Frank would come home for his dinner about twelve mid-day and she had barely begun the morning chores. He would cuss and swear at her saying she was a lazy bitch and she should try and remember she had her duty to the family to have the jobs done and a meal on the table instead of being so fucking selfish. Sadie cried a lot and couldn't understand why Frank was being so mean. She was sure if he knew how bad she already felt he would be more understanding. Eventually Frank stopped coming home during the day but Sadie dare not ask him where he was spending his time for fear he would have another outburst and clump one of the kids. Frank's temper had got decidedly worse of late, Sadie put it down to the pain in his leg but in truth she felt like she spent her life walking on eggshells.

Maud didn't hide her disapproval either, "You had better make this the last baby you bring into this world, my girl. You're looking like an old woman these days, black rings under your eyes, swollen ankles to match your belly, no wonder Frank doesn't come home much. Look how well Dot keeps herself, she's only three years younger than you but you're beginning to look more like her mother."

Sadie became more depressed at Maud's cruel words, Despite Sadie's efforts to get rid of the baby it would not budge, maybe God would intervene and take this baby away and she swore she would never let Frank lay a hand on her again.

Chapter 3

Flash back 1914-1919

Maud worried about Frank; he had been so depressed since he had come home from the war. Still she thought many never made it home at all, at least he was here. Thank God Dickie never got drafted to the front, dodgy ticker the doctor said, something about an erratic rhythm, not that Maud understood much, only that it meant her other son didn't have to go to the front to fight. Dickie got himself a job on the railways, there was a shortage of men and he quickly climbed the ladder and was in charge of transportation of munitions down to the coast. He would often travel down to Dover to oversee operations. That's where he met Dot. She was working in the station café. He would stop there for refreshments before returning to London.

There weren't many men around and Dot looked forward to Dickie's visits, she enjoyed the male attention. "When's your next day off?" he asked. "Why don't you come with me to London we could go up West maybe see a show." Dot thought it sounded marvellous, she was a little apprehensive as she had never been outside Dover before, but she couldn't contain her excitement and agreed to go with Dickie without a moment's hesitation.

Dot lived with her gran; she had been there since she was ten years old. Her parents had died from influenza both in the same year. Gran was a dear, she was getting old and a little bit absent minded but Dot loved the bones of her

Dot would make up a story and tell her she was staying with a friend and Gran would believe her.

Dot did have pangs of guilt about lying to Gran but the thought of a trip to London with Dickie soon wiped away all her qualms.

Dot sat on the platform seat, her small brown overnight case beside her. The clock seemed to tick unusually slow as she waited eagerly for Dickie's train to pull into the station. The tracks began to make a noise and she could see the smoke from the funnel as the train appeared from around the bend. Dot stubbed out her cigarette with the toe of her shoe and stood up to straighten her dress. The palms of her hands were sweating and she felt as if she could not breath, her heart began to beat faster as the train came to a halt and the carriage doors flew open. Passengers began to get off the train and she scanned the platform for Dickie. The platform was soon empty, the whistle of the train blew and it slowly pulled out of the station. She felt a rush of humiliation at being so gullible. Had Dickie just been stringing her along? Stupid little Dorothy Sheppard had fallen for his sweet-talking lies hook, line and sinker. Dot's heart sank, how could Dickie have let her down after all the planning that had gone into making this weekend possible and worst of all the lies she had told Gran. Now she would have to go home with her tail between her legs and make some lame excuse. Yes, she was hurt and humiliated and she never wanted to clap eyes on that Dickie Bullock again. Gran was surprised to see her back, "Lucky I hadn't asked a man back for the night," she teased.

"Sorry, Gran, I had a migraine come on. I couldn't go to the Billy Beere concert at the Town Hall with this head."

"You go and get yourself into bed and I'll bring some lavender and a cold flannel." Gran was such a dear and it made Dot feel even worse. Dot did as Gran had told her; she went to her bedroom and threw herself onto her bed, burying her head in the pillow to muffle her sobs.

Dot arrived at work the next day hoping that the red puffiness around her eyes was not too obvious. Still, she would just say it was the aftermath of her migraine; she might just get away with it. Ethel was busy washing the dirty dishes and talking ten to the dozen.

"Are you listening to me, Dorothy Sheppard? Or am I just talking to myself, you haven't heard a word I just said, have you? The South Eastern Line has been blocked at Warren, there's been a landslide, it caused a right old commotion yesterday, even London was affected, all the war traffic and hospital materials were sent on a later train. Oh by the way some bloke came in on the late train asking for you, said you was supposed to meet him. I told him I didn't know anything about it. I said you wouldn't be in till today, oh he left you a note, now where did I put it?"

Ethel began shuffling around trying to find Dot's note. "Oh here it is," she said pulling it from behind the cooking oil container. "Sorry love, it's a bit greasy," she said as she handed over the note scribbled on a serviette.

Chaos here due to landslide. All trains re-scheduled. Beyond my control. Will be down on Saturday at four o'clock, but have to return on the six o'clock train. Let's have dinner in the station café. Please be there, love you.

Signed Dickie.

Dot was still disappointed not going to London and having dinner in the place she worked was a poor substitute, but Dickie had said he loved her.

"What are you smiling about?" asked Ethel.

"Dickie didn't stand me up after all; it was all due to the landslide. He's coming down on Saturday and we're having dinner here in the café, and he loves me."

Ethel gave out a laugh, "Romance blossoming in the station café, someone should make a film about it," she declared.

Dot sat in the café on Saturday watching the hands on the clock tick slowly by. Four o'clock and the train was nowhere in sight. Just as she was about to give up again the train came rattling around the bend and pulled up alongside the platform. Exactly as she had done the week before she scanned the platform. This would be too much to be let down a second time.

"Excuse me, miss," came a voice from behind her, "have you got a light?"

She turned round and Dickie stood there with an enormous grin on his face. He put his arm around her, "Come on girl, let's get inside, it's brass monkeys out here."

The two hours that they sat in the café talking and holding hands was gone all too quickly. Dot lowered her head as Dickie stood up and said it was time for him to go.

"I don't like it any more than you do, it's killing me when we're apart." Dot was surprised Dickie felt this way. "Listen girl," he said, "I know we haven't known each other that long but these are uncertain times we are living in." He seemed to take a deep breath. "Let's get married?" Dot was taken by surprise. She had always expected a romantic proposal like in a Jane Austen novel. "How about next weekend? You make all the arrangements, book the town hall and a little B & B for the honeymoon. You can bring your gran, I know you want to."

"You seem to have it all planned out, Dickie Bullock, don't I get any say in things?"

"Not unless you have a better idea, we'll marry on Saturday, spend the night in the hotel and then we can catch the Sunday train back to London."

"Where will we live?" enquired Dot who felt a little breathless at the speed things were moving at.

"We'll stay at Mum's first of all until we sort out a place of our own."

"Well I suppose that's that then," and they kissed to seal the deal.

Gran wasn't too pleased to say the least. "You know what they say, Dorothy?" she always called her by her full name when showing disapproval. "Marry in haste, repent at leisure." She gave Dot a long hard look, "You're not in the family way are you?"

"No, Gran, certainly not," replied Dot.

Dot told Ethel the news, expecting a lecture from her as well. Ethel looked Dot straight in the face. "Well," she said, "if your heart is telling you its right then you've got to do it, the way things are these days none of us even knows if we've got a tomorrow. You've got to grab happiness with both hands while you can." Suddenly Ethel seemed to come to life at the prospect of helping Dot plan her wedding. "What you wearing then?" she asked.

Dot shook her head and said she didn't know. "Oh I suppose I've got me best Sunday dress I can wear, tart it up a bit, it'll have to do."

"No such thing as make do for my friend Dot when I've still got my dress tucked away in moth balls." I would be honoured if you would wear it." God only blessed me with boys so I've no one to pass it on to, so come on Dot what d'ya say?" Dot gave out a huge smile and nodded frantically. "You come round to my place tonight and we'll try it on you, just in case it needs alterations."

"Thanks Ethel you're a star, what would I do without you?"

Dot finished her shift at three o'clock and went straight to the town hall to book the wedding, the only time was four o'clock but it was take it or leave it, she could only hope Dickie could get there on time. Then she tried to book a bed and breakfast, but there were no vacancies as Billy Beere was in town again doing a concert and every boarding house was bursting at the seams.

Dot knocked on Ethel's front door. "Blimey girl, you look like you found a farthing and lost a sixpence."

"What's up couldn't you book the wedding?"

"Oh I did that OK, but all the bed and breakfasts are full due to Billy Beere."

"Cheer up, at least you can get married. Maybe you could even take the train back to London the same night. That would be quite romantic if you ask me," said Ethel trying to save the situation. Dot began to cheer up; Ethel always had a way of making her smile. Ethel ushered Dot into the parlour and proudly pointed towards the wedding dress. It wasn't exactly what Dot would have wanted, but it would look better than her own dress. "Come on don't just stand there, let's get it on you." When Dot finally got the dress on and was looking at her reflection partly in the mirror that hung over the fire place and partly in the window opposite she thought she looked passable. Ethel said it fitted like it was made for her. Ethel was rummaging in the box frantically looking for what she said would finish the outfit off. "There it is" she said and pulled out a dainty veil. Dot had to admit she didn't look half bad.

Dickie managed to telephone Dot at the station café the next day. He apologised to her once again for changing their arrangements but they wouldn't be able to stay in the bed and breakfast after all as he was needed in London first thing Saturday morning. There was a train going back to London at nine o'clock Friday night and he had to be on it, so they would catch that and have their honeymoon in the East end after all. He'd let his family know they'd be home and to have their room ready. Dot was a little nervous all of a sudden. Dickie was going to take her to a strange place and then just leave her with strangers. Surely he could at least take a couple of days off while she settled in.

"Don't worry," reassured Dickie, "there's only Mum and Edie at the house. Frank's away in France and his missus and two girls live ten minutes away. We won't bombard you with any more family until you've settled in."

There was a bit of a silence. Dickie wasn't sure if Dot was getting cold feet but he wasn't going to be deterred. "I'll be at your Gran's house to pick you both up in a taxi a three o'clock Friday, now go and get packing girl it'll be our wedding day before you know it."

Friday 5th May 1916

Dot stood there in her wedding dress, all lace and finery, her little case packed with her belongings in at her side. Gran had made her a small posy to hold and Dot could not have been more pleased. Gran kept wiping her eye every time she looked at Dot, said it was a cold in her eye but Dot knew gran was going to miss her terribly and felt almost guilty at leaving. Suddenly a car horn made her jump and brought her back to reality. Dickie was banging on the front door, she heard Gran open it and Dickie swung her poor old Gran in the air and she could hear them laughing. Dickie grabbed Dot's case and all three of them piled into the taxi, Ethel and her husband were waiting outside the town hall when they pulled up. Ethel and her husband had agreed to be their witnesses. It was a simple ceremony and was over quickly, Dickie had managed to lay his hands on a small gold band, quite a luxury as most women had to make do with a brass curtain ring. "Nothing's too good for my girl," he grinned. It was a little loose but Dickie said they could sort that out at a later date.

The wedding buffet was just the five of them in a small fish bar on the seafront and then in the local pub for a drink to wash it down. They all went down to the station and Gran, Ethel and her husband, all huddled together on the platform, waved them off. The train slowly pulled out of the station, Dickie pulled up the window and they both sat down in their seats ready for the journey back to London. Ethel had told Dot not to worry about her gran and that she would keep an eye on her. Maybe when she was all settled in her new home in London the three of them could come for a visit. Dot had tried to put on a brave face as they said their goodbyes but her heart was breaking. How could you be happy and sad at the same time she thought? The train had travelled a few miles down the track when Dickie announced that he needed to make himself a little more comfortable. He took his jacket and tie off and unbuttoned his shirt collar. He sat back down on the seat next to Dot and took her hand, he began to kiss her neck and slipped his hand inside her dress.

"Dickie, what are you doing?" she protested, "someone might come in and we're not far off the next station."

"No one will come in, the train is empty, the guards are up front in the first carriage and this train is nonstop to London."

"But…" Dot started to protest some more.

"Shhhh," came Dickie's voice, "we're all alone here let's make the most of it, when we get home Mum and Edie will be in the next room and walls have ears."

Maybe it would be thought quite romantic in some circles to lose your virginity on the fast train to London, maybe a tale to tell her grandchildren, or maybe not.

Dickie carried on removing Dot's dress, then her underclothes. The whistle of the train gave a sharp hoot and with that Dot lost her virginity.

Dot needn't have worried about meeting Maud and Edie because they made her very welcome and said they were sorry they weren't at the wedding but these were strange times. Maud said in a couple of weeks they would have a good old-fashioned East End Bullock knees up to celebrate their wedding. She said it would be like a second wedding only much better.

Dot met Sadie and the girls and thought how lucky she was to have a beautiful family.

Then, true to Maud's words, two weeks after she arrived, the Bullocks gathered in the King's Head for a party. Maud stood up and gave a little speech which was slightly slurred due to the gin. She said Dot was a lovely girl and how lucky her Dickie was to have her and she hoped that they would be as happy as her and Ron had been God rest his soul.

Dot thought she would never remember all the names as people were introduced to her. Maud had three brothers-in-law. Edward who was married to Joyce and they had two sons, Edward Jnr, who was affectionately known as little Ted, and Vinney. Albert who was married to Rita and had two girls Alice and Louise, and Lawrence who said he was fashionably single. The youngest of the aunties was Matilda known as Tilly. Dot thought she was very flamboyant with her painted face and bright red lips. When Lawrence sat down at the piano and began to play Tilly got up and stood beside him. She had an amazing voice and began to sing *If you were the only boy in the world and I was the only girl* followed by *What do you want to make those eyes at me for, if they don't mean what they say.* There were Barry's cousins Dave, Terry, Lorraine Ray and Vernon she could hardly keep count of them all.

When the traditional songs had been sung Lawrence suddenly changed the tempo and the pub came alive with the most vibrating music and people began to dance. Tilley looked at Dot and laughed at the amazed look on her face. "It's Jazz," she said, "all the rage in the USA," and she began to gyrate around the room. Dot was more than amazed, she had never seen or heard anything like it in her entire life. The people in the east end sure knew how to live and have a real good party, she was going to like living amongst these people, it was great being a Bullock.

The first time Dot met Frank was when he returned home from France as a wounded soldier. Dot thought Frank was a moody sod and told Dickie what she thought.

"Listen, Dot," he said. "Frank wasn't always like this. His leg gives him a lot of jip and he has seen some terrible things over there. For Christ's sake he had even seen some poor sod's head blown off, that's enough to make any bugger depressed." Frank told Dickie the tale but never mentioned it was Cyril. Just couldn't bring himself to say it. He would always carry the guilt that he had ruined his sister's life. If she knew the truth he would never be able to look her in the face again.

Dot felt a little ill at ease when she was around Frank. He was far too handsome for his own good and she felt he was always watching her, this gave her goose bumps and made her cheeks flush.

Sadie seemed to be continuously pregnant, although she miscarried most times, still the latest pregnancy seemed to be holding up. Maud showed her disapproval at all the goings on, "My poor Frank," she would say, "she's pregnant again."

Sadie went into labour in her eighth month and delivered a boy, Sadie never managed to go full term, it became a bit of a joke amongst the Bullocks and everyone said Sadie should learn to count properly. Frank's mood seemed to improve all of a sudden, funny what a son can do for a man.

There was a knock on the door and Dot went to answer it. "Why, Frank, what are you doing here? Our Dickie's at work." Dot thought Frank smelled like he had been drinking.

"Never mind," said Frank, "I'd rather see you anyway."

"You been out celebrating the birth of your Barry again?" she said as she was trying to back away. "Why shouldn't I?"

"I'm on top of the world." Frank didn't make any attempt to leave; he swayed a little and perched on the edge of the kitchen table for support. "Why ain't you and Dickie produced a sprog yet? Is my little brother firing blanks?" Dot felt her cheeks redden with embarrassment; she really didn't want to be having this conversation with Dickie's brother.

"It'll happen all in good time and not before," said Dot trying to defend them, after all it wasn't for the want of trying she thought to herself. If Dot was honest she was wondering the same thing, maybe she had something wrong with her. Frank moved closer and Dot could feel his breath on her, her heart began to beat faster and she could feel the familiar goose bumps. "Go home, Frank," she said Sadie needs you there. Frank ignored her remarks and he brushed his lips against her cheek. Dot's head was saying no but her body was crying out for Frank's touch. She really didn't have it in her to refuse Frank as he led her to the bedroom. She saw him wince as the pain in his leg caught him and then he seemed to forget as their passion took over. "Oh my God," she said after they had finished, "that was amazing."

"Not like that with Dickie then," he grinned as he slapped her on the bottom.

Dot felt so guilty when Dickie came home for tea that night she could barely look him in the eye but it didn't stop her from making love with Frank for the next three months. It was only when she discovered she was pregnant it stopped her in her tracks. When Dot told Frank she was going to have a baby he just laughed. "What's your problem, isn't that what you wanted?"

"But what if it's not Dickie's?"

"Whichever way you look at it, it's still a Bullock and that's all that matters," Dot raised her hand to slap Frank's face but he caught her by the wrist and pulled her towards him, kissing her lips. He didn't feel any resistance so he held Dot closer, parting her lips with his tongue. This time it was Dot unbuttoning Frank's trousers and leading him to her bedroom. Why couldn't it be like this with Dickie she thought as their bodies thrust toward one another.

Dickie was over the moon when Dot told him he was going to be a father. The whole family gave their congratulations and said it was about time.

Frank would torment her when he thought the others were out of earshot. "So I'm going to be a daddy again am I?"

"For Christ's sake, Frank," she would say, "don't let anyone ever hear you say that. Any way it might not be yours."

Frank would just smile, "Have it your own way it makes no odds to me either way."

Dot gave birth to a baby girl after a long and hard labour, Dickie was a pleased as punch with his new baby daughter, but said he couldn't put Dot through that again and as luck would have it Edie brought home some free samples of birth control sheaths from the Mothers' Clinic where she was working. Dickie was only too pleased to try it out.

Life settled down into a regular routine, Dot was busy with baby Irene, Dickie was still working on the railways and he had got Frank a job selling newspapers outside the station.

Sadie still managed to get pregnant and miscarry. Dot, deep inside was a little envious of Sadie when she thought of her and Frank together but nothing would come of dwelling on it.

Dickie religiously used the contraception, which Dot hated but was afraid to complain about in case her little secret should get exposed.

In 1922 Sadie had another daughter, Geraldine. Frank was disappointed it was another girl and he didn't seem to hide it. Frank seemed to put all his concentration into Barry, he was the golden boy and Frank spoilt him something rotten. How things were with him and Sadie she wasn't sure. They seemed alright on the outside, but Dot wondered if they were just keeping up appearances. There were no more pregnancies until 1926 when Sadie was convinced she was in an early menopause and it turned out to be their Markey.

Chapter 4

Bullock house 1926

Sadie used to watch Frank asleep in the chair snoring his head off after he'd had another skinful in the King's Head. She seemed to have lost all the feelings she once had for him and wouldn't have cared less if he had dropped dead. Then she would be sorry for her thoughts and begged God not to punish her for them. She felt the baby move in her stomach and was counting the days till it would leave her body. One part of her longing for it and another dreading that her labour would be as bad as Geraldine's birth.

The day started like any other, Sadie got the kids off to school, the older ones went to the factory to work and Dot popped round for a cup of tea. Sadie and Dot chatted while Sadie scrubbed the clothes on the washboard.

"What's that on the back of your frock, Sadie?" asked Dot. Sadie pulled at her clothes and tried to look.

"Oh my God it's blood, oh it's too early for the baby to come, Dot, I've got another six weeks to go."

"Let's get you to bed then, maybe it's rest you need. I'll go and get Maud and be as quick as I can."

By the time Dot came back with Maud Sadie was lying in a pool of blood. Maud pulled back the covers to check on Sadie. "Bloody hell Dot the baby's head is almost out and Sadie had lost a lot of blood, go and get the midwife and hurry up."

This birth was nothing like Geraldine's, by the time the midwife had arrived and the water had boiled the baby was born. Maud and Dot held Sadie's hands as she cried out in pain. They didn't leave her side until it was all over.

"It's a boy!" announced the midwife with a grin on her face

"My Frank will be as proud as punch," said Maud as she looked at the baby, Maud's grin began to disappear when she looked at the baby more closely. "He's got a strange look about him" she said, trying not to alarm Sadie. She tried to cover her alarm up. "Oh I'm sure it's nothing, he's just a bit squashed, it'll be alright when he's ironed out "Maud carried on tidying up as the midwife handed Sadie her new son.

Sadie lay back on the soft pillows cradling her new baby in her arms. He did look different from the others but she kissed the top of his head and they both drifted off to sleep.

Dot had gone downstairs to make them all a cup of tea. Dot looked at Maud's face as she came into the scullery. "What's wrong?" asked Dot, Please Maud tell me what's wrong, you're scaring me."

"There's something wrong with him. I've seen that look of him before.

"What are you babbling on about, Maud?" Dot could feel her own hysteria building up.

Maud put her hand to her mouth, "How are we going to tell Frank? He'll blame Sadie." Maud's hysteria was increasing to fever point and Dot was getting frightened. Maud lowered herself into the chair, her face had an ashen white colour to it. Maud could barely bring herself to say the words, how could they take him out? What would people say? Would they have cruel words, would they look on them with pity? "He's a Mongol" she whispered "A Mongol, she put her hands over her face and wept.

From the time Mark was born the relationship between Frank and Sadie went into deep decline. Sadie spent her days nurturing her family and Frank spent his time avoiding them, spending more and more time in the King's Head public house. He always defended himself by saying having a drink was the only way to help ease the throbbing in his leg, he said alcohol dulled the pain. Sadie knew Frank blamed her for the way Mark was, maybe it was her fault. When she first knew she was pregnant she hoped she would miscarry again, but when it was looking like she wouldn't she tried all the ways she could think of to abort it but nothing worked. If she had admitted to herself sooner that she could have been pregnant maybe she could have got rid of it, but she was half way through and it seemed determined to stay put. She tried a syringe that Edie had given her to administer a salt and soda solution but that didn't work. She had tried the gin and a hot bath method which almost left her scarred for life, but nothing would shift it. She was too afraid to resort to the crochet hook so she eventually resigned herself to the situation. She knew that aborting a baby at twenty weeks would have been a mortal sin, it may even have stayed alive for a while and she would have had to live with that picture for the rest of her life

Frank wouldn't even look at the child, he barely acknowledged he existed. Whenever Mark cried he would just yell at Sadie and say the kid's crying, sometimes even his words were cruel and he referred to him as the brat.

Mark was a good baby really, luckily for them all he very rarely cried because Frank had no patience with him at all. Mark would crawl over to Frank and pull at his trouser leg for attention. Frank would just push him away and this would hurt Sadie deeply. He would laugh and gurgle and love it when his other siblings played with him. His only problem was that he constantly seemed full of congestion which meant Sadie always had kettles on the boil to keep the moisture in the room to ease his breathing. This used to annoy Frank who complained the house always felt damp let alone the money that was being wasted he would yell. Frank slept most nights on the sofa, he and Sadie only spoke when necessary these days, usually to discuss the children or household things. Frank would sell his newspapers outside the station and then go to the pub. If Dickie was around they would share a pint together if not Frank would just stare into his beer alone. Sometimes he would spend the afternoon in the betting shop with his cousins Ted and Vinny. Ted and Vinny worked down the docks and were often finished early enough to have a quick bet before they went home for their tea.

Frank decided to knock off early as it started to rain. Not many people were stopping to buy a newspaper as they were in too much of a hurry to get home out of the bad weather. Frank poked his head in the ticket booth.

"Fancy a pint, Dick?" he asked.

"Sorry, mate, got some overtime tonight. It's hours before me shift finishes."

Frank didn't want to go home, where had it all gone wrong he asked himself as the pain in his leg began to throb again.

The bloody war's to blame he cussed as he made his way through the doors of the King's Head public house. He was only staying for one drink he said to himself, but before he knew it, it was nine o'clock. Frank got up to leave and stumbled onto a chair. Better sober up a bit before I go home he thought. Even though he and Sadie were estranged he still didn't want to receive the sharp end of her tongue.

Frank found himself standing outside Dot's front door, he decided not to knock but instead he went round the back of the house. He pushed the back-yard gate and it swung open. Dickie really ought to fix the latch on that gate any one could walk straight in he thought. He almost scared Dot to death when she saw him standing in her kitchen doorway.

"Jesus," she said, "what the bloody hell you doing here?"

Frank's words were still a little slurred. "Just come to see my favourite sister in law."

Dot tried to ignore Frank and she carried on washing up the dishes. He moved towards her and accidentally kicked over the chair. "For Christ's sake, Frank, do you want to wake Irene up."

"Oh how is my little girl then? I haven't seen her for a while."

Dot turned around, but Frank was too quick for her and he was standing closely in front of her. She could smell the beer on his breath, "Frank go home," she said. Frank began to kiss her neck, then her lips. Dot feebly tried to push him away, but deep down she really didn't want to. Frank pulled up her frock and undid his fly. Their lovemaking was fast and furious, Dot felt Frank's legs go weak at the very moment she saw Irene standing in the doorway rubbing her eyes.

"Irene," she yelled, "what are you doing up? Get back to bed right now."

"Mummy I want a drink" she cried sleepily.

"Go back to bed this minute and I'll bring you a drink." Irene did as she was told. "Oh my God," said Dot. How long had Irene been standing there? How much had she seen? Frank was mumbling and Dot was getting cross. "Frank, will you just go home for Christ's sake. NOW!" Frank left and Dot took Irene a glass of water to her bedroom. She tucked her back into bed.

"Mummy why was Uncle Frank here?"

"Shhh," she said, "go back to sleep, it's nothing for you to worry about."

Dot went back downstairs and got the Christmas port out of the cupboard and poured herself a large one. Oh my God if Irene ever told Dickie about this there would be blue murder, what was she thinking of letting Frank in her knickers. Oh what a mess!

The house was in darkness when Frank arrived home. He pulled of his shoes and slumped down on the sofa. Soon the effect of the alcohol took over and he started to snore. Barry had heard his father come in and could hear his snores echoing up the stairs. He climbed out of bed and went downstairs, he saw his father laying in a big heap, his head bent to one side, He kept thinking of how he had laid in bed listening to his mother crying herself to sleep. He hated the sight of the man he called

Dad. He wished him dead, if only someone would answer his prayers.

The whole family were in shock over Mark being born the way he was. There had never been anything like it on either side of the family before. Mark had a weak chest and seemed to be ill an awful lot and was a constant worry to Sadie. Sadie didn't think Frank gave two hoots about the boy, he found him more of an irritation. Mark seemed to get a cold at the drop of a hat and within no time at all his chest would begin to wheeze. Mark had been coughing all night and Sadie couldn't settle him." I'm going to take him to the London Hospital," she said as Georgie came into the kitchen. Georgie was rubbing the sleep out of her eyes.

"I'll come with you, Mum, just wait and I'll get dressed." To be honest Sadie was grateful Georgie was going with her, she felt so alone these days and was glad of her support. Georgie went upstairs to dress, she gave Ronnie a shake. "Oi wake up, Markey's ill and mum's taking him to the London."

Ronnie struggled to wake up. "Do you want me to come with you as well?" she asked.

"No," said Georgie. "You stay here and keep an eye on Barry and Geraldine. Maybe you could let Gran know what's happening."

Sadie put Mark into the pushchair and wrapped a blanket around him, she grabbed a bottle of baby milk and a clean nappy and shoved them in her bag. Georgie pulled the door closed behind them and they hurriedly made their way to the London Hospital.

Ronnie fell back to sleep and didn't wake until she felt Geraldine shaking her and asking for breakfast.

"Where's Barry?" Geraldine asked Ronnie.

"I don't know ain't he in bed?"

"No," said Geraldine.

Barry had a bad habit of going off somewhere and not letting anyone now where he was going. Ronnie dragged herself out of bed and took Geraldine downstairs to the kitchen to make some breakfast. There was evidence of Barry trying to cut a slice of bread and a knife with the traces of jam and butter on it. "Looks like Barry's had breakfast and gone out," sighed Ronnie as she put the kettle under the kitchen tap and began to fill it with water to boil for tea.

Geraldine began to cry. "I want mummy."

"Go and see if Daddy wants a cup of tea," Ronnie told her, trying to distract her from thoughts of their mother. Geraldine tried to shake her father but he just grunted and turned over on the sofa, her nose was running and she wiped it on the cuff of her nightshirt. Geraldine was still crying as she walked back to the kitchen.

"Daddy's asleep and won't wake up," she said. Ronnie guessed he'd had a skinful again and was nursing a hangover.

"Come on let's go and get dressed and go to grans," she said, hoping this would cheer Geraldine up. By the time they were dressed the kettle had boiled and Ronnie made some tea and toast for their breakfast.

Ronnie and Geraldine sat eating their freshly toasted bread and drinking a weak warm tea when they heard some movement and some vulgar noises from the hallway as their Father passed wind. This was a result of the best bitter beer he had consumed the night before.

"Get us a tea, gel," he shouted. "Where's yer mother?" he asked.

"Markey wasn't too good in the night, her and Georgie have gone up the London Hospital with him."

Frank shrugged his shoulders, "She'll be bloody hours up there."

"What about me breakfast and dinner?"

"That kid's a bloody liability." Frank ate the breakfast Ronnie put in front of him then he announced he was going to have a shave. He stomped about for a while shaving and getting dressed. Ronnie told him that her and Geraldine were off to Gran's to let her know what was happening and she had no idea where their Barry had gone. Frank said he would be off to do the lunchtime papers shortly so it was Barry's own fault if he was locked out of the house and had to wait on the doorstep. The little sod should tell someone where he was going. Frank was in a foul mood today and the girls thought the sooner they went out the better.

Ronnie and Geraldine put on their coats and shoes then headed off to let gran know Markey was up the hospital yet again with bronchial congestion. Gran just shook her head when Ronnie told her the news. "You girls might as well stay here and have a bit of dinner. Yer mother will be gone for hours." Ronnie was pleased as it gave her a chance to use Gran's old piano, in fact she was getting very good and Gran said how much she enjoyed listening to what she played.

Frank sat outside the station selling his newspapers, the effect of the night before beer was wearing off and his leg was throbbing. He looked at the station clock which just struck two. If he packed up now he could get a few pints in before closing time. As he walked through the King's Head door he heard someone yell to him. "Oi Frank over 'ere mate." It was his cousins Ted and Vinny. "Long time no see," said Vinney. "Where yer been hiding? How's that kid of yours?"

Frank began to unburden himself, saying how he wished Markey had never been born, how he blamed Sadie for his condition. Ted thought Frank was gonna start to blubber, especially by the time he got to his fourth pint and third whisky.

"Come on, Frank," said Vinny, "it's about time we got you home." The boys escorted Frank to his front door and helped him inside. "Go on, mate, you go and sleep it off before yer old lady gets in." The two boys closed the front door. Frank took out one of his woodbine cigarettes and lit it. Barry was sitting on the wall in the back yard, he saw his father's cousins through the window and then he heard the front door slam and knew they were gone. Barry sat watching his father through the window for ages. Barry saw the smoke in the front room and watched it thicken. His father didn't seem to stir. He sat there until he could see the flames dancing up and down the curtains, then he jumped down from the wall into the back alley. He began to kick an old tin can along the cobbles as he walked away with a smile on his face and a feeling of satisfaction in his stomach.

The flames had taken hold before anyone noticed them. Someone had called the fire brigade but by the time they arrived the fire was well under way. Barry came round the corner just in time to see his father being wheeled out on a stretcher. Barry didn't know much but he did know that if a body's face was covered it must be dead and he couldn't have been more pleased.

Word travelled fast and neighbours sent a message to Maud about what had happened. No one knew where Sadie and the kids were until Maud confirmed everyone's whereabouts. The only one who couldn't be accounted for was Barry.

Barry was down by the canal throwing stones into the water and watching the ripples. How pleased he was that his father was gone. He would never have to listen to his mother crying again because that bastard had upset her. He was man of the house now and would take care of them all.

Maud arrived at the hospital, gasping for breath, she had to sit down on the steps to regain her composure. Her limbs were heavy and her chest was heaving. "You alright love?" enquired a porter.

"No I bloody well ain't" she cried. "Help me find Sadie Bullock, will you? She brought her boy in here a few hours ago. There's been a fire at her house and I need to find her." With that Maud became hysterical and the porter had to call for assistance. They finally found Sadie and Georgie in the children's ward where Markey was having a nebuliser and was now in a stable condition.

There was no easy way to break the news of what had happened and what happened next could only be described as hysteria and chaos. The nurse pulled the curtain round Markey's bed and asked them to keep the noise down as they were upsetting the other patients.

Mark was now stable and was responding to the medication the doctors had given him. They wanted to keep Mark in overnight just as a precaution, he was sleeping peacefully and reassured Sadie he was going to be fine. Sadie agreed to come back the following day to get him. Sadie wanted to go back to her house, if only to get a few belongings but Maud told her it was a bit of a state and may still be unsafe. As they all stood on the steps of the London Hospital the reality of what had happened hit Sadie like a locomotive. Maud was in just as much of a state but managed to convince Sadie to go back to her house, after all Ronnie and Geraldine were already there. Sadie was now frantic as to Barry's whereabouts. The local bobby was outside Maud's when they arrived back there and updated them on what had happened at Sadie's house and how they thought the fire had started. He told her that only her husband had been found inside the house and was sure Barry would turn up soon. In the meantime he would keep a look out for him. Barry didn't turn up till late but no one asked where he had been, no one even noticed how unaffected he seemed to be by the whole thing and how he had known to come to Maud's.

The whole Bullock clan called at Maud's house, one by one to offer their condolences. Ted and Vinny told them how they had taken Frank home because he was worse for wear from the drink. Nobody blamed anyone, it was just a senseless accident that Frank was smoking and dozed off and his fag burnt the bloody house down.

Dickie was a tower of strength and took over making all the funeral arrangements. He was very sympathetic to Sadie and her lot, but quite frankly Dot's continuous snivelling was beginning to irritate him. After all he was her brother in law not her own flesh and blood.

Dot tried to pull herself together, she was in a terrible state but there was not a living sole she could share her secret with of how her and Frank had been lovers. Frank's funeral was a big affair; every Bullock for miles around came. There were Frank's aunts, uncles, cousins, second cousins and as they say 'Uncle Tom Cobley and all' The wake was held at Maud's house; the place was bursting at the seams, the little back yard was full with mourners and they spilled out into the street. Everyone had brought a crate of ale, and true to tradition in Bullock style the party began to give Frank a right good send off.

"Your Dot's looking a bit peaky," commented Auntie Joyce to Dickie.

"We'll it's probably because she's in the family way again. We wasn't going to mention it just yet on account of the funeral. We couldn't tell everyone our good news with all this shit going on."

"Maybe it's just what everyone needs, a new Bullock on the way, you know what they say, Dickie, one goes out to make room for another to arrive. Congratulations, boy, I'm pleased for yer."

Dickie gave a weak smile he was still trying to fathom out how they had made a slip up as they had always used the condom. Still Dot tried to point out you can always slip up, nothings fool proof, it only takes a little dribble. Still she was pregnant alright so that must have been the case.

Sadie and the kids went to stay at Maud's house as there was no other option. Everyone knuckled down and were trying to do the best they could, all except Veronica, who in spite of having the piano at her beck and call constantly moaned about how squashed and cramped it was there. Dickie said he would have helped out if he could, but Dot was feeling like a sock full of wet shit at the moment and it was all she could do to look after him and Irene.

The truth about Dot feeling so bad, which she had to keep to herself, was that she was so consumed with grief for her lover coupled with guilt at what she had done she couldn't snap out of it. When her time came to deliver her child it was hell. Her labour was even harder than the first time. She thought that it must be her punishment, thank God she would never have to do this again, what with Dickie, unknowing to himself, being infertile and her sperm supply being dead. The baby finally arrived after fifteen hours of labour and Dickie was as proud as punch to announce he had a son. Dot said they should call him Frankie, she was sure it would please Maud and Sadie. Dot said it would show them how much they thought of Frank to name their son after him. Dickie was extremely proud of Dot for such an unselfish act as to name their baby after his dead brother. So Frankie Richard Bullock was welcomed into the world.

The two years that followed were hard for them all. Money was tight, Maud became sick and Sadie struggled to take care of them all. By the winter of 1931 Maud had taken to her bed and sadly never recovered. Everyone said it must have been the Cancer that had got her, going on how much weight she had lost. The family were devastated to lose her, all except Barry who immediately though that with Maud gone there would be some extra space in the house.

Veronica started to go missing for hours at a time and would always be vague on her whereabouts when she was questioned.

The truth was she had started to go down to the wharfs where there was a little club where unknown musicians would gather to make music together.

They played everything from jazz to blues. They would try to imitate people like Duke Ellington and George Gershwin. They played Ragtime and danced the Charleston.

One night she arrived at the club and it was empty, it was a little early for members to arrive but the door was unlocked so she went inside. She walked over to the piano and ran her fingers along its rich wood, caressing it and aching to play. She lifted the lid and began to tinker with the keys; she could not resist the temptation to sit down on the stall and to imagine she was a famous pianist. She soon got the feel of the instrument and started to play Alexander's Ragtime Band. She was totally unaware that from the shadows of the doorway she was being watched. Solly the saxophone player had arrived and was amazed to hear the little lady play the piano with such accomplishment. He walked over to pick up his instrument and began to play along. This startled Ronnie but Solly motioned her to continue and they made sweet music together.

That is how Veronica started to play with the musicians down on the wharf. She would stay out all night as they played into the small hours. Sometimes she would go home with Solly who rented two rooms five minutes' walk away. Sadie was beside herself with worry at Ronnie's disappearing acts but eventually exhaustion took over and she said she washed her hands of it all and Ronnie had made her bed and would have to lie on it.

With Maud gone Sadie took over the house, most of the time it was just her and Markey there. Barry used it as a base but came and went without a bye or leave to anyone. Veronica had moved in with Solly and his crowd and they spent their time making a living out of playing the clubs. Georgie had followed Edie into the nursing profession and had joined the crusade for contraception for women. Geraldine landed herself a nice little job at the borough council offices, the only fly in the ointment was Barry. Dickie tried to keep an eye on him, if only for his late brother Frank's sake. Barry was forever in fights and all sorts of trouble. Sadie would despair, but Barry couldn't tell her most of the fights were because of the horrible things stupid ignorant people would say about Markey. People would call him mongrel and spastic and Barry would hit them. Markey was the kindest most lovable person you could want to know, but people just wouldn't give him a chance, they just couldn't see beyond their own prejudice.

Dickie even got Barry a job on the railway but Barry continuously failed to turn up and in all fairness they had no choice but to let him go. Barry found proper work a bore; he spent his days hanging around street corners mixing with what his mother would call "the wrong kind of people." By the time Barry reached the age of sixteen he had entered the world of illegal gambling and had become a bookmaker's runner. Barry for all his faults knew where his bread was buttered. He soon gained the reputation of being undoubtedly reliable, loyal and having nerves of steel, and was quickly and easily being drawn into the underworld of the East End criminals. Gambling was illegal but Barry would work the street corners and the factory gates and collect the bets for his boss. He never forgot the day he nearly got his collar felt when he was collecting bets outside Taylor's clothing factory. He was sure one of them Taylor boys had grassed him up to their father and he had called the old bill. Their card was marked, he swore, he wouldn't forget this little incident and one day they would get their comeuppance. The truth was he had always carried a dislike for the Taylor's, just because their old man had his own business they thought they were better than anyone else.

Barry learned his craft well and by 1938 he was collecting the protection money from pubs for the local hoods.

Barry was making a fair bit of money for himself. He had nice clothes on his back and cash to flash around. He would get all spruced up on a Saturday night in his pin stripped suite and trilby hat and make his way up west to a night club. Yes, Barry these days was known as a bit of a wide boy. But nevertheless he always made sure Sadie and Markey didn't go without anything, but most importantly he was saving for a rainy day. One day he wanted to be his own boss, he had no intention of being a petty criminal, maybe he would have his own bookmakers of even a club with upstairs gambling rooms. Yes, he could visualise it all in his mind's eye. There would be lavish furnishings, beautiful girls to help the punters buy their overpriced drinks, and him, yes Barry Bullock, lord of the manor.

Barry had a good eye for business and this was soon noticed by his boss, Barry soon found himself taken into the fold and at the heart of planning robberies and hoists and was proud to say they almost never got their collar's felt. Even if someone did have the misfortune to get a tug they had started to entice politicians and judges into their web and they were soon on the pay roll. Even though they kept the long arm of the law in their pockets the internal shit was dealt with by themselves. God help anyone who crossed them. They had the occasional scrap with rival gangs from south of the river but both sides always tried not to step on one another's toes.

Barry had been edgy all day. By early evening he could feel his mood darkening. He tried to shake it off but when they got a grip on him he would sink to the depths of despair. He had been the same as a child; sometimes he would do bad things. His mother would always make excuses for him and say to his father that he hadn't meant to do whatever it was he was accused of, and that he was truly sorry for being such a foolish boy. He would let his mother plead his case so that his father wouldn't take his belt to him, but in truth he never felt any remorse at all, in fact he enjoyed the feeling of power and was happy when his victim squirmed beneath him.

Barry was tempted to get the bottle of scotch out of the cupboard and drink himself into a stupor but at the last minute decided to take a cab up west to his favourite drinking club. Maybe a drink with some pals would pull him out of his black hole. It was either that or down The Kings Head with Vinney and Ted. Barry added the touch of his Gucci after shave to his face, put his wallet in his pocket and closed the door of his flat. Sadie hadn't been too pleased when Barry told her he was leaving home.

"What's the point of paying out rent for a place when you have a perfectly good roof over your head already?" she would say. Barry made up a bundle of lame excuses, he could hardly tell his mother it was so that he had a place to take women back to. Some nights him and the boys drank and played cards into the small hours. For fuck's sake there comes a time when a bloke needs some privacy. Still he loved his mother more than anything and spared her feelings the best he could. He would pop his head in every other day or as often as he could, he would always take her a little something and always something for Markey. He smiled to himself when he thought how glad they always were to see him, he felt sure his mood was lifting already and was glade he had made the decision to go out.

"Taxi," he shouted and climbed into the back of a black cab.

Billy and Jack were already in the club when Barry arrived. These men had moulded him and taught Barry all he knew, Barry had been a bookmaker's runner for them in the early days and now he was a player in their other illicit money-making ventures.

"Barry over here, mate," Billy waved to Barry to come and join them. There was a good-looking woman sitting at their table with them. Barry guessed she must have been about thirty years old, great figure and quite well spoken compared to the usual crowd. "Barry Bullock, I want you to meet Grace Greene." Grace looked up at Barry and offered him her hand. "Pleased to meet you," she said. Barry looked at the gorgeous creature, "Not half as pleased as I am to meet you," he said with his cheeky grin. "I can see you gentlemen have business to discuss," and she stood up to leave. Every movement was as graceful as her name and he couldn't take his eyes off of her.

Barry lifted his hat, "Until we meet again beautiful lady."

Grace looked Barry straight in the eye, and very casually, as if she really couldn't care less, said,

"Maybe," and Barry had never been so besotted in his entire life.

Jack watched Barry closely. "She's out of your league, boy, you don't stand an earthly chance with that one." Barry just turned to him and smiled. "Never say never," he said. "Never say never."

The men carried on drinking for a while and made arrangements to meet the next day to finalise matters for a little job they were planning. Barry wasn't sure if he had decided to leave or he had been dismissed but it was still early so he decided to catch the last tram home, maybe catch last orders at the King's Head. The streets were pretty empty, people were either in the theatres or clubs. He looked at his watch and just as he was wondering where the fuck the tram was a cab pulled up beside him. He was just about to tell the driver he didn't want a cab when the window wound down. He couldn't quite make out the figure sitting in the back seat but the voice was very much unmistakable.

"Can I give you a lift somewhere?" came the voice. Barry was just about to say no mate you're alright, when he realised it was Grace Greene sitting in the cab. Barry opened the door and jumped in.

"Guess I'm going your way," he said with his boyish grin spread across his face. Never say never he thought, never say never!

They drove for about twenty minutes before they pulled up outside a plush apartment block. Barry opened the taxi door and held out his hand to help Grace onto the pavement. "Pay the man," was all she said as she made her way to the entrance of the building. Barry, who was still in shock at the whole situation promptly did as he was told and hurriedly followed Grace into the building before she changed her mind or he pinched himself and woke up to find he had been dreaming.

Once inside the apartment Barry glanced around at its stylish décor. He wondered what she would have thought about his little flat, which consisted of two rooms in an old tenement building. It wasn't that he couldn't afford a better place but its location suited him and it was cosy enough thanks to his mother who continuously added scatter cushions and rugs and almost anything she knew he wouldn't throw out immediately. Most importantly he was still close to the family to keep a watchful eye on them and it was a good place for business. Besides he was saving his money for bigger ventures, it really didn't matter where he crashed each night.

Grace threw her coat across the chair and kicked of her shoes. "Pour me a drink would you?" she ordered. This woman intrigued Barry and he was ready to jump however high she told him to. He walked over to the decanter and poured them both a large drink into the crystal glasses.

"Don't you think it's a bit risky picking up strangers at bus stops?" he asked, Grace looked at him and smiled.

"You're not a stranger, Barry Bullock, I know quite a lot about you already and would like to know a great deal more." With that she took Barry by the hand and led him into her bedroom. Barry was used to being the dominant one in lovemaking but Grace was the one who took control showing him how to give her pleasure. He was eager to enter her but she would not allow it until she was ready for him. Barry wasn't sure how he felt about this; he was a control freak and could feel the start of his mood darkening again. Still he wanted this woman from the moment he had clapped eyes on her, but what surprised him was why she wanted him.

After their passion was spent Grace lit two cigarettes and handed one to Barry. "You do smoke don't you?" she asked, Barry felt like she was patronising him. Maybe she was, after all she must be about ten years older than him, maybe he should cut her a little slack or maybe he should just get the fuck out of her apartment and crawl back where he belonged. He inhaled the smell of her perfume as he stumped out the butt of his cigarette in the ashtray. What the hell, he thought, let's just go along for the ride and see what happens.

Grace would expect Barry every Thursday evening without fail. They would go to the theatres and have dinner. Then go back to her apartment and make love for hours. It was like Grace dangled him on a piece of string and there was nothing he could do about it. She was like a drug to him and he couldn't kick the habit.

Chapter 5

World War Two

Barry's immediate plans were rudely interrupted when Adolf Hitler invaded Poland. People were still betting, it took their mind of the horrors of war, but with a large proportion of men away at the front revenue took a nosedive. Still you know what they say one door closes and another one opens.

Barry was never one to let the grass grow under his feet. The government started to ration most things and he, as an up and coming entrepreneur was going to capitalise on the whole affair. He soon discovered that if you sold clothing as seconds you didn't need a ration coupon. He knew that Taylor's factory were mainly making parachutes and uniforms but he managed to get a nice little side line going with the youngest brother. He never approached him in person; he sent a go between to the factory to do the business and this kept his face out of the picture. They would buy the clothing for a good discounted price and Barry got a pitch in Romford market where his mate worked the stall for him. Once Barry got a little taste of the black market he decided that he had a golden opportunity in the palm of his hand. This war was going to be the making of him and he could see The Bullock Empire within his grasp. He thought that Joe public wanted more than anything was their fags and booze, so where else would you get these commodities but down at the docks. His first thought was to hijack the goods as they were on their way out, he would intercept the lorries and relieve them of their wares. This run the risk of getting their collars felt. He soon discovered that the captains of the ships were more than willing to sell contraband to him at a very reasonable price. Barry stood on the quayside pondering on what to do next when he saw an old run down building with a TO LET sign on it. A wide grin spread across his face, let's have a legitimate front to the operation and keep things above board. Barry felt pleased with himself. He wasn't one to let the grass grow under his feet, so he set his plan into action.

He rented the little office, he moved some of his trusted associates in and they began to sniff around to see who they could approach. Once they got started they found it was a piece of cake. The foreign ships pulled in and out of the docks, they unloaded their main cargo and the captain would have a special delivery ear marked for Barry Bullock Enterprises. Once all the wheels were in motion the whole business took on an air of legitimacy and they did not have to behave like common thieves. It seemed Barry Bullock wasn't the only one feathering his own nest, everyone was at it, but he was pleased with his set up and the whole operation was almost legal.

Night after night the air raid sirens went off and the bombs fell flattening London to the ground. Day after day families were burying their dead. Windows were blacked out and Anderson shelters were erected in back yards. The underground stations, as soon as the last train had gone through for the evening, became safe havens to shelter from the havoc and carnage reeking all over London. Amongst all this chaos Barry was doing just fine thank you very much. Edie and Georgina signed up with the Red Cross, working opposite shifts. They still ran their well women's clinic in their spare time, educating local women on the benefits of contraception, but demand seemed to have dropped off as all the men were leaving for the front.

Barry employed a woman to work in the dockside office just to make everything look more legitimate. She just filed a few documents and answered the telephone but mainly she was a bit of window dressing. By 1942 The Bullock enterprise was well under way, Barry's sister Geraldine was working her way up the career ladder at the local council. She had gone from office junior to a substantial position in the planning office. She kept Barry informed of interesting things that were taking place. She told him how Mr Churchill had commissioned William Beverage to do a report on how London should be rebuilt after the war. He proposed a new welfare state where every working man would contribute a proportion of his wages so that health care could be free to everyone. Barry was more than interested in the rebuilding part and so with Geraldine's help he started to put together plans to tender for the rebuilding contracts as soon as the war was over. Yes sir, you just need to plan ahead and be one step ahead of the game.

Barry's plans looked like they were about to get a fly in the ointment when he arrived home one night to find a brown envelope on his door mat with a large stamp marked On Her Majesty's Service. "Fuck me," he said when he opened it; it was only his bloody call up papers. There was no way he was going to go to war and get fucking killed, maybe he could call in a few favours. He had better do something and be quick about it; he had to report for his medical in less than a week.

Grace and Barry were still seeing one another occasionally. Barry knew that it was a relationship that was never going to go anywhere. Things had petered off a little between them lately, Barry's business was more demanding and sometimes he wouldn't see her for a couple of weeks at a time, partly because of his business commitments and partly because on a few occasions he had called at her apartment and there had been no one at home. Barry couldn't control his jealousy when it came to Grace. He started to get obsessed that she was seeing someone else. When he didn't know where she was his moods would become black and God help anyone who stood in his way.

Barry had called at Grace's apartment the previous night, only to find the place in darkness. He returned to his flat and opened a bottle of whisky. Barry was imagining Grace in the arms of another lover and he continued to drink until the bottle was empty and he eventually passed out. His mood was no better when he finally woke up the following morning, his head was pounding and he fell over the chair on his way to the bathroom cabinet to find some aspirin. "Bollocks," he said as he looked at the clock. He had to be down at the docks by eleven o'clock and it was already nine fifteen. One of the ships' captains had a little consignment of tobacco he had to collect. He looked at himself in the mirror that hung above the bathroom sink, Christ he thought, what a mess, he couldn't go out looking like a sack of shit. He turned on the tap to run some water for a quick shave. The pilot light on the ascot wouldn't ignite, "For fuck's sake," he cursed under his breath, there was nothing worse than trying to have a shave in cold water. The razor felt course against his face, "Bollocks," he swore again as the razor caught his chin and the blood oozed out. He was down to his last clean shirt and he didn't want to get blood all over it. He had better drop his bag wash in at the laundry for a service wash on the way out. Barry finished getting dressed amongst a sea of cussing and swearing, the blood still dripping from his chin adding to his irritation. He grabbed his car keys and slammed the front door. He jumped into the driving seat of his ford prefect car and started the engine "Shit," he said as he remembered his bag of washing still sitting on the bedroom floor. As soon as he got to the docks he would send Brenda out to buy him a couple of new shirts, it would give her a break from filing, the poor mare.

Barry drove up to the dockside gates, the security guard raised the barrier, "Morning, Mr Bullock," he said lazily as he tried to stifle a yawn. Barry was in no mood for pleasantries but felt it was best to keep on some people's good side, one never knew when one needed a favour.

"How's it going?" enquired Barry who was just going through the motions and wishing he could remember that poor bastard's name.

"Fine thanks, Mr Bullock."

Barry pushed his foot down on the accelerator. "Be lucky," he shouted as he drove off in the direction of his office.

Barry was supposed to make the exchange with the captain at twelve thirty and it was already almost twelve o'clock. He climbed the stairs to the office two at a time and flew through the door like a bull in a china shop. Brenda jumped out of her skin and Dave nearly fell of the chair he was swinging backwards and forwards on. "Blimey," said Dave. "You look like a sack of shit mate."

"If you weren't family I'd give you a slap for that remark." Barry made his way over to the safe to get the cash out to pay the captain. Barry chucked the bundle of notes at Dave and Dave put it in the inside pocket of his jacket. Dave made no attempt to move. "Well shift your arse then and go and get those fags. Time and tide waits for no man."

Barry almost chuckled to himself thinking he had cracked a little joke. Maybe his spirits were beginning to lift; it was probably the thought of making a bit of money. Fifteen minutes later the smile was wiped off Barry's face when Dave fell through the door covered in blood. Barry jumped up from his desk and ran round to help Dave up off the floor.

"What the fuck happened?" he yelled, Dave tried to answer as he wiped the blood away from his already swelling lip.

"A bloke asked me for a light and as I went to light his fag I got coshed from behind. Next thing I knew I was on the ground getting a kicking."

"What about the money? Have you been rolled?" asked Barry. "I'm sorry, mate, I tried to stop 'em but they had me good and proper."

Barry was furious and he could feel his headache returning. "Someone is taking us for fucking mugs," he swore. It has to be someone from the ship who got wind of what was taking place and thought they'd take the money for themselves. If they think they can take the fucking piss and get away with it they've got another think coming. Dave take my car and go get some of the boys. Go down the lock up in Bow and find Clint, he should be there now."

Dave tried to get out of the chair steadying himself on the side of the desk, he reached over to get the car keys and his face turned a strange colour as he was about to pass out. Barry was still rambling on about getting revenge and it wasn't until Dave ran to vomit in the washbasin that he came back to reality.

"Dave, mate, I'm sorry, maybe you need to go home, Brenda call Dave a cab," and with that he grabbed the car keys and headed for Bow himself.

Clint was just locking up as Barry pulled up outside the garages that they hired from a mate to store their contraband, he had just sold the last of the fags they had in there to a little Jewish newsagent down Whitechapel. "Job done boss," he said to Barry. "Just got the booze to move out this week."

"Never mind that," retorted Barry. "Some fucking bastard has just given our Dave a right good hiding and rolled him for the cash as well. Clint I want you to sniff around and find out who done it and then we'll work out how we are going to make them pay. And to top it all off I've only had me fucking call up papers. How come you haven't had yours?" Barry asked Clint.

"Clint just shrugged his shoulders. "I don't know mate, think I must be under the MOD's radar. When I came to England from France, I never asked for anything from anybody so I don't think the Brits even know I exist and that's the way I want to keep it. "You don't know how lucky you are, mate, I've got to work out how to get out of it, there's no way I'm going to war and get my fucking head blown off. Barry could feel his head begin to pound, he hadn't seen Grace for weeks and felt now was the time to pay her a visit, she would know how to make him feel better.

"Meet me at the dockside office tomorrow afternoon, maybe you might have some information by then," Barry said to Clint, and with that he drove off in the direction of Grace Green's apartment.

Barry pulled the car into Grace's private parking bay; he could feel the throbbing in his underpants at the anticipation of seeing her. He climbed the stairs two at a time and rang her doorbell. Maybe his day was going to turn out better than it had started. Barry waited a few moments but there was no reply. He rang the doorbell again and began banging loudly with his fist on the door. The door of the adjacent apartment opened and a short, stout, bald-headed man in his late fifties appeared. He looked at Barry feeling slightly annoyed at all the commotion. "There's nobody there," he said, "the lady moved out about a week ago."

"What do you mean? Moved out, moved to where? Barry continued shouting. The little man disappeared back into his own apartment, he reappeared a few moments later with a piece of paper in his hand and offered it to Barry. It was an address in the Walworth Road in Southwark, just off the old Kent Road. "She gave me that address in case any letters arrived for her, she asked me to forward them on."

Barry took the piece of paper, "Cheers mate," was all he said feeling slightly irritated as he made his way back to his car.

As he drove back to his flat his mood began to darken again. Christ, he thought, he knew they didn't have any commitment to each other but he thought she might have got word to him she was moving. Still, fuck the cow he thought, he didn't need her anyway.

Barry changed his mind about returning home, he headed back to the east end and the King's Head. As the car turned the corner he didn't see the bloke step out in front of him, he slammed on the brakes. How he didn't hit him was a miracle. "Look where you're fucking going you prick," he yelled out of the window. "Jesus Christ," he said when he realised it was his uncle Vinny he had almost mowed down. Barry jumped out of the car. "Are you OK, Vin? I'm so sorry, mate me head was miles away."

Vinny seemed a little shaken up. "Listen, Unc, jump in the car and I'll take us both down the King's Head and get you a stiff brandy. Vinny did as he was told.

"I was just on me way there anyway. I was meeting your Uncle Ted and Dave there. Ted said Dave had got a good hiding earlier and was in need of drink."

Barry told his uncle what had happened down the docks, how Dave and been the victim of a despicable assault and some bastard had stolen Barry's money. Vinny frowned, the rest of the family did not approve of Barry's way of making money. Ted was not happy at Dave's association with his cousin. "If you don't get your collar felt one day, my boy, it will be a bloody miracle," said Vinny.

Ted and Dave were sitting in the corner of the bar and Barry was annoyed to see that bloody Harry Taylor sitting with them. He went to the bar and ordered four pints of beer, Barry and Vinny carried the beer over to the table and put them down in front of each of the Bullock men. Barry made it blatantly obvious that Harry was not welcome. Harry could feel the atmosphere in the air. He stood up saying how sorry he was to see Dave had been mugged and wished him well. Dave and Harry Taylor had been in the same class at school and Dave thought Harry was a decent enough bloke and had an occasional pint with him. Barry lit a cigarette and slammed the box of matches down on the table.

"Was it necessary to be so rude?" asked Dave.

"I don't like the fucker, he thinks his own shit don't stink," Barry growled.

"He's a good bloke," said Dave "I think you're the one with the problem, mate."

Barry was annoyed at being spoken to like that, especially from his own cousin. He picked up his pint and walked away just in case he gave Dave a right hander and added to his injuries. Just at that moment Irene came through the bar door with a couple of girls in tow. That's more like it thought Barry a bit of female company. He painted his best smile on his face and made his way towards them. "Irene," he said, "let me buy you and your two gorgeous girlfriends a drink."

"Hello, Barry, that's good of you, we'll have a port and lemon each thanks."

Barry got the girls their drinks and sat down at the table with them. "Come on then, Irene, introduce me to your friends."

Irene took the headscarf from her head and shook her hair. "This is Vera Murphy and Pat Fuller meet my cousin Barry." Barry took each of the girls' hands and kissed them saying how pleased he was to meet such beautiful ladies.

Barry had never seen Pat before but he knew who Vera Murphy was on account of her brothers. He knew there were about half a dozen of them. They had lived down the next street to him before his house had been burned down and he had moved in with Granny Maud.

He especially remembered Vera's sister with long wavy hair called Margaret. He would have liked to buy her a few port and lemons, still like he always said never say never.

The girls downed their drinks and stood up to leave. "Whoo, where you lot think you're going?"

"We're off to the Ilford Palais," said Irene. Barry was a little disappointed the party was breaking up so early, it must be his night for getting blown out.

Barry let himself into his cold dark flat almost falling over the bag of dirty washing he had left there earlier. "Right," he said looking at the bag, "I think mum is overdue a visit, so tomorrow the both of us will pay her a call." Barry's hand felt around the wall in the dark until he found the light switch. The bare bulb hung from the ceiling lighting up the shabby little room. As much as his mother had tried to brighten it up for him you couldn't get away from the fact it was still pretty much a shit hole. She had bought him a nice shade for the ceiling and it was still sitting on the chair in the corner of the room. Barry made a mental note to put it up a soon as possible just in case she popped round and see it on the chair and thought he didn't like it. He would rather walk on hot coal than hurt his mother's feelings. Barry made his way over to the gas fire to light it. "Bollocks," he swore as the gas had run out, he searched around in his change to find a shilling for the meter. He pushed the coin in the meter slot and lit the fire. The heat it gave out barely made a difference to the room at all. He filled the kettle to make some tea, then changing his mind he poured a large whisky instead. Christ, he thought I have got to cut down on this booze. It's not even helping it's just making me feel like crap. Barry chucked his clothes over the chair and climbed into bed. The sheets smelt stale, *might as well take these to muvvers tomorrow as well just in case I get lucky sometime soon.*

Barry pulled up outside his mother's house in a fairly good mood considering he had to go for his medical at 3 o'clock that afternoon. He let himself in and made his way to the kitchen where he knew she always was. He gave her a peck on the cheek. "Where's Markey?" he asked. Since Mark had left his "special" school he had joined a day centre for young adults who, by society, were labelled as spastics. Markey loved going to the day centre as there were lots of people who were classed as different by the outside world. He soon showed everyone how clever he was in spite of everything and he was a helpful asset to the staff there. "He's at the centre, love," replied Sadie. "They have taken the group to the park today, think they are going to have a bit of a picnic over there." Sadie saw the large bag of washing Barry had brought with him and pretended not to notice. "So what do I owe the pleasure of your company then?" she asked.

Barry tried to look hurt. "I've just come to see my favourite girl," he teased.

"Umph, so whose is that big bag of washing then?"

"I was just on my way to the laundry with it when I suddenly thought, why give them good money when me old mum will do it for love?" Sadie lifted her hand to pretend to clump him round the ear and Barry ducked away. "You make a start on me washing and I'll make us both a nice cup of tea. As Barry poured out the tea he placed a ten pound note under the pot for his mother to find later on. He could never have given it to her outright as she was a proud woman and say she didn't want paying for doing her own son's washing. Barry made sure his mum and Markey always had what they needed, even though there was rationing he had his sources and on the black market, if you had the money you could get almost anything you needed, and Barry Bullock certainly had the money.

Sadie noticed a cloud come over Barry's expression. "What's wrong son? And don't say nothing because you can't lie to your old mum I always know when something's on your mind."

Barry wasn't going to say anything about his call up papers but he supposed he couldn't keep it a secret from her for long. "Got me call up papers, got me medical this afternoon." Barry watched the expression on his mother's face change as she grabbed the edge of the table and lowered herself into the chair. The words he had just spoken hung in the air.

Sadie drew in a deep breath, "Oh well ... I suppose it had to happen sooner or later, you wasn't going to be the only one who wasn't called up. She was petrified that something would happen to her beautiful son. There wasn't a day went by when you didn't hear of someone or other in a nearby street that had had the telegram boy knock on their door. Why just the other day that poor Mrs Murphy who lived round the corner from their old place heard her son, Wally, had been killed in action.

Just at that moment they heard a racket of clucking chickens coming from the back yard. Barry had taken Markey down brick lane one Sunday morning and he had fallen in love with the baby chicks. Markey's eyes lit up when Barry said he could take a couple home. By the time Markey had finished choosing the ones he wanted there were half a dozen in the little shoe box. Markey had seen his big brother's car parked outside in the kerb and he went running round the back of the house and into the yard to try and surprise him. Markey in his innocence hadn't anticipated the commotion the chickens would make. Barry smiled to himself and pretended to be suitably surprised as Markey bounced through the door. They pretended to box one another and Barry held up his hands in surrender.

"Are you staying for tea, Baz?" asked Markey with an eager expression on his face.

"Sorry, little bruv, maybe next time gotta see a man about a dog."

Markey began to laugh, he looked up to Barry and idolised him. It was half past two and Barry said it was time he made a move. He kissed his mother goodbye and ruffled the top of Markey's head. "Be back tomorrow for my laundry Ma."

"Ok, Son," replied Sadie with a heavy heart wondering how long it would be before her boy would be shipped out to fight the Germans.

Barry sat in the medical waiting room with a dozen other men watching the hand on the clock slowly tick by, each man waiting in anticipation for his name to be called. Some of the chaps were chatting saying how they couldn't wait to have a go at "Gerry" eager in their urgency to get out there and get on with it. Barry, on the other hand was still racking his brains on how he was going to get out of it. He was still milling over a couple of options that were forming in his mind when a nurse holding a clipboard called out his name. He stood up, dropped his cigarette butt onto the floor and stubbed it out with the toe of his shoe. He followed the nurse into a cubicle where she told him to strip down to his underpants. Barry did as he was told and sat down on the edge of the examination couch. He sat there for at least fifteen minutes and still no one came. Not only did he feel a prat sitting there in his pants but he was beginning to get cold and that was really pissing him off. Just as he was deliberating whether or not to get dressed and leg it out of there the curtain was pulled back and an elderly doctor stood in front of him, he had a stethoscope around his neck and a tray full of suspicious looking instruments on a trolley. The nurse followed the doctor into the cubicle and re-pulled the privacy curtain. The doctor looked at Barry, "I will do my examination Mr Bullock and the nurse will ask you some questions" The nurse began by confirming his name, address and date of birth. Then she asked him about childhood illnesses and family history. When she got to the section that asked if Barry had ever had treatment for any sexual diseases he got annoyed. "You've got a fucking cheek asking questions like that," the doctor looked up over the rim of his glasses.

"They're just routine questions, Mr Bullock, will you kindly mind your language and answer the nurse if you don't mind."

Barry was trying hard not to lose his temper. He looked straight at the nurse, "No I have never had a dose of the fucking clap, how about you?" The nurse blushed with embarrassment. The doctor was checking Barry's reflexes with a small hammer and Barry thought it was whacking him a bit harder than was necessary. "Fucking moron" Barry thought to himself.

"Could you stand up for me, Mr Bullock and drop your underpants."

"Are you some fucking pervert, mate? I don't drop me cacks for any bloke."

The doctor didn't wait for Barry to oblige he just grabbed him by the bollocks and told him to cough

"Mmmm, OK, get dressed and wait outside."

Barry got dressed still feeling humiliated and thinking that he may have to give that doctor a slap for what he just did; instead he lit himself a cigarette and went back into the waiting room trying to control his temper that was seriously rising. He was still sitting there thinking of how he could wangle his way out of the army when the doctor called him over. Maybe he could get one of the boys to break his leg for him. The thought of physical pain was not high up on his list so he quickly dismissed it. Barry followed the doctor over to his desk and sat in the chair the doctor motioned him to.

"Mr Bullock," he began "your general health is good, but you have flat feet so you are of no use to the army. Maybe the Air force or Navy might take you, but even flat feet may cause a problem for them." Barry laughed out loud and the doctor looked at him disdainfully and a little disgusted.

"Well there's a turn up for the books, Barry Bullock not good enough."

"I suggest that you find another occupation to help the war as a civilian, there are plenty of things that need doing at home as I'm sure you are aware of." Barry was still smiling, "Doc you can rest assured I will carry on helping the war effort in any way I can. My main concern is to make sure the folks at home have a comfortable war." Barry's whole attitude now changed and he wanted to kiss the doctor, but instead he kissed the pretty nurse who had annoyed him earlier full on the lips as she handed him his exemption papers. Barry laughed all the way back to the King's Head public house, flat feet, he couldn't believe it, what a fucking turn up.

Barry was full of high spirits when he arrived at the King's Head, he wanted to buy the whole bar a drink to celebrate his good fortune. He saw his uncle Ted and Vinny sitting in the corner just as his cousin Dave came out of the gents. Dave looked peeved, "Get the drinks in, Barry, we're over there." Barry felt like his bubble had been burst and wondered why they had such long faces. Barry got the drinks and sat down. "What's the matter with you lot?"

"Keep it down, Barry," said Vinney. "It's our Terry, he's gone AWOL from the army."

"Have you any idea where he is? Have you heard from him?" enquired Barry. "Yes to both questions, we've got him hiding out in Aunt Alice's caravan down on Canvey Island, but he can't stay there till the end of the war."

"Don't panic," said Barry, "we'll think of something."

"He's in a shocking state," said Vinny, "Terry said he would rather die than go back to the front."

"How the bloody hell did he get home?" asked Barry

"He managed to get back to Dover where he got word to your uncle Dickie. Dickie smuggled him on a train and got him back to London. It gave us a right shock when they came banging on our door in the middle of the night," answered his uncle. "Our house was the first place they'd come looking for him, so quick as you like we got him down the caravan."

Barry sat thinking for a minute.

"We've got to get him out of the country, maybe over to southern Ireland, leave it with me and I'll see what I can do."

Vinny looked a little relieved, "Thanks, Barry, we knew we could rely on you."

Barry had to be careful who he spoke to because you couldn't trust anyone these days, but he also knew Terry couldn't hide out indefinitely in the caravan. Still he was sure he was safe enough for the time being and he would start to make a few discreet enquires about getting him over to southern Ireland. Barry smiled to himself as he remembered the couple of times he had been to his aunt's caravan when he was a child. His aunt Alice had her rickety old caravan even then. As many Bullocks as possible packed up their belongings and left the dirt and grime of the hot sticky summer of the East End. There must have been a dozen or more of them all squeezed inside the caravan those couple of summers he could remember. They slept anywhere they could, on mattresses on the floor and on top of one another. They cooked their meals on an open fire outside the van; the adults drank beer and sang songs late into the night. During the day the children played on the beach and spent hours just catching crabs and building sand castles. Happy days he thought.

Barry got Dickie to arrange for Terry to travel by train to Liverpool where he would get the ferry to Dublin. He had a few contacts over there that he had done business with in the past. Dickie wasn't happy about getting involved. He knew his nephew sometimes mixed with undesirable characters and got involved in shady deals with the Irish and he didn't want any part of it. Barry had tried to draw Dickie in a while back by asking him to sell him some of the arms destined for the

British army to the Irish. Barry knew trouble was brewing in Ireland and as ever Barry saw a business opportunity. Dickie was adamant that he wouldn't have none of it, but did agree for the sake of his cousin Vinny to help get his boy Terry out of England. So it was all arranged, Terry was put on the train to Liverpool with money in his pocket and the name and address of a safe house in Dublin. A week later Barry got word from the Irish that Terry had never showed up. Barry didn't relish the thought of telling his aunt Grace and Uncle Vinny the news. Vinny said Grace had been in a permanent state over the whole affair and neither of their nerves could take much more. Where the fuck had his cousin got too? As much as family came first all this shit with Terry was taking up too much of his time and business was being affected.

Six weeks later Barry's aunt and uncle received a letter from Terry apologising for any trouble he had caused, but by the time he got to Liverpool he went right off the idea of Ireland and caught a ship to America. He bribed a ship hand who stowed him away for the duration of the journey. He was planning to hitch hike around the states and do casual work to pay his way. He said he was having a whale of a time and not to worry about him. What a mental bastard thought Barry, let's hope he didn't get picked up and arrested for being an illegal. Still this news pleased his aunt and uncle and peace was restored to the Bullock clan.

1944 Georgina = 34 years old still crusading for women's health and contraception.

Veronica = 32 years old her and Solly are an item and she is playing in the band.

Barry = 26 years old wanna be gangster and black market entrepreneur

Geraldine = 23 Working at the local council, married to a man with political ambitions

Mark = 18 years old lived with his mother as he was downs syndrome

Over the next few months Barry put his heart and soul into buying anything he could lay his hands on and selling it a tidy profit. The little dockside office became the nerve centre of the Bullock empire and Brenda was turning into a proper little personal assistant. She kept a ledger with detailed information of all Barry's dealings in a code which to the regular layman looked bona fide business transactions. Barry thought what a little diamond she had turned out to be and you should never judge a book by its cover. The soppy mare had a brain on her shoulders after all.

Dave had got himself a job as an ARP warden and looked quite respectable in his uniform. Dave said he was lucky that he failed his medical for the forces as well and could only thank Barry for the time when they were kids and he had shoved a pencil in his ear and perforated his eardrum. Dave being an ARP warden turned out to be quite an asset for Bullock Enterprises as well as he could give Barry the nod to any goods that needed redistributing after an air raid strike. Barry felt himself to be a bit of a robin hood on account of how he was helping the poor and needy in their times of hardship. Barry's motto was God helps those who help themselves and no one could blame a bloke for making a bit of profit for himself on the side.

Barry arrived at the dockside office about one o'clock. He had been at the lock up since six o'clock that morning with Clint shifting and sorting the orders ready for the deliveries as soon as night fell. All he wanted was a couple of hour's peace and a nice cup of tea to recharge his batteries before the evenings work commenced. He knew the boys were capable of handling the deliveries but a lot of money would be changing hands and he wanted to be there taking charge of it.

Brenda looked up from her typewriter as Barry entered the office. "Any messages for me?" he asked expecting her to say no in her usual flat manner.

"Mr Bullock, I have had your sister Georgina on the telephone half a dozen times today looking for you. She sounded very upset and said as soon as I found you I must tell you to go to your mother's house immediately as something terrible had happened."

"Oh for fuck's sake," said Barry under his breath. "Didn't she give you any idea what the problem was?"

"No Mr Bullock," replied Brenda "but as I have said, she seemed extremely upset, bordering on hysterical if the truth be told." Barry knew Georgina was not the type to have hysterics for no apparent reason so something must be up, but when would they all learn to sort things out by themselves, he asked himself, he might not always be around to do it for them.

"Brenda telephone Clint and put him in the picture just in case I don't make it tonight. Tell him to make some calls and get some reliable help, and I mean reliable, as he will have to take charge of the payments and I don't want any cock ups."

"Yes Mr Bullock, right away, Mr Bullock," said Brenda who was already dialling the number of the warehouse. Barry grabbed his car keys from the desk and made a quick exit. He drove towards the dock gates, his mind in overdrive wondering what the hell could be wrong. The traffic was heavy and Barry honked his horn with impatience. "For fucks sake get a move on," he shouted even though no one took a blind bit of notice of him. He could feel himself begin to sweat in the afternoon heat and he wound down the window. What the fuck was holding up the traffic this bad he thought. He reached over to the passenger seat and found his cigarettes in his jacket pocket; he lit one and inhaled deeply which made him instantly begin to cough. He threw the cigarette out of the car window and tried to control his coughing. It's a bad fucking habit he thought and vowed to give it up sometime soon. Finally the traffic began to move again and he put his foot down on the accelerator. The journey to his mother's house seemed to take forever but finally he pulled up outside the front door. Georgina had been looking out of the bedroom window and as soon as she saw Barry's car pull up she ran down the stairs to open the front door. Barry could see she had been crying.

"Georgie, what's wrong? Is Mark OK?" Georgina tried to answer Barry but the words just stuck in her throat and she began to sob again. At that moment Mark appeared from the back room. He saw it was Barry and immediately a huge grin appeared on his face. Barry ruffled the top of his head, "What's all this fuss about then?" he asked. Mark answered in a matter of fact manner.

"Mum wouldn't wake up; she was very tired today and yesterday. I thought she might be hungry so I made her some bread and milk but she still wouldn't wake up not even when I shook her. Now the man has taken her away, when will he bring her home again, Barry?" He asked in innocence. Barry pushed past Mark and went into the front room. He was more than surprised to see his aunt Edie there.

"What the fuck is Markey on about, Edie?" Edie was dreading the words she was about to say but there was no way to cushion the blow, Barry idolised his mother, ever since his father had died he had been her protector and provider. She was almost a saint in his eyes and had, in his mind endured terrible tortures at the hand of his father. Even though now he was a grown man he knew the noises he had heard as a child coming from his parents' bedroom were the sounds of adults in their lovemaking. He refused to admit his mother had willingly let his father do those things to her. His father was a beast and had forced his mother to submit to such indecencies. Edie walked over to Barry and took his hand. "Barry love, your mum's passed away, the doctor said it looked like she'd been gone a couple of days, probably her heart just gave out, Markey didn't understand, he thought she was just sleeping bless him. There was nothing anyone could have done." Edie's voice trailed off into the distance, Barry stood motionless for a few seconds while the realisation of what his aunt had just said sank in. Then he yelled out

"NO!"

He hit his fist hard against the wall until his knuckle bled, then he sank down to the floor and cried like a baby.

Barry was finding it hard dealing with his emotions. It was the first time in his life he was unable to buy or bully his way out of a situation. The week leading up to Sadie's funeral he spent his time in a whisky enhanced stupor. His temper was foul and his mood was blacker than it had ever been before. Edie and Georgie stayed at the house to take care of Markey and organise the wake. No one could find Ronnie, the last anyone heard she had gone on tour up north with Solly and the band. Barry put out the word amongst all his associates and contacts for her to get in touch with him but so far he hadn't heard a word. Barry organised the funeral alone. He wouldn't let anyone help him, not even his Uncle Ted or Uncle Vinny.

The day of Sadie's funeral arrived and Barry had half emptied a bottle of scotch by eleven o'clock. Georgie was fast losing her patience with her brother.

"For God's sake, Barry, take it easy on the drink, the way you're carrying on you'll drop the bloody coffin on the way into the church." Barry threw his glass into the butler sink and the glass shattered. "That's it, throw your toys out of the pram why don't you, act like a child." Barry clenched his fist as he was getting an overwhelming urge to clump his sister. Barry threw open the door to the back yard and went outside. He took his cigarette packet out of his jacket and lit one. He was cross with Georgie for talking to him like that. She spoke to him like he was ten years old, still perhaps he deserved it. She was right, today was not the time to wear your heart on your sleeve, they were all grieving. He took a deep breath, Ok, Mum, he said to himself, today I'll make you proud of me and tomorrow I'll cry.

Markey asked where his mum was and Georgie explained she had gone to be with the angels and his dad and grandma Maud.

"When will she come back?" he asked in his innocence. Georgie tried to be gentle in her reply.

"Markey, once you go to heaven you can't come back, you won't see Mum again till it's your time to go, when Jesus calls you." Markey seemed to think for a while trying to make sense of this information.

Markey looked worried, "Suppose I don't hear him?" he said. Georgie's eyes were so full of tears she could hardly see her baby brother's face.

"Don't you worry, when Jesus wants you he makes sure you hear him," and she put her arm around Mark's shoulder and gave him a big hug.

"Are you going to live here with me now, Georgie?" was Mark's next question.

"Me and your auntie Edie will stay for a while, at least until after mum's funeral is over and then we will sort out what we are going to do about you." Then the questions began all over again when Georgina had to try and explain what a funeral was.

"Barry could come and live with us again now mum won't need her bed," said Markey, and as he idolised his big brother he was getting quite excited and all thoughts of his mother were fading fast.

Georgie tutted and shook her head, "Yes, Markey, my darling and pigs might fly." The thought of pigs flying made Markey burst out laughing.

The Bullock clan began to arrive at the house. Each one offering their condolences before pouring a large whisky from the bottle on the table. Edie and Georgina had been busy all morning preparing food for the family for when they came back after the service, Barry's cousin Dave and his dad Ted had pilled the back yard up with crates of beer ready for the wake. The family made their way one by one into the front parlour where Sadie had been laid out two days earlier. They said their goodbyes and each placed a small memento or letter in the coffin in accordance to their family tradition. The carriage drawn by two very black stallions pulled up outside the house. Barry announced that they would be ready to leave in fifteen minutes or so when the flowers had been loaded onto the hearse. The house immediately began to empty as the rest of the Bullocks made their way to the church for the funeral service. Barry and his uncle Dickie were to be the chief pallbearers. In the middle was cousin Dave and Markey followed by Uncle Ted and Uncle Vinny at the rear. Georgina had her reservations about Markey being a pallbearer and said it was a recipe for disaster as he was bound to cock it up. She had a terrible vision of Markey dropping the coffin and her mum landing on the floor. Barry told her it was Mark's rightful place whether she liked it or not so shut the fuck up. There was a sharp knock on the door, "Oh well," said Edie. "This is it then, it must be the undertaker letting us know it's time to go."

Ted got up from his chair and went to open the front door, he stepped back hastily as the arrival flew down the hall like a white tornado. Everyone was more than surprised to see Veronica had made it to Sadie's funeral after all; they were even more surprised at the way she was dressed in her exquisite brown fur coat, red shoes and matching handbag. The hat on her head had more feathers on it than Markey's chickens.

"Nice to see you made it, Veronica," said Barry "although I thought you might have been more suitably dressed for your own mother's funeral." Veronica's mouth dropped open. "Come on, Ronnie, it's not like you to be speechless," spat Barry.

"What you talking about, I come to tell Mum me good news."

"Well I can't fault your timing I'll say that for you," continued Barry in his sarcastic manner. "Who do you think all that outside the front door is for, you stupid bitch." At that moment the undertaker poked his head round the door and said it was time to go.

"Well there's no time to change your clothes now," said Edie. "For Christ's sake lets go and bury your mother with a little pride and dignity, your poor father will be turning in his own grave at such a display."

The mention of his father's name on today of all days made Barry's blood boil; he stormed out of the house and got into the front seat of the first black limousine. The rest of the family followed and the cars pulled off to make their way to the little church and Sadie's final resting place next to Frank.

The little church was heaving with people and the scent of the hundreds of flowers filled the air. Father O'Malley stood up to conduct the service. Barry was a little worried about this new priest, he only looked about the same age as himself and wondered if he had, had enough practice at funeral services. He would have much preferred old Father Flanagan conducting the service but he had suffered a stroke a few months earlier and it had affected his speech. Geraldine stood up and said a few words, how Sadie was a devoted mother and selflessly strived to look after her family when her husband tragically died. Geraldine broke down as she tried to continue and had to be helped back to her seat. Father O'Malley took over and said prayers; he conducted the readings, homily and eulogies. When he had finished he nodded to the pallbearers that it was time to take Sadie to her resting place beside her husband. Veronica slipped quietly from the pew. Georgina gave her a steely look but not a word was said. Veronica had one last thing she wanted to do for her mum. She felt guilty about all the worry she had given Sadie, the times she disappeared down to the jazz club where she played with Solly and the band. She crept up to where the organist was playing and whispered in her ear. Father O'Malley took his place in front of the coffin ready to lead the procession. Right, thought Ronnie, it's now or never, she hoped to God she hadn't forgotten how to play the church organ, after all she hadn't played since she was a girl and Father Flanagan had been their priest.

Ronnie hit the keys and played this especially for her mum and with each note the tears streamed down her face as she played *We'll meet again.*

Ronnie needn't have worried because she played beautifully and by the time she had gotten to the end of the first line the whole church was singing along saying goodbye to Sadie.

Sadie was laid to rest and the whole Bullock clan went back to the little terraced house and the wake began. Edie said it was the only time everyone got together either a christening, wedding or a funeral; she supposed it would be her turn next. Dot told her to shut up being so bloody doom and gloom and that it was just as likely to be her or Dickie's turn. Irene and little Frank found their conversation slightly amusing and said it must be the drink talking. Little Frank was now nearly six foot tall and everyone said how he was the spitting image of his uncle Frank. Barry and Ronnie sat in the back yard smoking their cigarettes and reminiscing about their childhood, Ronnie was still wrapped in her fur coat. Her hat had somehow ended up amongst Markey's chickens and blended in with no trouble. The hens thought it was a new rooster and were each showing out to it as a potential mate. All the anger Barry had felt before they had left for the church that day had disappeared and they were talking and laughing together.

"So what brought you back then, sis? If you had no idea mum had died?"

"I came to tell her me and Solly had tied the knot and he had made an honest woman of me. Thought it would please her and she would forgive me for all the grief I had given her over the years. Still, she'll never know now will she?" Ronnie felt a lump rise in her throat.

"So where is the big guy then?" asked Barry.

"He wanted to come with me but I wanted to see mum alone first, just to prepare her like, you know, what with him being Jewish and all.

"Ronnie, just because we were brought up catholic like Dad, Mum never forgot her own Jewish upbringing. She did what she did to please Gran; I don't think she would have had a problem with it. Tell him from me he's now an honorary Bullock."

Ronnie kissed Barry on the cheek, "Thanks little brother; that means a lot."

Barry saw Ronnie shudder. "Come on let's go inside it's getting chilly, we could both do with another drink and I'm sure that lot in there are about to lift the piano lid, you had better go and rescue us from aunt Joyce's terrible playing … Oh too late," said Barry as the heard Joyce playing the first few keys of 'Maybe it's Because I'm a Londoner'. They both laughed and went to join the wake.

Barry woke up the next morning with a terrible thumping head and a tongue that had grown a layer of fur. His body was stiff from spending the night on the sofa and his limbs were heavy as he tried to move them. The house was quiet but Barry couldn't remember much about anyone leaving. He struggled to stand up kicking over an empty beer bottle in the process. He needed a pee and made his way to the back yard. He opened the toilet door and heaved at the smell. Christ it must have been a good night for the lavatory to smell that bad. He pushed the door shut and relieved himself on the only flowerbed in the yard instead.

He came back inside just as Georgie was putting the kettle on. She looked around the room at the mess. "It's gonna take me all morning to clear this lot up you know."

"If I were you," said Barry, "you had better chuck a bucket of disinfectant in the toilet it fucking stinks to high heaven."

They both fell silent, "You know there are things we need to discuss and sort out don't you, Barry," said Georgie. "For one thing who's going to look after Markey now mum's gone?"

"I can look after myself," said Mark as he came through the kitchen door.

Barry pretended to wrestle with him, "Course you can champ, course you can."

Georgie gave Barry a steely look. "I've told Ronnie and Geraldine to meet back here tonight at six clock to discuss things and I suggest you do the same."

Here she goes again thought Barry talking to him like he were a child. He took a swig of his tea from the cup. "Ok," he said as he made his way to the front door, "see you later." Barry had to go down to the office at the docks to check up on business but first he had to go home for a wash and a shave, he had a busy day ahead of him. On his way to his flat he kept thinking about what Georgie had said and in truth he wasn't sure how to solve the problem of Markey. As much as it pained Barry he may have to do the one thing Sadie had strived to avoid and put him into an institution. Maybe Geraldine could make some enquires through the council for suitable places. Even as he was thinking these thoughts he was apologising to his mother in his head.

Barry had some black market goods coming down from Liverpool and was eager to get the stuff sold on. He had a shipment of tobacco coming in from Spain with the possibility of some alcohol as well. Business was doing well but even Barry listened to the newsreel reports and could see the war was coming to an end. He had to look to the future; no one was going to accuse him of letting the grass grow under his feet. It was time to change direction and with Geraldine's help he was going to rebuild London and make himself a packet.

The day sped by and before he knew it, it was five thirty. I suppose I'd better get a move on and get over to mother's he thought before Georgie gave him another bollocking. Even at the thought of Sadie's name the wave of sadness swept over him. Still, it was early days and as everyone kept telling him with time it will get easier. God he hoped they had some food on the go he was starving.

Barry pushed open the front door to the delicious smell of cooking. They were all sitting round the kitchen table and his aunt Edie was dishing up a lovely Sheppard's pie. Edie looked up, "Grab yourself a seat and sit down before this lot gets cold, first we eat, then we talk." Barry sat down at the table and a feeling of warmth engulfed him. For one brief moment he felt that he had been transported back to his childhood where the innocence of youth prevailed and all was right with the world and he smiled.

They finished their meal and Edie cleared away the plates, stacking them on the draining board ready for washing. "Well then," began Edie, "it's time to get on with what we are gathered here for, to decide what is to happen to Mark now that Sadie's gone. Has anyone got any suggestions?" she asked. The room suddenly fell silent and they all seemed to be looking everywhere but at Edie.

Geraldine was the first to speak, "Well I've been checking out a couple of homes like Barry asked me to. There's one out at Epping that looks OK."

"So, that's the answer is it," scowled Edie. "Let's put Markey in a home, out of the way so that none of your little lives are interrupted? What about you looking after him yourself?" asked Edie.

"I can't do that," she quickly replied.

"Why, is your precious career more important to you than your own brother?"

"it's not that at all, Eric is running for Mayor at the next elections and if he is elected as the Mayor's wife I will have to entertain and all sorts."

"What do you mean as the mayor's wife? You're not bloody married."

Geraldine became quite indignant "Eric has proposed and I have accepted, in a few months' time I will be Mrs Eric Baptist. Edie turned her glare to Veronica.

Ronnie stared straight back at her, "Don't look at me," she said, "my life is playing with the band and a life on the road is no place for Markey, we're not always in one place and we've got a tour lined up for a few months' time already.

Barry held up his hands, "Auntie Edie I would love to take care of our Markey, but come on now be honest, do you really think I am the best person for the job? After all who would put the bread on the table and pay the bills here?"

Edie turned to Georgina, "What did I tell you, Georgie, just as I predicted each and every one of them." Edie sat herself down and placed her hands on the table. "Well then let me tell you all what's going to happen. I'm not getting any younger—" mouths started to open and she raised her hand to silence them. "Let me finish," she said. "I am going to give up my job at the Mother's clinic, Georgina is going to come back home as well and together we will care for Markey and start promoting contraception for the women of the East End right on our own doorstep."

"Well," said Barry with a genuine hint of relief in his voice "Auntie Edie that's the best idea I have ever heard," and at that statement they all joined in with enthusiasm and enormous relief.

"That's nice," came a voice from the corner. They had all forgotten Markey had been sitting in the corner polishing his new shoes and listening to his family discuss how each one of them couldn't look after him. He stood up and took the bowl of left over Sheppard's pie out into the back yard to feed his chickens.

Veronica and Geraldine stood up and said they had best be off as it was getting late. Barry said if they wanted he would give them a lift in his car. "OK, that's great," said Geraldine "it will give me a chance to tell you about this nice little property that is coming up for sale, it's a bit bomb damaged but the site would be fantastic for that little club you were talking about starting up and you could get it for almost next to nothing with my help."

Edie and Georgina moved back to the little terraced house to take care of Mark and life seemed to settle into what you would call normality. It wasn't as easy as the women had expected to launch their new contraceptive clinic. Georgina had tried to secure premises but found herself hitting brick walls. It seemed it was still a taboo subject and the local council feared it would cost them precious votes to give the scheme their backing. Still, they were determined not to give up hope. As proud as they were, there seemed no other alternative but to see if Geraldine could pull a few strings. Geraldine blatantly refused to have anything to do with it all. She said that it could affect Eric's chances at becoming mayor if anyone got wind of it. Edie became very annoyed. "Oh it's OK to do back-handed deals with property developers for our Barry but you can't give us a helping hand for something as important as women's health and to bring the likes of us out of poverty." Edie was fuming, "All you're interested in, miss high and mighty, is yourself. You can poke your help, me and Georgie will do just fine on our own and we won't have to thank you for anything." With that she stormed off wondering just what the hell she was going to do. Maybe she should just give up on the whole idea, but it was her life's work to educate women that it was not necessary to have a baby every year. Georgie was sorry that Edie had argued with Geraldine and did not know how to heal the rift.

Days turned into weeks and Geraldine did not come to visit like she normally did. It seemed the line was drawn and a crack had appeared in the unity of the

Bullock family. Barry said they both needed their heads examined and were both being fucking stupid but he was far too busy with his own affairs to be bothered with their petty quarrels.

Barry made a couple of official trips to the town hall to check out possible club locations. What had started as just a distant idea was beginning to consume his entire waking thoughts. Barry had big ideas and he had a stark realisation that he didn't have nearly enough cash to make the dreams a reality. Geraldine suggested he look for potential investors. Who the fuck did she think would give him any money. Honestly sometimes that girl talked out the hole in her arse. No, he was going to have to think of a way to make some big bucks or he would miss the boat.

Try as he might Barry knew the only way to make money on the quick was to deal in the illegal substances that were being bought and sold from the incoming ships. The boats that came in from places like South America or Africa often carried opium and heroin but these sources were mainly linked with gangs on the other side of the river. If you were wise you didn't get caught up in that world, the dealers were hard and ruthless bastards. They would sell their own grannies up the river for a shilling. Still he would put some feelers out and see what fell into his lap. He would have a word with Clint, he had eyes and ears everywhere, see what he could come up with.

Barry could feel one of his headache coming on as he shaved and washed. He grabbed the aspirin bottle and poured himself a glass of water from the kitchen sink. The pipes began to rattle as the tap ran and he filled the glass. He didn't want his mood sinking tonight; he had arranged a meeting with Clint and his cousin Lorry in the King's Head. He was hoping that after their little chat they would have some good news for him. He needed a clear head; there was no room for error if they were branching out the business to pastures new. They would have to keep their eye on the ball and not upset any one by treading on their toes. If things went to plan they would dip their toe in the water for a few months, just to get a little bit of extra cash, then pull out. No one need know and no one would get hurt. He would layer the chain of selling so that it couldn't be traced back to himself. Small amounts over a wide area should be the safest bet.

Chapter 6

Clint

Clint arrived at the King's Head public house, he looked at his wristwatch, he was early, the place was pretty empty but that suited them as they didn't want anyone overhearing their business. Clint sat there mulling over the past as he often did. Thinking of his mother and his early childhood in France. There had just been the two of them. He had asked his mother about his father with a natural curiosity of a growing boy. She had told him stories of how he should be proud of his father who had been a soldier and had fought bravely to liberate France from the German occupation. She told him he was a British soldier and at the end of the war he had been sent back to England. He promised he would send for her, but first he had a few things to sort out to prepare for her arrival. She waited in vain for his letter and when she discovered she was to have a child she had no alternative but to turn to her parents for support. His mother had tried to trace his father for a while but did not have any luck so she decided that it wasn't meant to be and consoled herself to a life with just her and Clint. They lived in a small village with his grandparents and he had nothing but good memories of his childhood. He later learned from his mother that she had told her parents a small lie so as not to embarrass them. She told them that she had met and fallen in love with a soldier, they had married quickly before he left for the front and that he had been killed in action. It was so easy to lie in those times. Places were bombed and documents were lost. If his grandparents had any suspicions they never said. When his grandparents passed away Clint and his mother carried on living in the house and life went on. It wasn't until his mother died and he was clearing out her belongings that he found a name and address on an old faded piece of paper amongst her private papers. There was even a photograph of her in her nurse's uniform standing between two soldiers. He wondered if one of these could be his father. It was an English name and address on the back of the photograph. Clint felt that his mother had known all along where to find his father but had kept this from him. He could only guess that he had been married and would never have left his English family for his mother. So with no ties to hold him in France he decided to make his way across the channel to see if he could trace his English family. Clint was fluent in English with just a trace of a French accent when speaking it. With just the few possessions he could carry he set out on his journey to England. He arrived on British soil and caught the train to London not knowing what to expect, only that he thought it would probably be a little like Paris. By the time Clint arrived at Charing Cross station he was exhausted. He asked the guard if he knew of any where he could stay, and as luck had it he directed Clint to a local YMCA. The room was small and stark but adequate for his needs. It had a bed, a washbasin and a chair. The bathroom and toilet facilities had to be shared with the rest of the rooms on each floor. The most important thing was that it was cheap, because until Clint found a job he had to be careful with his money. He had no idea how long it would have to last him. His intention was to move on the next day but instead he stayed a couple of weeks in the hostel exploring the local area. There was a considerable amount of bomb damage, far more than Paris. He took quite a few tram rides up to the West End. He loved the hub and the atmosphere and felt like he belonged there. There were many nationalities in the centre of London and this made Clint feel less of a foreigner. Still the time came to pack up his little holdall and make his way to the address in East London in search of his family. Clint couldn't describe his disappointment when he discovered the house and the family that had once lived there had since moved on. There had been a fire and the man he hoped was to be his father had died. Still, he was here now so he may as well find out what happened to the dead man's family, after all he could have brothers and sisters. Curiosity had got a hold of him and he wouldn't be satisfied until every stone had been unturned. He made his way to a little newsagents he had passed earlier to see if there were any ads for a room for rent. The newsagent eyed Clint up and down. "You can try the couple of places that are advertised, mate, maybe one of them will be desperate enough to take in a foreigner "Clint didn't think of himself as a foreigner. Somehow he thought he would automatically be accepted as he spoke the language. Right he thought to himself, as he made his way to the address the newsagent had scribbled on a piece of paper for him, I've got to ditch the accent. Clint stood outside the door of the little terraced house. It looked like it hadn't seen a coat of paint in years. He took a deep breath and banged on the door. He saw the curtain pull back just a little and someone peeping out eyeing him up and down. A short stocky woman opened the door. She had curlers in her hair covered by a string hair net.

"What can I do fer yer?" she asked.

"I've come about the room," Clint enquired.

"Where yer from?" the woman wanted to know. Eyeing him suspiciously.

"I've been living in France for a while, I have even picked up a bit of an accent," he said trying to blag his way along.

"Me ole man fought out there during the first war," she sniffed. "Now me sons are off to fight in this bleedin' one."

"'Ow are we supposed to manage? I ask yer?"

Clint thought he had better get a word in quick before she sent him packing. "I can pay three months' rent up front if that's OK."

At the thought of all that money the room was his. "No funny business though. No women back ere either. I will have to 'ave the three months up front now, then each month in advance, is that understood? Or yer be out on yer ear."

Clint handed over the money and he was shown to his new room. The wallpaper had seen better days and the woodwork was painted brown, the rug on the floor was threadbare. You could see it was pretty poor but to give the woman her due it was clean. For a couple of extra schillings a week the old dear offered to do Clint an evening meal and a bit of tea and toast in the morning before he set off job hunting. With the local men going off to fight he found it exceptionally easy to find casual work. He was well built so could do a bit of manual work, the pay was cash in hand and if any one started to ask questions he would just move on. Clint felt invisible, no questions, no taxes, it was as if he didn't exist. Sometimes in the evening he would sit and chat to the old couple, Percy would smoke his pipe and reminisce telling stories of his time on the Somme. How they had spent their time in water-drenched ditches, the sound of cannon fire ringing in their ears and the sight of the dead corpses lying where they fell, rotting because it was too dangerous to go and get some of them. The blue bottles laying their eggs on the decaying flesh. There were young men, barely boys, crying with fear, calling out for their mothers as they knew certain death was near. He even saw them shoot some for cowardice. Percy would shake his head and his eyes would become glazed as he remembered the terrible times he had endured. Percy said he was one of the lucky ones getting injured and ending up in the military hospital in Flanders. He stopped talking and his mind wandered back to the pretty French nurse who had looked after him and how one night when he had a nightmare she pulled round the screens and laid on the bed next to him. How she comforted him and allowed him to make love to her in the quiet of the night. What was her name now Claudette? Yvette? Ah well no matter it was a long time ago now. "Funny thing was I ended up in a bed next to a chap who lived a few streets from here." Percy closed his eyes and drifted off to sleep. Clint would smoke a roll up while Percy's wife pottered in and out the kitchen washing the dishes and making tea. He even got up courage to ask them about the fire at the Bullock house.

"Oh that was years ago ducks," said Lizzie. "The silly old sod burnt himself to death, he'd had a skinful in the pub and dropped his fag on the sofa, set fire to the place. Suppose it was lucky no one else was in the house at the time. His muvver took the family in, it was good of 'er as there were a lot of them, Five kids and the muvver. There was already 'er and her daughter, not sure if she had her son and his wife there as well.

"Still what else was she supposed to do? She was a good sort was Maud Bullock, didn't know her too well but you could tell she was the salt of the earth.

"They only live five minutes from here, some of them are still there as far as I know, d'yer know 'em then?" she asked.

"No," said Clint. "But my mother was a nurse in France during the last war and she met the man Frank Bullock, thought I might look them up."

"Well Ducks, you'll need a medium to talk to him, but his wife Sadie might be able to 'elp yer." Clint's heart began to race, he couldn't believe the people he had been looking for were right there on his door step. It's a funny thing," she continued. "It was the silly old sod who burnt the house down who was in the military hospital with our Percy, small world ain't it."

Clint couldn't believe his luck; all this was right here on his doorstep and within his grasp. Should he just go up to the Bullock house and knock on the door and say your husband was my father. No he couldn't bring himself to do that. The shock might be too much, anyway why should any of the Bullocks believe him. Maybe he could just hang around and watch them, maybe try and get to know one of them, a friend like. Just bide his time.

He made it his business to find out as much as he could. He discovered there were three girls, a boy who seemed a wild kid and a boy who most would considered not quite right. He weighed up the situation and after deciding he didn't want to go courting to get in with the Bullocks he would make a play for befriending the boy Barry. He watched him for a while and thought the kid had a lot of bravado. He discovered him running for a local bookie and made a point of putting on a bet and being friendly to the kid. His lip curved into a smile when he thought this was probably his brother. They soon got on first name terms. Clint actually admired the little fucker who seemed to be developing big ideas of his own and was becoming a bit of a name in the local area. Clint made it his business to keep a close eye on Barry Bullock. He would shadow him and at the hint of trouble he would be there to help bail him out. It wasn't too long before they became a pair ducking and diving around the local area. Clint soon got the reputation of being Barry's minder and right hand man. Barry trusted him and as the Bullock empire grew Clint was at the top of the pecking order.

Chapter 7

Barry, Clint and Lorry took their pints of beer to a quiet table in the corner of the saloon bar in the King's Head. They didn't want any nosy buggers overhearing their discussion.

"Well, Lorry," asked Barry, "how did you get on down at the docks about the you-know-what?"

"It wasn't easy, Cousin. But I think I can get us a little bit of what you asked for."

"Good," said Barry "how much money does he want?"

"WHAT..." shouted Barry a little too loudly "is he taking the fucking piss?"

"Listen, mate," said Lorry trying to calm Barry down. "Had to offer him a little bit more than our brothers across the river was paying or it would have been a no go, the way I see it is we take it or leave it." Barry rocked back and forth on his chair for a while. Everyone knew the war was coming to an end and he needed to make some big money fast. The bombed damaged land was ripe for the taking at a cheap price. He wanted to get his hands on as much as he could and with Geraldine in the know he could start to rebuild London single-handed. After all he was doing a service to King and Country and most important lining the pockets of Barry Bullock.

"OK then let's do it," he said. "Clint, you go with Lorry and do the deal. If you need Dave let him know."

So with business concluded and Barry in high spirits he turned his thoughts to the rest of the evening. Barry sat in the bar finishing his pint of beer feeling much better than he had in a long while, in fact he felt like celebrating and just at that very moment who should come through the pub doors but his cousin Irene with her two mates Pat Fuller and Vera Murphy, now who better to celebrate with than three beautiful girls. Irene spotted Barry sitting in the corner, "Hi, Baz, all alone tonight?"

"Not now I'm not" he grinned, "let me buy you beautiful ladies a drink, port and lemons if I remember rightly." They all had a few drinks in the King's Head and decided that it was time to move on up west to dance the rest of the night away. The girls went to spend a penny while Barry made his way outside to hail a taxi. The girls came out of the pub giggling and laughing just as the cab pulled up. They piled inside and Barry pulled down the window of the Taxi. "Paramount Dance Hall, Tottenham Court Road, mate." Then off they all went.

The dance hall was heaving when they arrived, there were soldiers, RAF both English and American. The atmosphere was amazing they were dancing to all the greatest music, Glenn Miller, The Andrew Sisters and Louis Jordan. The girls had no trouble finding dance partners so Barry headed straight to the bar to get the drinks in.

"What's a nice boy like you doing in a bar like this" came a voice.

Barry turned round, "What the fuck are you doing here?" he asked surprised to be face to face with his sister Veronica.

"Oh me, Solly and the band are playing here tonight."

"Well I've definitely gotta stick around to see that if nothing else," teased Barry. He noticed the dark rings around his sister's eyes. He grinned his wonderful Barry grin at her to mask his concerns. "Joking aside Ronnie, haven't seen you for a while, are you OK?"

"Sure," she replied, "having a ball, the music is good, the money's flowing in, but living in hotel rooms up and down the country takes its toll. Solly said America's the place to be, all the best Jazz is there. He's after getting us out there as soon as he can fix it." Barry felt a bit put out when he heard this. "Oh, when was you planning on letting the family know your plans? Or was you just gonna send us a postcard from the states?" Ronnie shrugged her shoulders and climbed down from the bar stool, she leaned across and kissed him on the cheek.

"Gotta go now, were on in ten minutes, I promise I'll send you a postcard from every grubby little town we play in, little brother" and she waved her hand in the air as she walked away.

Barry went to find the girls, they saw Ronnie and the band play and they all danced to rag time until the small hours. It was almost 3 a.m. when the four of them stumbled out of the dance hall onto the pavement. Barry hailed a taxi and they all made their way back to the East End. They pulled up outside his cousin's house first. Irene put her finger to her lips

"Shhhhh," she said, "mustn't wake up the olds."

Barry helped her open the front door and watched her stumble inside. Someone's gonna have a sore head in the morning he thought as he quietly closed the door behind her. Barry got back inside the cab. "OK, Vera you're next," and he gave the driver the address. Vera began to fumble in her handbag for her key.

"I can't find me door key," she said in a slightly slurred voice.

"For Christ's sake, Vera," said Barry as he grabbed her bag and tipped it out on the seat of the cab. "There's no fucking key here, Vera. You're gonna have to knock at the door." Vera and Barry got out of the car and he went to lift the knocker. "No, no," cried Vera in a loud whisper. She bent down and found a stone in the gutter. She threw it at the upstairs window, no one came. She threw another stone, the curtain flew back and the sash window went up.

"Who the bloody hell's making all that racket?" came a voice.

"Maggie, Maggie is that you? Come down and let me in I've lost me key."

"Hold on a minute will you, and keep the bloody noise down." Vera's sister Maggie opened the front door.

"Oh my God," she said, "look at the state of you." Maggie looked directly at Barry "I suppose this is all your fault," she snapped.

"Don't blame me, princess your sister's a big girl."

Barry couldn't take his eyes off Maggie. The last time he'd seen her she had been just a child, now she was a beautiful young woman, His mind went into overdrive trying to think of a way to get to know her better and take her out for a drink or dancing. Perhaps he could have a word with Irene and see if she could arrange it.

Barry stood there long after the door closed. The taxi window came down and a voice said, "Are we going or what, mate?" Barry had almost forgot that Pat was still in the cab. Barry climbed back inside and Pat snuggled up to him. The next address he gave the driver was his own.

Barry had to admit that he had never fancied Pat Fuller much in the past, but since changing her hair to blonde she had developed quite a sex appeal. He'd seen some pictures in a magazine of some young American model when he was in the dockside office. Brenda was always thumbing through a new magazine she acquired from her American soldier friends. Women were certainly changing their looks since the Yanks arrived, maybe they weren't all bad after all.

They arrived at Barry's flat and he helped Pat out of the taxi, she gave him a huge smile and didn't put up any argument as he led her into his flat. Barry flicked on the light switch, the 40-watt bulb didn't give out much light which was just as well as he wasn't that big on housework. The room was cold, "Fancy a night cap?" asked Barry.

Pat shivered, "Tea would be nice if that's OK?" Barry grabbed the kettle and began to fill it with water from the tap. He struck a match and lit the gas stove. "Where's the bathroom?" asked Pat "I need a pee." By the time Pat returned Barry had made two cups of steaming hot tea. The top button of Pat's blouse was undone revealing the crevice of her breasts. Barry had to admit to himself he had bedded better-looking women and his thoughts turned to Grace Greene. But right now he was as horny as hell and Pat looked like the best thing since sliced bread. Barry pulled Pat closer to him and finished unbuttoning her blouse letting it fall to the floor. He kissed the top of her heaving bosom as he unfastened her bra. He continued to suck at her nipples as he undressed her and she was standing naked in front of him. She made no attempt to stop him as he led her to his bed and she laid down. Pat watched Barry as he removed his own clothing and she could see how much he desired her. Barry continued to kiss and fondle Pat and she continued to respond. He reached across to his bedside table and began to search for a rubber. Thank God for Auntie Edie and her contraceptives. Barry lowered himself on top of Pat and momentarily wondered if she was a virgin. Still judging by her response he quickly dismissed it and was soon lost in the pleasure of her body.

Barry opened his eyes to the sound of the milk float coming down the road. Good it was early, he had plenty of time to get ready for the meeting with Geraldine and the council bods. All he had to do today was hand over the deposit and sign on the dotted line. Everyone knew the war was almost over, he would just bide his time until that day and then the rebuilding programme would get underway. It was good as money in the bank. By the time they needed the rest of the money his little illegal business activity would have provided the balance and he could get out before anyone turned nasty. Pat was still fast asleep, he wondered if she would still be there when he came back, perhaps she would give the place a tidy up before she went.

Barry arrived at the council office at ten o'clock. He parked his car in the space marked Geraldine Baptist, which he knew would piss her off when she arrived and had to use the public car park. Geraldine's wedding to the soppy Eric had been quite a lavish affair. There had been a lot of council people on the guest list and Eric's family had all been invited. Geraldine was a bit of a snob and omitted to send out invitations to any of the Bullocks except himself. She excused herself by saying that since Sadie's funeral day none of them had spoken. Barry told her it would have been the ideal opportunity to heal the rift, but she chose to ignore his advice. Geraldine said the family were more likely to have a punch up and there was no way on this earth she was going to risk that happening.

Barry continued to make his way to the main entrance, he nodded to concierge on the reception desk.

"Good morning, Mr Bullock, Mrs Baptist sends her apologise, she will be about half an hour late, she said go on up to her office and help yourself to a coffee."

"OK thanks," said Barry and he made his way to Geraldine's office. He was slightly irritated that she was keeping him waiting. When would she realise that the whole world didn't revolve around her. She spent too much time looking in the mirror every morning. Barry smiled to himself. It couldn't have been the boring little shit, Eric, wanting a leg over before she left that had delayed her. By the time Geraldine fell through the door breathless and flustered another two council officials had arrived at her office to join them, politely introducing themselves and helping themselves to coffee. Barry immediately got out of the chair, walked over to Geraldine giving her a hug. At the same time whispering in her ear, "What kept you little Sis? A quick shag with the enigmatic Eric?" Geraldine's face turned scarlet and she fumbled for words trying to make her apologises. Barry was a great believer that everything happens for a reason. While he was waiting for his sister he flicked through the file lying on her desk. He didn't feel in the least bit guilty, after all if it was confidential it wouldn't be lying there for all and sundry to see. He was gobsmacked when he read its contents. Some other bidder had offered a higher price. Geraldine had said their arrangement was signed and sealed, it was a done deal. What was she playing at? Geraldine sat down at her desk and tried to regain her composure.

"Good morning, gentlemen," she began. "Firstly I would like to say how sorry I am for keeping you all waiting. It seems we have two tenders for the same plot of land and I have had to seek instruction from my superior." She looked at Barry with an apologetic face. "Both parties have put forward some extremely good development proposals, both in cost, environmental and improvement to the social life of the East End residents. There will be open grassed spaces, primarily play areas for children and much needed sanitation improvements. Each dwelling will have its own bath and toilet facility. There would be modern electric heating, thus complying with the cleaner air proposals. So gentlemen what does it come down to? Quite frankly the council needs to raise funds for projects of its own so in a nutshell as both parties are offering parallel proposals the land must go to the highest bidder."

Barry thought that if Geraldine didn't stop waffling on he was going to strangle her. He had seen the file and the other prats had put in a higher bid. He was definitely going to smack his sister.

"So, gentlemen," she continued the higher bidder by a small margin is Bullock Enterprises."

Hands were shaken, congratulations and commiserations were exchanged and the losers left the room disappointed. Barry let out a long sigh, "Thought we'd blown it there, Gerry."

"I saw the file, they outbid me by 10percent."

Geraldine looked at him through narrowed eyes. "That'll teach you for snooping, Barry Bullock," she said. "I've laid a lot on the line for you here, you had better not let me down. By the way you had better get a new offer on my desk quick smart with an increase of ten percent."

"Where the fuck am I gonna get that from?" moaned Barry. Geraldine looked at her brother in dismay. "I thought that thanks would have been coming my way, I could have let them have it you know."

"Sorry, Sis. I am grateful really I am, but don't forget the back hander you'll get out of it." Geraldine chose to cock a deaf ear.

"Oh and, Barry, don't forget to send your tender in on the new logo headed paper, you're officially Bullock Enterprises now so don't let me down."

Barry walked out of the council offices into the warm summer sunshine. He wasn't sure if he had just won or lost a battle, all he knew was that he had to lay his hands on some more money and pretty fast. He pulled his car keys from his pocket and opened the door. There was a rough scribbled note tucked under his windscreen wiper it read. 'NEXT TIME YOU PARK IN MY SPACE MISTER I'LL LET YOUR FUCKING TYRES DOWN.' Barry laughed, he was glad Geraldine hadn't got too far up her own arse to have a good swear.

Barry headed for the dockside offices for his meeting with Clint and Lorry. They were none too pleased with Barry wanting them to up the ante with the drug consignments. Clint said there was no trouble getting rid of the gear but if the boys across the river got wind of it there might be hell to pay and they were ruthless bastards.

"You worry too much, Clint, a couple of months and we drop it altogether."

Clint stood up to go, "Come on, Lorry, you heard the boss, we've got work to do."

"Right then, Brenda, I've got a little job for you," said Barry "I want proper headed paper, everything that goes out of this office from now on will officially be from Bullock Enterprises, oh and register it at company's house, were going legit." Barry was feeling in a good mood, he even remembered the antics of the previous evening with fondness. "Oh Brenda, get some flowers sent to Pat Fuller's house for me will you, I'm not sure of her address, but our Irene will know it."

Summer turned into autumn and autumn into winter. Business was ticking over and the cash fund was growing nicely. Barry almost had enough money to complete the deal on the land purchase. The completion date was drawing near and Geraldine had been hounding him for the past week for the balance of the money. He couldn't wait to get it all finalised himself and he could get her off his back.

Geraldine didn't come to the house any more, not since the family argued about who was going to take care of Markey when his mother died. Sometimes Barry would meet her in the local greasy spoon or the King's Head but neither of these suited miss-high and mighty very much. Barry found it strangely amusing the way she wore a head scarf and dark glasses as a disguise. They continued to do their deals, Barry buying up the land ready for the rebuilding to begin just as soon as the

Nazi's were kicked into touch. Geraldine had telephoned his office and Brenda had taken a message, she had told Brenda to make sure Barry was in the King's Head at seven o'clock this evening and make sure he knows it's important. Brenda was as good as her word and Barry was there bang on time. He walked into the King's Head dead on seven o'clock and Geraldine walked in five minutes later in one of her disguises. Barry thought she reminded him of Audrey Hepburn in a scene from an American movie "We've got to finalise the deal before the Christmas break otherwise the council could withdraw its offer," she implored.

"For fuck's sake, Geraldine," said Barry. "You've got to stall the bastards, I've almost got the money, I've not come this far to see it all go tits up."

"I'm just telling you how it is, you just be in my office no later than 23rd December or I can't be held responsible."

"OK, OK, I'll have the money."

Geraldine stood up to leave, she hesitated for a moment. "How is everyone?" she asked.

"Like you're interested," came his reply.

"Please, Barry, don't be like that, of course I care about them, I just can't be there like they want me to be. I bet they don't give Ronnie such a hard time."

Barry hesitated for a moment before he replied. "Ronnie only cares about one person and that's herself, the last time I saw her she was talking about going to America, I doubt if she'll even let us know she's gone."

Geraldine straightened her coat and made sure her head scarf was firmly in place. "Give my love to Markey for me will you?"

"Why don't you stop by and give it to him yourself, he'd like that."

Geraldine gave out a little sigh, "We'll see, we'll see," she said and with that she left. Barry sat there for a while mulling over what to do about the money and how to make the completion date, whatever happened he had to get his hands on it somehow. He promised himself that all the stuff with the drugs would stop. Each deal was going to be the last, but each time another golden opportunity would come along that he couldn't pass up and it was easy money.

"Penny for your thoughts," came a voice.

Barry looked up, "Bloody hell, Clint, you must be psychic, you're just the man I want to see."

"No, Barry, definitely no, you must be bloody mad and I'd be just as mad if I went along with it."

"Clint, I'm desperate, mate, I promise this is the last time and we'll have enough money for the land, by Christmas we'll be home and dry."

Clint looked at Barry shaking his head in despair. "OK, but this is the last time, if they come looking for us from across the river we're dead meat. I'll go down to the docks Friday when the ship should be in, leave the readies with Brenda, don't come looking for me for a few days I'll be off the radar while I get rid of the stuff."

"As good as done," said Barry who was sufficiently pleased with the way things had turned out. "If you and Dave need any extra help take Lorry with you he hasn't got much on and I'm not too pleased paying him for sitting around the office on his arse doing nothing all day." Clint didn't answer he just got up and walked out of the pub. You know what, thought Barry to himself, that bloke is getting too big for his own boots I'm gonna have to take him down a peg or two.

Just at that moment he heard the familiar voices of Renne and her mates from the other side of the bar. "Girls, were gonna have to stop meeting like this, what are we doing tonight then?"

"Don't know about you, Barry, but were going to the pictures," said Irene. Barry looked straight at Pat and caught her eye, her face went red as she blushed. He guessed she was remembering their night of passion just as he was. Tonight she looked hot in her pencil skirt and tight fitting jumper. He walked over to Pat and whispered in her ear.

"How about ditching these two, I know a nice little place where we could get a meal and a bottle of wine?" Pat looked at him with a guarded expression.

"I've already eaten, thanks all the same. Playing hard to get is she thought Barry, what else could he tempt her with so he could get in her knickers before the night was over. Barry slid his arm around her waist; he moved close and whispered in her ear again.

"I know a nice little place down by the riverside; we can grab a few drinks and a little gambling. You can be my lucky charm tonight." He brushed the side of her cheek with his lips. Pat knew she would not be able to resist, she also knew that before the night was over she would be in his bed again. He was handsome, confident and smelt gorgeous with his Gucci aftershave, what girl in her right mind would turn him down.

"Listen girls," said Pat "I think I'll give the pictures a miss tonight, I can feel a headache coming on."

"Oh that's a shame," said Vera "do you want us to walk you home?"

"No don't be silly you'll miss the start of the film, you two go on and have a good night, I'll be fine, the fresh air will do me good." Pat left Irene and Vera in the King's Head finishing their port and lemons, she walked down to the end of the street and turned the corner. Just at that moment a taxi pulled into the kerb and the window came down.

"Can I offer a girl a lift" came a voice. Pat opened the passenger door and jumped inside, snuggling up close to its occupant. Barry gave the driver the address and they headed off to the riverside club.

Pat seemed to be quite a hit in the club; Barry had to admit she was a sexy tart. The blonde hair suited her and she had started to wear makeup, much to Barry's surprise she even knew a couple of the Canadian fellows. For some strange reason Barry didn't like her talking to them, he thought they seemed a bit too familiar.

"Where did you meet the pricks?" he wanted to know.

Pat tried to make light of it. "Oh a little while back, me and Vera took the bus to Billet Lane in Hornchurch, we went to a dance at the army barracks, they just remembered me that's all." Pat didn't want Barry getting one of his moods on. She had heard from Irene all about her cousin Barry and his unpredictable behaviour, especially when he had been drinking. Local people like to gossip and Barry Bullock had a reputation on how he could turn nasty at the drop of a hat. Barry grabbed her hand and Pat winced at the strength of his grasp.

"Let's play the tables for a bit, see if you can bring me some luck." Barry always said that gambling was a mug's game. He had seen too many men collect their wages on a Friday night and gamble it all away by Saturday afternoon on the gee gees. But tonight, tonight he couldn't stop himself. They sat down at the roulette table, Pat crossed her legs and adjusted her skirt just enough to show off her knee. The croupier's eyes were transfixed for a moment, then he called, "Place your bets." Barry placed some of his chips on black twelve and the wheel was spun.

"Banker pays red twenty-four."

"Bollocks," said Barry. He took a five-pound note from his pocked and shoved it in Pat's hand. "Go and get us a drink baby." Barry could see a few familiar faces at the tables. He had wheeled and dealed with a few of them in his time, they caught each other's eyes and nodded in acknowledgment. Barry sat for a moment drinking in the atmosphere of the little club. One day, he thought he would open his own club. He could see it in his mind's eye. A plush bar on the ground floor and upstairs elite gambling rooms. His thoughts were interrupted as Pat returned with their drinks. He looked her up and down and decided that he would have some posh tarts as well just to entertain the men that required it. It would be a members' only establishment where behind closed doors it didn't matter who you were. Villains, lawyers, members of parliament even royalty would be welcome. He wondered if Pat would consider being one of his escorts, maybe he would ask her nearer the time, but for now they would have some fun together. Barry smiled to himself, you got to think big in this world or you'll get nowhere. He looked up at the croupier, "One hundred notes on number thirteen if you please."

The croupier was taken aback. The whole place was on CCTV cameras and he knew he was being watched. The croupier waited for confirmation that the bet would be accepted. Barry knew this was normal practice but couldn't help passing a comment, "What's wrong is my bet not good enough for you?"

The croupier ignored Barry's remark and waited in silence until he got the nod to proceed, "One hundred pounds on number thirteen, any more bets?" The wheel was spun and the ball released, everyone around the table was watching, was holding their breath in anticipation. The ball seemed to cascade around the wheel for an eternity and then came to land on number 13. Barry looked at Pat.

"What did I tell you, baby, you would bring me luck tonight." Barry stood up, "Let's grab our winnings and get out of here baby." Barry went to the kiosk and picked up his winnings. Not a bad night's work he thought as he stuffed the wad of notes in the inside pocket of his jacket. A bouncer stepped in front of them as they went to walk through the exit doors of the club.

"Leaving us so soon, Mr Bullock, just when you are on a winning streak?"

"That's the best time to leave," replied Barry, pushing the bouncer out of his way with Pat close on his heels. They stepped out on to the pavement and the cold icy wind bit at their faces. "Never a cab when you want one, come on let's walk up to the main road."

The cobbled street made it difficult for Pat to walk in her high heel shoes and she was lagging behind a dozen or so steps. Pat hoped Barry had managed to hail a cab by the time she had caught up with him. Just before Barry reached the main drag someone stepped out of the shadows and blocked the way. A hard punch knocked Barry off his feet and he felt the kicks in his ribs. The bloke was twice his size so he never stood a chance. He felt a hand in his inside pocket; a final kick in his back and the assailant was gone. Pat came staggering up to Barry shocked at what she had just witnessed, one heel of her shoe broken off. She bent down beside Barry who by this time was trying to lift himself up onto his feet. He leaned against the wall for a moment wiping the blood that was trickling down his face with his handkerchief. His ribs hurt as he tried to regain his breath and he knew he would have more than a few bruises in the morning. He felt winded but with Pat's help he was able to make it the last few yards to the main road. They felt like they waited for ages, but finally a cab came along and they knew they were safe and on their way back to Barry's flat. Pat snivelled all the way home in the back of the cab, "You OK, lady?" enquired the driver. No one answered and Barry watched the driver watching them through his rear-view mirror. They pulled up outside the flat and got out, Barry paid the driver and he drove off. Barry ached all over, "Pat get my keys out of my trouser pocket will you?" Pat fumbled around in Barry's pocket trying to get the keys out. "For fuck's sake, Pat, get the bloody keys out and stop playing pocket billiards will you." Barry choked on a laugh and his body hurt like hell. Pat finally managed to open the front door and they climbed the stairs to Barry's little flat. Barry made it to the bed and collapsed. Pat was concerned when she actually saw the state Barry was in.

"You need a doctor," she said.

"NO," replied Barry. "What I need, Gel, is a nice cup of tea, go stick the kettle on."

Pat came back with two steaming mugs of tea and sat down on the bed next to Barry. "What the hell just happened to us, Barry? We could have been murdered."

"If they had wanted us dead we wouldn't be sitting here now, no it was a warning."

"From who? Why?" asked Pat.

"Ssssssh, don't you worry your pretty little head about it, I'll sort it all out, now come over here and help me get my shirt off and rub some balm in these bruises."

Pat began to help Barry and heard a rustle of paper. Barry put his hand down the front of his underpants and pulled out a wad of money. Pat looked at him astonished. "Well you don't think I'd be that stupid to put it all in one place do you? They saw me put it in my jacket pocket so as soon as we were out of sight I shifted some."

The night hadn't turned out quite the way Barry had thought it would but he still had a wad of money on his bedside table and a girl in his bed. He leaned over to take a gulp of his tea and winced with pain from the cut in his mouth. Pat saw this, "Shall I go and leave you in peace?" she asked.

"Are you kidding," said Barry "I need a little care and attention, now take off your clothes and come and make love, just be gentle with me."

The next morning Barry was even stiffer and could hardly move, he was finding it hard to breathe and wondered if he had cracked a rib. He managed to pull himself up and slid his legs off the side of the bed. He lit a cigarette and inhaled causing the pain to engulf his chest. Pat felt Barry moving, she opened her eyes and could see the condensation running down the inside of the window. Barry was glad she was awake, he could murder a cup of tea but wasn't sure if he could make it to the kitchen.

"Be a good girl will you? Light the gas fire and stick the kettle on."

Pat did as she was told and then ran to the bathroom for a pee. She came back shivering. Barry chucked her one of his old pullovers, "Get that on and you'll feel a bit better. Pat put on the pullover and went back to make some tea, she opened the cupboard to see if there was anything to eat. The cupboard had some stale bread, a tin of spam and a couple of eggs.

"Where do you keep your frying pan?" she yelled. Barry wasn't sure he had one.

"Under the sink maybe," he yelled back. By the time Barry had managed to dress himself Pat had fried the spam, eggs and bread in the pan and made something edible for breakfast. Barry was impressed. "Quite the little housewife aren't we." Pat ignored his sarcastic comments. "You know what? This place does need a bit of a woman's touch and I can't expect you to stay here much the state it's in." He put a few notes on the table. "While I'm out see what you can do with this place." Pat was surprised that Barry was fit enough to go out at all, but going by what he had just said he was expecting her to stay there again so she didn't want to rock the boat. I guess this meant they were courting she thought.

Barry gingerly climbed into the driver's seat of his car, he had to get over to meet Clint to pick up the cash to give to Geraldine today. Tomorrow was Christmas Eve and he wanted to celebrate getting the development contract, after all this was going to fund his ultimate dream, his club. Barry pulled up outside the warehouse, he went inside and could see his cousin Dave sitting in the office.

"Where's Clint? asked Barry with an unreadable expression on his face.

"Don't know," said Dave "he just said he had to see a man about a dog."

"Has he left me the money I needed?"

"Sure it's in the safe." Sometimes Dave really annoyed Barry the way he was so laid back or was he just stupid. He seemed to do anything Clint asked without question or thinking.

"Will Clint be coming back today or not," Barry wanted to know.

"Don't think so, Barry, he said have a good Christmas before he left.

"Go on then you get off home or I'll have Aunty Wynn on my case." Barry pressed a few notes into Dave's hand. "Have a good one, mate; see you in a couple of days."

Barry removed the picture of the scantily dressed girl from the wall to reveal the small safe. He picked up the plastic envelope containing the money. He opened it and looked inside, it was bulging, good man, Clint, thought Barry, there looks more than enough to clinch the land deal with the council. Now he would lay off the drug wheeling and dealing before anyone got wind that it was him involved. Barry closed the safe and hung the beautiful lady back on the wall. He had a quick look around, satisfied all looked well he locked up for the Christmas holidays. Clint would be back to open up on boxing day for a little light work, they had a deal with a bloke in the rag trade and they wanted to get the clothes down to Romford Market for the January sale. Barry got back in his car and leaned over to open the glove box. He winced when the pain in his ribs caught him, a grim reminder of the night before. He placed the plastic envelope in the glove compartment and closed it. He checked his face in the rear-view mirror. His cheek was turning purple as the bruising from the punch was coming out. The blood had congealed inside his mouth sealing the gash. He hoped that he didn't see too many people at the council office because today he definitely didn't look his best. He readjusted the mirror and started the engine, once again the pain wracked his body, thank God it was Christmas and he could have a couple of days' rest. He was glad he had agreed to spend Christmas day at the house with his Aunt Edie, Georgie and Markey. He would do his bit of business with Geraldine then stop off at Brenda's to pick up the gifts that he had sent her up West to buy for the family

Barry pulled into the council car park, thank God it was almost empty, you could always rely on the council bods to get away as early as possible. He could see Geraldine's car parked in her reserved space. He took the plastic envelope out of the glove box and went to tuck it inside his jacket pocket. Second thoughts he tucked it down his underpants, you never can be too sure, not even in broad daylight. Geraldine was sitting at her desk, she looked up as Barry came through the door. She was shocked to see the state of his face. "What the …"

"Don't even ask," was his reply.

"Anyway, you're cutting it bloody fine," she said. "Have you got the money?"

"Of course I have or I wouldn't be here."

Geraldine opened the desk drawer and pulled out a file. She opened it up in front of Barry. "I have marked all the places that you need to sign so let's get on with it, Eric and myself have a very important dinner arrangement in a hotel up west with the backers for his future career in politics."

Barry raised his eyebrow, "That's excellent news, Gerry, someone in high places linked to the family, that's a good asset." Barry signed the final document.

"Aren't you forgetting something, Barry?" she asked "The money."

"Oh yeah." Barry reached down the front of his trousers and pulled out the plastic pouch. "For Christ's sake," she looked in disgust. "Did you have to put it there?"

"Stop fretting you don't have to touch it." He opened the wallet and placed the money on the table. "I think you will find it's all there."

"Barry Bullock you've got the luck of the devil."

Barry walked round the desk and planted a kiss on Geraldine's cheek. "Merry Christmas, little Sis."

Geraldine went to hug Barry, but he stepped back quick. "Sorry, Babe, but the body's a little delicate today." Geraldine shook her head and Barry closed the door behind him on the way out.

Pat wanted to please Barry, now they were lovers she hoped he would ask her to marry him. She knew he had a bit of a bad boy reputation but this added to his attraction. She went down to the market and bought some scatter cushions for the sofa and a nice eiderdown for the bed, she even managed to find a couple of table lamps. She was hard pushed to get them all back and gave a young lad sixpence to help her carry it. After she had arranged all her goods her thoughts turned to food. There wasn't a thing in the cupboards. She didn't think she had the energy to go back down to the market so she checked her purse and decided she had enough to go to the local shop at the corner of the road. She pushed open the shop door and a little bell rang. There were a couple of women already in the shop. Pat saw them look at her sideways and whisper behind their hands. She hadn't realised that she was the subject of gossip. Still, she thought that's what people did when they were jealous. Pat held her head up high and gave the shopkeeper a list of all the things she required. When he had finally packed them into her bag and totted up how much she owed him Pat smiled to herself. Now I'll give them something to gossip about as she laid a five-pound note on the counter. The shopkeeper examined the note suspiciously, Pat overheard one of the women pass a remark, "ILL gotten gains I expect." "Probably for services rendered I bet," whispered the second woman Pat was a little hurt by this but she continued to hold her head up high as she picked up her grocery bag and left the shop. One day she thought I'll make them eat their words when I'm Mrs Barry Bullock.

By the time Barry had picked up the Christmas presents that Brenda had got for him to give to his aunt Edie, Georgie and Markey, he arrived back at his flat to the wonderful smell of sausages and fried onion cooking. Pat was surprised to see Barry laden with parcels and thought that one of them was for her. Barry looked at her face and thought, Oh fuck I haven't bought Pat a Christmas present and she looks like she is expecting something.

"This lot's for me to take round Christmas Day to Edie's. My best girl can't have hers till tomorrow night where she'll find it under her pillow." With this he slapped Pat playfully on the bottom and started to kiss the back of her neck. He slid his hands under her arms until they cupped her breasts and he began to fondle them, he turned her round and started to kiss her hard on her mouth. "Not now Barry the sausages will burn."

Barry stopped and thought for a moment. "You're quite right, girl, let's get our priorities right."

Pat stayed the night again at Barry's flat. His body was still battered and bruised but it didn't deter him from wanting to make love. He showed her how please him in ways she had never dreamed of. She wasn't even sure if it was quite normal as she had never been with a man properly before. She had experienced the usual fumbles in the dark but this was something quite different. A quick wham bam thank you mam type of thing was the extent of her knowledge, and these things just didn't come up in conversation with the girls. He showed her how to use her tongue to arouse him until he was hard enough for her to lower herself on top of him. He liked to please her too. He sucked on her nipples until they throbbed. He licked her in her most intimate parts, places that no one had ever seen before – not even herself properly without a mirror. Pat was falling in love with Barry hook, line and sinker. She was sure he felt the same way and thought the Christmas present under the pillow tomorrow night was sure to be an engagement ring. After they lay in the dark, completely spent Barry made a mental note to stop off the next day at a little Jewish pawnbrokers in Whitechapel to grab Pat a present.

Pat hadn't been home for two nights, she knew her mother would be furious with her, while Barry was out on Christmas Eve she would show her face and try to pour oil on the troubled waters. She knew Barry was spending Christmas Day with his family and she wasn't invited so she would have to go home then anyway. Still, when she showed her mother her engagement ring she was sure it would ease the situation.

Pat opened her eyes and the bed was already empty, she found a scribbled note on the kitchen table with some money. Get what you need, we'll grab some fish and chips tonight and go down the King's Head for a few drinks, should be back about six o'clock for a wash and change, signed BB.

Pat sang as she got herself dressed. She was in love and elated. How could her mother not be pleased for her when she knew how happy she was? Maybe she would stop off at the market on the way to her mother's to see if she could pick up a wireless for the flat.

Pat put her key in the front door of her mother's house and opened it with anticipation. She could hear her mother clanking around in the kitchen. "Is that you, Pat?" she yelled.

"Yes, Mum," was Pat's very humble reply.

"Oh so you've decided to show your face then, I've been out of my mind with worry not knowing where you were."

"Mum, I'm sorry, I've been with Irene and Vera."

"Oh no you haven't, my girl, I saw Irene Bullock and she told me you were gallivanting around with her cousin Barry. He's a bad lot that one and no good will come of it. Still you make your bed and you've gotta lie on it."

There was no point trying to interrupt her mother and reassure her, she was just going to have to listen and take what was coming. Pat lowered herself onto the kitchen chair and waited until her mother had run out of steam.

"Mum, me and Barry we're in love, in fact we're going to get engaged tonight, I'll be able to show you my ring tomorrow."

"Oh so you're coming fer your dinner are you? I'm not happy about having that man in my house, Pat."

"It's OK, Mum, I will be on my own, Barry has already made arrangements to go to his sister and it's too short notice to cancel."

"It's a funny carry on if you ask me, is he ashamed to take you with him then?"

"No, Mum, it's not like that at all, his brother can't have things sprung on him, it upsets him so we got to get him used to me a bit at a time."

"That's another thing," spat her mother. "They've got a spastic in the family, you could end up with a baby like that yourself if you stay with him."

Pat had had enough of listening to her mother's ranting and got up to leave, she didn't want to argue any more, enough was enough for one day. "Mum I've gotta go, were going out tonight so I've got things to do. I'll see you tomorrow for lunch." Pat let herself out of the house and stepped onto the pavement. She breathed in a big gulp of fresh air, why did parents have to be such a pain in the arse?

Barry and Pat ate their fish and chips in the fish bar. Everyone was bustling around getting the last-minute bits for the big day tomorrow. Barry was in a great mood, he had done the deal for the bomb-damaged land and he was set to make a fortune when the development was done. In fact Geraldine had a few more deals in the pipeline for him. Barry had always managed to make a few bob, the war years had been kind to him but 1945 was going to be a terrific year, he felt on top of the world. Just as they were about to leave Clint came through the door. He didn't see Barry and Pat first of all, not until he had ordered his meal and was looking for a place to sit down. Barry waved his hand and showed out to Clint, calling him to come and join them. Clint sat down and gave a little nod of acknowledgement to Pat.

"What you doing in here all alone," joked Barry. Nothing was going to dampen his high spirits.

"I was supposed to meet Dave down the pub about an hour ago for a pint but he didn't show."

"You know Dave," replied Barry. "He's got no sense of time."

"Still, that's where we're heading now, a couple of drinks in the King's Head then off to bed." Barry gave Pat a nudge to get up. "Well merry Christmas, mate, I'll see you down the dockside office boxing day. There's a ship due in that we might be interested in."

"OK, you have a good one, too," replied Clint. "See you Boxing day then."

Pat was a little disappointed as she thought that her and Barry would spend boxing day together, when you hung around with a bloke like Barry you shouldn't expect things and she knew never to lay down the law. She had seen how quickly Barry's mood could change and up to now she had not been on the receiving end of it. By the time they arrived at the King's head the party was in full swing. The pub was full of familiar faces; probably fifty percent of them was Bullocks. Barry done the rounds wishing his aunts and uncles a merry Christmas, even Dot and Dick had put in an appearance;

they were all gathered together in one corner. His uncle Ted came over to him.

"Barry, do you know where our Dave is, is he on a job for you? Cause he ain't come home and his muvver's worried about him."

"No, Unc. He's not on any job for me, you know Dave he's probably picked up with some tart, he'll be back when she kicks him out of her bed."

"I'm sure you're right, boy, but he's never been gone this long before."

I'm not Dave's bloody keeper thought Barry and wanted to tell his uncle so. "She must be a good lay that's all I can say," trying not to fuel his uncle's concerns. He'd better show up on Boxing Day thought Barry or he'd cut his bloody balls off. Barry could see another group of his cousins and they looked like they were having a good time so he made his way over to them. He could see Pat sitting on her own, she looked like she had swallowed a wasp. If it hadn't have been Christmas he might have thought about dumping her, still why should he worry, after all he wasn't her keeper either they were just having some fun together. She could join him or not it was her choice and if she didn't buck her ideas up he would definitely dump her before New Year's Eve. Irene and young Frank seemed to be heading the singing and they had been joined by Vera Murphy and a very pretty young girl was with her. Barry made a point of going over and talking to them. Vera introduced her younger sister Maggie to Barry. Barry pretended that he didn't know who she was, he took her hand and kissed it politely. He wondered if he was in with a chance and should he ditch Pat after all. Maggie's parents had reluctantly agreed for her to come out on the proviso that Vera would watch her like a hawk and only let her have lemonade. Barry took the opportunity to chat Maggie up a little. To give her a little taste of the Bullock charm. He decided that in the New Year he would try his luck and ask her out on a date.

Pat felt like a bit of a wallflower in the pub, Barry was his usual sociable self, buying all and sundry drinks and being king of the hill. Still finally the bell for last orders was rung; she couldn't wait to get back to the flat to get her present. Pat stood up and began to put her coat on, Barry didn't look like he was in any hurry to leave. Pat went over to see if she could encourage him to get a move on.

"Are we going now? Last orders have been rung."

Barry leaned over and whispered in her ear, "Most of the punters will be gone in a minute and the landlord has promised us a lock in for a few hours."

Pat was mortified, she couldn't think of anything worse. "Barry I've got a splitting headache."

"You go back to the flat I won't be too long." Pat couldn't hide the disappointment on her face. "Open your Christmas present, it's under the pillow, and baby, stay hot for me."

Pat left the King's Head and walked all the way back to Barry's flat. By the time she arrived she was chilled to the bone and tears were rolling down her cheeks. She went into the bedroom and threw herself onto the bed and her tears erupted in full flow. When her emotions were spent she sat up, wiped her eyes and blew her nose. She put her hand under the pillow to feel for the box her Christmas present was in. It was a square flat box, she tore of the paper and opened it. It was a beautiful necklace, normally any girl would have been ecstatic, but she, Pat Fuller just burst into tears all over again with disappointment. How could she face her mother tomorrow now without and engagement ring, how could Barry humiliate her like this?

Pat hadn't heard Barry come to bed, his promise of hot love had obviously succumbed to too much alcohol. Barry rolled over when he felt Pat moving about in the bed. He definitely felt worse for wear. "What time did you roll in then?" she asked.

"Don't know, couldn't tell you," he groaned. "Get us an aspirin would you my head's fucking killing me."

Pat got Barry his aspirin and brought it back to bed. He swallowed it and laid back on the pillow for half an hour until the hammer in his head subsided. He looked at Pat's face which hadn't improved much from the night before. Thank God he was getting rid of her today; he was in no mood to put up with the moody cow, perhaps it was that time of the month. Another few minutes passed. "Did you like your Christmas present?" he asked.

"It was very nice thanks," answered Pat. Very nice thought Barry, is that all she could say the ungrateful bitch. Don't know what she was expecting but it was about time he put some distance between him and Pat Fuller he thought. If she was hearing wedding bells she could think again, that was the last thing on his agenda. Besides, he had ideas about Maggie Murphy lined up for the New Year.

Barry offered to give Pat a lift to her mum's house but she said she wanted to walk if it was all the same. She supposed she would have to tell her mum she hadn't had her present yet otherwise all she would get all day long was, I told you so, and she didn't think she could stand it. She did consider not going to her mother's and staying in the flat on her own but a slice of spam and some mashed potato didn't seem very appealing.

Barry arrived at his mother's house about twelve o'clock Christmas Day. He sat outside in the car for a while reminiscing about bygone Christmases. Remembering that his mother would usually cook a chicken that smelled delicious, as the years went by and Barry brought more money into the house they even had turkey. The children would be playing and laughing until his father walked through the door, full of ale and half cut, then the atmosphere would change and a silence would engulf the room. He was trying hard not to remember the Christmases in the old house before his father burnt it down. It was so much better after he died and they came to live with Granny Maude. He hated his father for the way he blamed his mother for how Markey was. It still pained him when he remembered Markey being pushed away by his father as if he were a disease. One more cigarette and he would go inside. He could feel his mood darkening and he didn't want this to happen today. He wanted this Christmas to be a good one for his little brother's sake. Barry flicked the fag butt out of the window and got out of the car. He banged loudly on the front door and Markey opened it, "Come on champ," he said. "Help me get all these presents out of the car boot."

Christmas Day went well, Edie and Georgie cooked a wonderful meal, they all ate so much they could hardly move. The mood was easy and Markey enjoyed every moment, which after all was what they all wanted. They played charades and snakes and ladders all afternoon. They laughed at Georgie's stories from the hospital about bedpans and women in labour. Edie added a few stories of her own and even Barry shared a few things with them that he made them promise never to repeat outside of the four walls. They had even got a few bottles of brown ale in for him which he thought was very acceptable. He opened a bottle for Markey, ignoring Edie's frown. Markey was eager and took a large swig from the bottle. "That was yuk," he decided, "think I'll stick to lemonade."

Barry smiled, "You do that, champ, and you won't go far wrong."

Georgina had picked the bones of the turkey and Markey went into the back yard to feed his chickens. Barry sat by the fire cracking a few nuts open. The sudden banging on the front door made them all jump. "Who the hell could that be on Christmas Night?" said Georgie as she went down the hall to open the door. Barry could hear the sound of his Uncle Ted's voice.

"Barry I was hoping to find you here, Wynn's going out of her mind with worry, our Dave still hasn't shown up and I gotta be honest with yer I got a bad feeling about it. He's never been gone this long."

"It's getting late now, Ted, and I've had a skinful of beer, first thing tomorrow I'll get Clint out looking for him."

"Thanks Barry," replied Ted, "I appreciate it, I'll be off then and try and calm his muvver down; if he turns up I'll let yer know."

Markey came back in from the yard. "Who was that then?"

"Only your uncle Ted, he's had to shoot off now. Guess I'd better be doing the same," said Barry.

"Oh don't go," pleaded Markey.

"Why don't I make you up a bed on the sofa and you could stay tonight?" offered Edie.

Barry thought of the cold little flat and it was holding no attraction for him. He wasn't sure if Pat was going back there or not tonight and he wanted to put some distance between them. It was like she had moved in and he wasn't sure how that had happened. He would have to try and get her key back off her before she got too comfortable.

"That would be great, Auntie," replied Barry. Suddenly he felt like a small boy again and had a strange longing for his dog scrappy.

Barry had the best sleep he'd had in a long time, he only woke up because he could hear Markey clanking around. "You been out and fed them chickens already?" He asked. "They're quiet this morning." Barry tried to get up from the sofa but his limbs were stiff from being curled up all night.

"They didn't want anything," replied Markey in a matter of fact way. "They're stuck on the fence."

"What you talking about? Stuck on the fence, let me take a look." Barry opened the back door with Markey close on his heels. "What the fuck ..." exclaimed Barry as he looked at the sight before him. The chickens had been slit from neck to parson's nose. Their insides were spilling out and blood had dripped and dried down the fence onto the concrete floor. They had been nailed to the fence and left to hang.

"What's all the bloody fuss about," said Georgie as she joined them in the yard. "Oh my God what happened to the chickens?"

Barry looked at Georgie as if she must be mad, "They committed suicide in the night," replied Barry sharply. "I don't bloody well know, someone's killed all the fucking chickens, the sick bastards."

"Can you and Edie get this lot cleaned up? I need to get down to the office and see if I can find out what's going on, what with Dave on the missing list and now this."

Georgie shrugged her shoulders. "Do we have a choice?" she asked. Barry didn't answer he was too busy getting his clothes on. "No, I thought not," she continued.

With that Barry put on his shoes, grabbed his coat and slammed the front door as he left. The roads were empty, the world and his wife were sleeping off their hangovers from Christmas Day. It was mild for the time of year, Barry wound down the window to get some air. The security guard acknowledged Barry as he drove through the dockside gates. Barry walked through the door to see Brenda sitting at her desk filing her nails.

"Have there been any messages for me, Brenda?" Snapped Barry. "And where the fuck is Clint?"

Brenda chose to completely ignore her boss's bad temper, "Shall I make you a coffee, Mr Bullock?" she asked as she lifted the kettle from the stove and went to the sink to fill it up. "Oh, Mr Bullock, a parcel arrived for you first thing, I put it on your desk."

Barry opened his office door, what the hell was that smell? Barry opened the package and looked inside, the bile rose in his throat and he leant over the waste paper basket and vomited.

"What is it?" came Clint's voice from the office doorway. Barry couldn't answer as he felt another wave of nausea sweep over him. Clint looked inside the box and he saw five decomposing toes. Barry could hear bells ringing in his head. Brenda popped her head around the door.

"That was your uncle Ted on the phone, he's at the London Hospital, he said can you get there as quick as you can."

Barry told Clint about the chicken incident at the house earlier on as they drove to the hospital, "It's a warning, Barry, it's a fucking warning, I told you to pull back on the dope, but you wouldn't listen, now none of us are fucking safe." Barry didn't like the way Clint spoke to him, after all he was only an employee but for now he would have to lump it.

Barry and Clint found Ted sitting in the main entrance with Renne and her brother little Frank. He still got called little Frank even though he was six foot tall now. Barry never liked him much, not even as a kid. He supposed it was because of the uncanny resemblance he had to big Frank, Barry's father. When Irene and Barry were kids they were pretty close. As they grew up they still had a sort of soft spot for one another. They even did a little teenage experimenting with each other. One Day his aunt Dot caught them on the sofa and she went mad. Irene tried to explain that cousins were allowed to marry and everything, but his aunt banned Barry from coming to the house and she made a right song and dance about the whole thing. His Uncle Dickie thought she was overreacting, but as Dot had worked herself up into such a frenzy he said maybe it was for the best and Barry should keep his distance for a while.

The waiting area was full of people but Barry made no attempt to keep his voice down. "What's going on, Ted? Is it Dave? How is he?"

Ted raised his head from his hands and looked at Barry. "He's in a pretty bad way, boy, he's lost a lot of blood, lucky to be alive they said."

"They've sedated him and tried to fix him up, said we might as well go home as he will be out for a while.

"Do you know if he said anything about what happened?" asked Barry.

"Don't know much about anything, boy, the doctors told me he had a foot injury and that's about it."

"What's he been up to? That's what I'd like to know, have you got any idea?"

Barry didn't think that now was a good time to tell him about the parcel that had turned up at his office full of toes which probably belonged to Dave. "How about we go home and get some rest, Unc. I'll come back with you tomorrow and see what Dave's got to say for himself" The last thing Barry wanted was for Dave or Ted to go spouting their mouths off and get them all killed. He knew Dave was going to be a cripple now, that's if he even survived, he knew it was his fault and felt sick at the thought of it. He'd see Dave alright, make sure he never wanted for anything; that was the least he could do.

Clint and Barry drove Ted home. They wished him luck when telling his wife her son was lying in the London Hospital in a critical condition, wait until they found out half his foot had been hacked off.

"We'll pick you up about three o'clock tomorrow, Ted," said Barry. "We'll catch the afternoon visiting and hopefully know what happened by then."

"Thanks, Barry," said Ted. "You're a diamond." Clint put his foot on the accelerator and they drove away.

"You get down that hospital first thing in the morning and see what's what, and for Christ's sake don't let Dave say anything stupid or we'll have the old bill on our backs, and Clint," added Barry, "be discrete."

Edie and Georgie cleared up the back yard of mutilated chickens, they were having a hard time consoling Markey who couldn't understand who had done such a terrible thing to his much-loved chickens that he had nurtured from baby chicks. Edie continuously tutted saying it was sick and evil and was sure Barry was behind it somewhere. She would be glad when the new year had been and gone, desperately wanting to brush the entire incident under the carpet. The noise from the flap of the letter box stopped them mid flow.

"Go and see what that was Markey," said Georgie "it's probably a Christmas card from someone who forgot to send us one or worse some more uncooked offal. Thankfully Markey returned with a white envelope with blue edging. "It's an airmail letter" exclaimed Georgie with excitement "It's from our Veronica, look its stamped USA." She opened the envelope with shaking fingers.

Dear All, it began. We arrived in New York safe and sound. We went to Greenwich Village where you could hear such wonderful jazz and blues music. We listened to a black singer called Billie Holiday, who was fantastic. The music had such soul to it. We are trying to get some bookings and are spending a great deal of time practising the new style of music. Solly is trying hard to get us some work but there is a lot of competition. We're being sensible with our money and are staying in a proper fleapit so as not to be extravagant. Love to you all and will keep in touch. Signed Ronnie and the band.

Georgie slipped back in the worn armchair just as a moonlight serenade by Glen Miller began to play on the wireless. What an adventure Ronnie was having. No worries, no ties. She mentally scolded herself for being a little jealous. Yes she had a very worthwhile job educating the women of the East End about contraception and she knew how working with the Red Cross nursing core was equally important. But sometimes the days would wear her down and make her weary. She knew she would never walk away from her lot in life. She would never let Auntie Edie down, and there was Markey to consider. He would always need to be cared for and no one else seemed prepared to step up to the plate. She'd given up ever finding a man of her own and was resigning herself to be the spinster of this generation of the family following in Edie's footsteps. Georgina and Edie would spend a few hours each day down at the east end maternity hospital handing out their leaflets to the women who managed to attend the anti-natal clinics. They would give each lady who was about to give birth a sample of the male contraceptive. They would listen to the women bantering about it. "I've got five of the little bleeders now, they would hear them say, if my old man don't wear this overcoat he ain't coming near me no more. Edie and Georgie knew that most of them wouldn't even try to protect themselves. Their husbands would see it as going against their manhood and most of the women would be back the same time next year and be heading for an early grave.

Clint walked into the London Hospital. The smell of disinfectant was powerful and made him catch his breath. He hoped he would find Dave conscious and be able to tell him what had happened. Clint knew the sister wouldn't let him in as the official visiting was in the afternoon. It was lucky Dave was in a side room so he waited till the coast was clear and he slipped in and sat down by the side of the bed. Dave opened his heavy eyelids. They had sedated him and he was still woozy from the effects of the drugs. "Christ, Dave," said Clint. "You look like a sack of shit mate, what the fuck happened and who done it?" Dave's tongue felt too big for his mouth and he was having trouble forming his words. Clint leaned closer trying to make out what he was saying. Canal club, dark, didn't see, back of van, my foot, my foot hurts." Dave was getting a bit hysterical, Clint pushed the emergency cord and slipped out quietly. He wasn't going to get any sense out of Dave at this point in time, he just hoped he didn't remember anything and start shouting his mouth off and dropping them all in the shit. He thought he had better go and find Barry, see what he wanted to do next. He would check to see if he was still at home as he had to pass his door on the way to the dockside offices. He knocked on the door but there was no answer. He knocked again and could hear some movement, the door opened and Pat was standing there in her baby doll negligee. She must have been cold as he could see her pert little nipples poking through the flimsy material. He felt a stirring between his legs and thought he wouldn't mind keeping her warm on a cold night. Pat looked half asleep "Clint, what do you want?"

"I'm looking for Barry, I take it he's not here."

"No," replied Pat. "I was still asleep when he left, you could try the office," she said as she closed the door on Clint. Clint thought Pat was a stuck-up bitch and he told himself he didn't like her much, but the large erection that had formed in his underpants said otherwise. The streets were deserted as Clint made his way towards the office, he pulled the van over into the kerb outside a little newsagents. He needed a packet of fags, his nerves were in shreds. God knows he had tried to warn Barry that he was treading on the wrong people's toes and now they had made their point by chopping off Dave's.

Clint pushed open the office door to find Barry sitting all alone in the chair. "Where's Brenda?" he asked. Barry raised his head showing his face with an unreadable expression on it.

"Told her to take the rest of the week off and come back after new year, poor mare has had a bit of a shock."

Clint heard a strange whimpering noise coming from a cardboard box under the desk. He was surprised to see a small greyhound pup.

"What the?"

"Oh some old codger owed me some money and he didn't have it, said would I take the dog as payment, reckons he comes from a good stud. With the sort of week I've had he caught me at a weak moment."

"What the bloody hell you gonna do with it?"

"You know what, Clint, I'm gonna take it round and give it to Markey, he needs something to take his mind off them fucking chickens."

"You never know, if we get him a trainer he might turn out to be a winner."

"You know what, Boss, you're fucking mad you know that."

"You may be right, anyway let's lock up here and go, its New Year's Eve tomorrow and I'll be down the King's Head, not sure we'll be celebrating, more like drowning our sorrows." Barry got his keys out to lock the door and Clint was right behind him. "Clint ain't you forgetting something?"

"Boss?"

"The dog, mate, the fucking greyhound."

Clint went round and picked up the box with the dog inside and the bottom gave way allowing the puppy to fall to the floor.

"What you fucking up to, Clint?"

"The little bastard's peed in the box, it's all soggy and the bottom's dropped out." Clint picked up the whimpering puppy and tucked it under his arm and it began to lick him.

"I'm not putting THAT in my car, you chuck him in the back of the van and follow me to mum's." Barry felt a sudden pain in his chest as he realised what he had said.

Markey was over the moon with his new dog. Edie didn't seem too keen but Georgie said it was just what Markey needed and said they had better choose a name for him. Barry told them he had a certificate and his name was Boscoe. "I like that said Markey, I ain't never heard a dog called Boscoe before, that makes him special."

Barry had promised to take his aunt and uncle Ted to the hospital to see Dave and time was cracking on. He pulled up outside their little terraced house and honked his car horn. Ted and his aunt Wynn came out immediately. His aunt was red eyed and looked like she had been crying all night. Barry got out the car and opened the back passenger door for his aunt to get in the car. She poked him sharply in the ribs "This is all your fault Barry," she said. "I shall never forgive you for this; my boy is lying in hospital because of you, who knows if he will ever walk again he could be a cripple the rest of his life thanks to your irresponsible behaviour." Barry wondered how much his aunt and uncle knew about what had happened.

"What's auntie Wynn talking about, how come I'm getting all the blame?" he asked raising his hands in the air.

"It's always been your fault," scowled Aunt Wynn. "Whenever our David got into trouble it was because he had followed you on some hair brained scheme."

Ted shrugged his shoulders and climbed in the car beside his wife. They drove to the hospital in silence, the only noise was the sniffling of his aunt as she wiped her nose.

They walked into the side room where Barry had last seen Dave and the bed was empty. He thought that his aunt Wynn was about to faint when just at that moment a pretty young nurse came through the door. "Are you looking for Mr Bullock?" she enquired.

"That's right, love," said Ted. "I'm his father."

"He was a little more awake today, so we moved him into the main ward; sister thought that being with other people would do him good."

"Thanks, love," said Ted as he tried to support Wynn under her elbow. Dave was sitting up in bed and gave them half a smile when he saw them approaching. Wynn started wailing all over again, Ted got cross and told her to quieten down before she got them all chucked out. Barry pulled the curtain round the bed to give them a bit of privacy.

"How are you mate?" asked Barry. "Can you remember anything about what happened?"

"I keep getting flash backs," replied Dave. "I came out of the club, it was dark, someone jumped me and I was chucked in the back of a van. They put a hood over my head before I was taken from the van and back inside. I think it was some kind of warehouse as it was echoey and there was a smell."

"What damp like?" asked Barry.

"No I think it was coffee. I heard voices, mostly London accents. There was one though, sounded foreign, maybe Russian or something. When they took the hood off my head they had a light shining in my eyes. They dimmed it just enough for me to see the axe as it chopped off my toes. Aunty Wynn began to wail again and Ted tried to comfort her. Then I must have passed out cause the next thing I remember is waking up in here." Then it was Dave's turn and he began to sob very softly. Barry pulled a couple of notes out of his wallet and pressed them into Ted's palm.

"Get a cab home will you, there's something I need to do." Just as Barry was about to leave Dave looked up.

"Barry, it's not all your fault, I was skimming off some of the gear and selling it meself, don't do anything stupid on my account will you."

This threw a different light on the subject. "Listen, mate, you've been a stupid bastard but I'll make sure you're OK, now just get some rest and get out of here, the food will kill you if nothing else will." Barry left the hospital, he'd get to the bottom of this and if it was a low life dealer who did this to Dave he was fucking well gonna pay for it. He Jumped in his car and headed off to find Clint.

Clint made a few inquiries south of the river; he had a few people he had built up a bit of trust with who were willing to share information with him. It turned out that the Russian was a relatively new face around. He acted like the big I am and was not liked much over there either. It was agreed by all that the Bullocks had been wronged and should be the ones to take revenge. The truth be known the south side of the river gangs wanted the Russian out of the way as well and Barry would be doing them all a favour. The Bullocks would have the privilege of disposing of him whichever way they saw fit. Barry nodded in a knowing fashion when Clint relayed all of this to him and Barry knew Clint would deal with it. "I want him to suffer, I want him to feel the pain and I want to read about it in tomorrow's papers, now go make it happen."

Clint let himself into the Russian's flat. It was furnished relatively comfortable for a new arrival to the country so he must have been making a few bob. He found the bathroom and went to work on the taps. He fitted two small capsules into them that would dissolve when the water ran through them as the bath was filling up. He put the taps back together and quietly let himself out of the flat, fait accompli, as they say. The slimy bastard would get his comeuppance.

The Russian had indeed only been in the country for about a year, but it was long enough to worm his way into the dealers' market. It was not easy getting out of Russia but he had made it against all odds. He wanted to bring his wife and daughter to join him but his wife didn't make it. Still, he was grateful that his daughter had joined him a few days ago and she was safe now. Anna had been out all day and she felt dusty and dirty. She went to the bathroom to run the bath. Her father had got her some nice jasmine bath salts and she added them to the running water. The steam began to fill the little room and Anna peeled off her clothes and stepped in to the bath. She laid back to relax and she could feel her skin begin to burn.

Barry picked up a copy of the morning paper.

BATH TUB BURN UP

Freak incident as chemicals enter the water system of a London flat. Female badly burned, but she has yet to be identified. No one has come forward and little is known of the foreign gentleman who has been renting the premises. Some reports say she may be the man's daughter but this has yet to be confirmed.

Barry walked into the office and threw the paper at Clint to read. "We killed the wrong fucking person you prick." Clint didn't like Barry's tone of voice, who the fuck did he think he was talking to and who always did the dirty work anyway. Clint tried to keep his voice steady.

"Firstly no body's dead, you said you wanted him to feel the pain and suffer, well there was just enough acid in the capsules to make that happen. I didn't know anyone else would be in the flat, and yes it turns out it was his daughter. I expect he is suffering a whole lot more than if was himself that had got in the bath. There's worse things than dying you know." said Clint.

Barry thought for a moment and as usual Clint was right. It would be bad enough having an acid bath yourself but to watch your own flesh and blood burn for something you have done, that's got to be a bastard.

"You're right, Clint, OK let's call it a day and knock off, I think we deserve a drink after the week we've had." They locked the office and Barry slapped Clint on the back. "Happy New Year, mate."

Clint knew that was as near to an apology from Barry he was going to get.

Chapter 8

King's Head New Year's Eve.

You wouldn't think there was a war on. The celebrations were in full swing and the drink was flowing. Some people were seeing in the New Year and there were a few drowning their sorrows. There had been a couple of local funerals, once upon a time you wouldn't have had a funeral New Year's Eve but with so many dead it was just another day.

Barry knew he'd had too much to drink but he'd had a bastard of a week. He knew Pat was annoyed with him but he didn't really care much. Just at that moment he saw the lovely Maggie Murphy walking his way. Maybe it was time to blow Pat out and get Miss Murphy to warm his bed. She looked like she was heading for the ladies and he stepped in her path. "Hello gorgeous," was his unimaginative comment. "How about me buying you a little drink?" Maggie tried to look the other way and push passed him but Barry moved as well and continued to block her path, he grabbed her arm. Barry wanted this girl badly but the drink was talking and all his usual charm had gone out of the window. "You know Pat don't you? Maybe we could go back to my place and have a three some. The moment the words had left his mouth he regretted it. Maggie was a lady and didn't deserve such smutty talk. Maggie didn't want to make a scene.

"Let me go," she said quietly under her breath. Barry was about to pursue his attentions and try to lay on his Bullock charm when a man in uniform stepped between them.

"You heard the Lady," came his voice. Barry was getting annoyed.

"What's it to you pal?" retorted Barry and he took a swipe. He was unsteady on his feet and fell to the ground in total humiliation. He lifted himself up trying to regain his dignity. "You'll pay for that, mate, just you wait and see," growled Barry.

"And you, mate, should listen when a lady says no. John Taylor would have liked very much to give this low life scum a bloody good hiding, but as he was in uniform he would have gotten into a whole load of trouble if the police had got involved. Instead he held onto Maggie's elbow, looking Barry straight in the eye and said, "As my fiancée has just told you she's not interested, now get lost." With that John and Maggie left the pub and Barry was left seething.

Barry spent much of New Year's Day nursing a headache. Pat had left him a note saying she was staying at her mum's for a couple of days, and quite frankly he was glad. By tea time he was feeling a bit more human and he was famished. There wasn't much in the way of food in the cupboard and he thought it was about time he popped round to the house, which he had started to refer to it as, and see how Markey was getting along with Boscoe. The dog was causing havoc but Markey adored him.

"How about when he's a bit bigger we take him to the Dog Track for some trials? Maybe we could get him a trainer."

Markey thought that was an excellent idea and said he was going to go to the library and get a book all about training greyhounds. Barry said that was the best idea he'd heard all day but what he would really like right now was a sandwich. After Barry had eaten and played with the dog for a while he thought he would just have enough time to catch the last half hour of visiting time at the hospital. He thought he had better check on Dave and see what was what. Barry knew it wasn't entirely his fault that Dave had ended up in the situation he was in. He also knew that he was family and he would have to see he was properly taken care of. A few ideas were kicking around in his head to give Dave a purpose to get out of bed every day. He also had to be careful how he put it to him. He didn't want him to feel like a charity case. Still, first things first, they had to get him back on his feet so to speak. They were having some special boots made that would give him some balance. They cost a bloody fortune, but Barry could never tell Dave it was he who had paid for them, no, they would just let him think it was all part and parcel of his rehabilitation through the hospital. He had to let poor Dave keep a bit of pride and self-respect.

Barry still hadn't got over the humiliation of New Year's Eve in the King's Head. The Taylors thought they were above the rest. He may wear a uniform and speak a little posh but he'd be fucked if he was going to let him get away with making him look a prat. He would have a word with Clint and get someone to give him a spanking and tell him it was from an admirer.

1945

Barry was busy trying to put his house in order. The last few months seemed to breed nothing but trouble. The war looked like it was coming to an end and he had new seeds to sew, Barry was optimistic about the coming year. Geraldine had been promoted to head of all new planning and development of the bombed-out sites in the area. He would get first refusal of any good deals that were coming up. Geraldine would even give him the wink on any out of town developments that could be good business proposals. Now Barry's business was growing he thought it was high time he thought about investing in a proper office. The warehouse down on the docks served its purpose, but it was hardly the place he could bring respectable businessmen and women to. So with Geraldine's help he bought a nice little property in a prime location at a giveaway price. Brenda was very excited about the move, especially as she was to hire an office junior to help her. Barry decided to keep the dockside office, partly out of nostalgia and partly because it would still be a front for the fags and alcohol he got off the ships. Dave had been discharged from hospital but was still a long way from recovery. The special shoes had arrived and Barry was pleased to see how much Dave was determined to get back on his feet. Barry was actually proud of Dave for not wallowing in self-pity. In fact, Barry put it to Dave that he would be doing him an enormous favour by helping Markey train Bosco over at the dog track. Dave said he didn't know the first thing about training a greyhound. Barry wasn't about to pussy foot around so he told Dave he had better get off his arse and start to bloody learn.

Barry put his key in the front door of his flat and opened it to the smell of dinner cooking. "Is that you Barry?" came Pat's voice from the kitchen. Damn, thought Barry, he thought she had left for good. He walked into the kitchen and all his negative thoughts disappeared when he saw her standing there in her tight-fitting sweater and figure hugging pencil skirt. Pat looked directly into Barry's face. I know what you're thinking and I'm sorry I've been gone for too long, but mum wasn't well so I stayed to look after her, now sit yourself down and eat your dinner."

Never mind about dinner thought Barry, Pat looked good enough to eat. All thoughts of giving her the elbow went out of the window and he dragged her into the bedroom. Pat had been concerned about returning to the flat; she felt that she and Barry had drifted apart and that he was pleased she had gone to her mother's. She had made a special effort with her appearance and wore the figure hugging clothes that she was sure would turn him on. Pat knew this was not going to be a tender reunion. Barry pushed her on to the bed pulling down her underwear as he unbuttoned his trousers. Her body was not prepared, as she saw Barry standing over her, his penis fully erect and pulsating she knew it was going to hurt. Barry struggled to enter her and he began to swear. Pat was frightened that his mood would darken. When he was in a bad place he wasn't always responsible for his actions, but more than that she was afraid he would finish with her and send her away. Barry had become like a drug to her, he was in her blood and she would do anything to hold on to him. She reached down between her legs and guided him inside her. She went to remove her hand "no" shouted Barry leave it there. Barry's excitement seemed to accelerate and then he pulled out of Pat abruptly. His semen ejected over Pat's stomach.

Pat just lay there for a moment, afraid to utter a word. Barry's face broke into one of his cheeky grins.

"Sorry babe, no johnny on. Don't want any slip ups do we? Still don't mind me, I'm going to eat my dinner, you can finish yourself off, I'm starving."

Pat straightened herself up, she knew it was just a matter of time before Barry grew tired of her, she loved him deeply but knew he would never feel the same about her. Barry was handsome, and when he wanted to be he could be charming as well. Pat was well aware that he could have his pick of women if he chose. Something Barry had just said gave her food for thought. No slip ups was what he had said. Maybe that was a way to at least keep Barry in her life one way or the other. But Barry was always careful, always in control just like tonight. Most men would have been lost in the moment, but oh no, not Barry, he pulled out of her, himself satisfied with not a care for her. There seemed to be a lot of clanking noises coming from the kitchen which she presumed was Barry putting his plate in the kitchen sink. "I'm off out for a bit. Don't wait up," came his voice and with that the front door slammed. Pat sat at the dressing table for a while, pondering over her previous thoughts. She opened the drawer and took out her little sewing box. She opened the lid and sat and stared inside for a while contemplating the wicked thoughts in her head. Pat stood up and walked over to Barry's bedside cabinet and took out his packets of condoms. With her sewing needle she put little tiny pin pricks in each one. Satisfied that nothing looked out of place to the naked eye she placed them back in the drawer and said a little prayer. In fact, every time they made love Pat said a little prayer and each time Barry put a new packet of condoms in the drawer she opened her sewing box and repeated her little ritual.

The New Year was looking better already. Dave was adjusting to his situation, he was still in pain a lot of the time and swore to God he could still feel the tingling of his toes, but, he would grit his teeth and get on with things. He had taken Markey to the dog track and they had made arrangements to give Bosco a trial just as soon as he was old enough. Barry had taken Clint up west to show him a little property Geraldine had put his way. He wanted Clint's opinion on its suitability for a possible location for the club. Barry was excited about the new venture and when they saw the site Geraldine had ear marked for them to view he thought it was pretty much perfect. Barry looked at Clint's face and felt he didn't approve. God, thought Barry to himself, it was like taking Jonah on an outing. "OK," said Barry to Clint. "What's the problem with it then?"

"It's a bit out the way," replied Clint, "and that blue light flashing above the door could get on your nerves."

"So it needs a new bulb," defended Barry, come on let's take a look inside. Barry immediately saw why they were getting it at such a bargain price. It was completely run down but at the same time it was surprisingly spacious considering the entrance was so small. The downstairs was adequate for a bar, tables and chairs and an intimate dance floor. There was also room for a small stage to accommodate a three-piece band.

"Come on mate let's take a look upstairs." Barry was on the first floor landing before Clint had taken a single step. Clint put his hand on the stair rail and it rocked beneath his grip. He was half way up and his foot went through a rotten stair tread making him swear. Barry poked his head over the banister rail to see what the commotion was. Barry laughed at the sight of Clint dangling through the gap. "Get up you silly prick and come and see this place, it's a real treasure." There was room for an office combined with some private quarters and a couple of large rooms which Barry could see one as a gambling room and the other for private functions. The real icing on the cake was a little stairway leading up to a couple of attic rooms, these he thought would be ideal for a bit of hanky-panky for the punters. They looked out of the attic window on to a courtyard. Barry's mind was working ten to the dozen. "You know what Clint? We don't need a fucking garden, mate, I'll get Gerry to pass the plans for an extension."

"I want this signed and sealed by the end of the week and maybe we can get cracking on the refurbishment.

"I'll get Brenda to find us a tip top designer and architect." They were just about to make tracks and leave when an enormous bird flew in from a slipped tile in the roof. Clint ducked as he had a distinct dislike to any type of bird unless it had been roasted and was on his plate. "What the fuck was that?" yelled Barry as he shooed it away.

"A fucking eagle," retorted Clint under his breath, it's a bad omen."

"Don't be fucking stupid, it's not big enough for an eagle, it's a crow or maybe a raven from the Tower of London that's lost its way, it took one look at your ugly mug and its gone, anyway its getting dark, let's get back to the East End and put some wheels in motion. Once more outside on the pavement Barry locked the doors and stepped back to survey the building. The blue light continued to flicker above the door, Barry turned and looked at Clint and a big smile formed on his face "Clint, mate, welcome to The Blue Raven."

On the drive back to the East End Barry's mind was in top gear, he would need reliable staff. People that would know how to be discreet, people he could rely on. His thoughts turned to Grace Greene, she would be perfect to run the girls, yes it was about time he looked Grace up. His thoughts turned to Pat. Barry wasn't one for nostalgia, they had, had fun together and now it was time to call it a day. There was no point in delaying things, as soon as he got home he would ask her for her key back and tell her it's the end of the road.

Barry opened the front door of the flat and it was in darkness. He flicked on the light switch and almost jumped out of his skin when he saw Pat sitting there. "What the fuck you sitting in the dark for?" Pat looked up at Barry.

"Sorry I didn't notice how dark it had got, I was just sitting here thinking about us."

Barry didn't like the sound of Pat's words, maybe getting rid of her wasn't going to be as easy as he thought. Don't be daft he thought to himself how hard could it be to tell her to fuck off. Instead he said, "That's funny, I've been thinking about us today as well."

"Have you, Barry? that's nice because I've got some news for you, I'm pregnant." Barry thought he had misheard Pat.

"Sorry, did you just say you're pregnant?" Pat just nodded in reply. "But you can't be, we always use a johnny, you sure it's me that knocked you up?" With that Pat began to cry and Barry regretted what he had said. All said and done Pat wasn't the type to play around, but how the fuck could this have happened. Barry's head was swimming, this was the last thing on his agenda, maybe she would consider getting shot of it. He put his arm around her shoulder, "Don't worry gel. We'll put it right, we'll go and see my aunt Edie, she'll know someone who can help." Pat looked up at Barry's face and knew exactly what he wanted his aunt Edie's help to do. Pat didn't know if she was more scared of Barry's mood turning ugly or what he had proposed for her. Maybe she would be wise to disappear for a while. She had an aunt who lived out in the sticks of Dagenham, she could go and visit her for a while until the dust settled. Maybe Barry would see things differently if she wasn't around; you know the old saying 'absence makes the heart grow fonder'. Yes she would spend a few months with her aunt and by the time she came back to the East End it would be too late to terminate her pregnancy.

Barry was fucking furious that Pat had got herself pregnant. He went to have a word with his aunt Edie who said yes she did know someone in Harley Street who could help them at a price. Barry said he would get back to her and let her know when they could meet Edie's friend because at the moment Pat had done a disappearing act. Edie told him not to leave it too long as the further along she was the more complications could arise.

Markey was pleased to see Barry and couldn't wait to tell him how him and Dave had been exercising Bosco over the park getting him ready for his trial debut in a few weeks. Barry was surprised how quickly the dog had grown and told Markey to take good care of him as he was going to make them a lot of money. Barry tried to put all thoughts of Pat out of his mind. Maybe someone could go and have a word with her mother; surely she would know where Pat had gone. Fuck Pat, he would have to deal with her later because at the moment he had other fish to fry. His top priority was The Blue Raven, He had signed on the dotted line and it belonged to him lock stock and barrel. The architect was hired and the designers were chucking around a few ideas for the interior. He wanted it to be classy and there was only one person who could help him achieve this. Yes, Grace Greene was the girl for the job. He had hunted high and low in his flat to find the piece of paper with the address on the old man had given him the night he went to visit Grace and found her gone. He wondered if he should take a bunch of flowers with him, he was sure that would impress her and maybe take her mind off the fact that he hadn't tried to contact her all this time. He crossed the river and made his way towards the Old Kent Road, he pulled the car to a halt outside the first florist he came across and bought the biggest bunch of flowers he could find. That should do it, he thought laying them gently on the back seat of the car. Barry continued to make his way to the address on the piece of paper. He was surprised at how run down and dingy the houses looked and was more surprised that Grace would be living in such a dump. He found the street and pulled the car to a halt outside number thirteen, Oh, unlucky for some he thought. Barry lifted the knocker and tapped twice on the door. He could hear some noises coming from inside and waited patiently for the door to open. His stomach was doing a little flip at the thought of seeing Grace again. The door opened and a young girl of about twelve or thirteen stood there. The girl with long wavy hair and the face of an angel just stared at him waiting for him to speak. Barry cleared his throat, "Is Grace there, princess?" he asked.

"Who shall I say is calling?" she asked in a rather polished voice which was totally out of place for the area she lived in.

Just at that moment a voice called out, "Who is it?" The girl turned around as a woman began to walk down the hallway.

"It's a man asking if mum is here, he hasn't said his name, Auntie." The woman looked at Barry suspiciously.

"Who might you be then, asking after our Grace?"

"My name is Barry Bullock, I'm an old friend of Grace's."

"That's funny," she replied. "Grace has never mentioned you, anyway she's out at the moment can I take a message?" Barry pulled one of his newly printed business cards out of his pocket and handed it to the woman.

"I'm opening a club up West and I may have some work for her if she is interested."

The woman looked straight into Barry's eyes, "I think you had better sling your hook, mister, our Grace is a respectable woman."

Barry returned her gaze with a hurt little boy look. "You do me an injustice, madam, I need Grace to take care of choosing all the interior designs and then if I am lucky to be my manager because of the lady that she is." With that he handed over his bouquet of flowers and politely tipped his hat in a farewell gesture. Barry got back in his car, he didn't drive off immediately, he sat and looked at the shabby little house and wondered what had brought his beautiful Grace Green there. He would give it a few days and if she hadn't contacted him he would call again just in case the woman threw his card in the dustbin.

The following week went well. Geraldine had fast tracked the plans for the club's extension and work was scheduled to begin in a couple of weeks. Brenda had a list of some pretty stylish interior designers to take a look at the club and submit their tenders for the work. He desperately wanted Grace to take over this part of the operation but he still hadn't received any word from her. He hated to go back to her begging bowl in hand, maybe he would give it a little longer, besides he wanted to check on Dave and Markey's progress with Bosco's training. Barry went round the back of the house and let himself in to the yard. There was no sign of the dog so Barry guessed Dave and Markey had taken him out for a walk. He opened the door to the kitchen to find Edie sitting in the chair beside the fire. Edie looked up but didn't smile.

"I'm glad you're here, Barry, I've just had the woman from Markey's day centre here, it seems he's got himself a girlfriend."

Barry let out a short laugh "You're kidding me."

"Wish I was," replied Edie. "The woman said she didn't mention it before as she thought they were just friends, but yesterday she caught them kissing and cuddling."

"So when has that been a crime?" asked Barry.

Edie was getting annoyed with Barry. "I don't think you realise the seriousness of the situation, suppose it goes beyond kissing and the girl becomes pregnant, we should put a stop to it right now."

"Well, Auntie Edie, I thought contraception was your department."

"I'm sorry to disagree with your ideas but Mark's a man now and he has feelings and desires like any other male."

Just as their discussion was getting a little heated Dave and Markey came through the kitchen door. Barry and Mark had their usual pretend rough and tumble. Bosco went to his bowl to take a drink of water and Dave lowered himself into the chair to take the weight off his aching foot.

"How's our dog shaping up then?" enquired Barry

"He's doing good," replied Markey. "Dave said we can run him in a proper race in a few weeks' time."

Silence hung in the air for a few moments. "What's all this I hear about a girlfriend then, Markey?"

Markey looked from one of his elders to the other and then smiled. "She's beautiful and soft to touch."

"You do know what can happen when you touch girls don't you, Markey?" asked Barry.

"'Course I do," he replied. "I'm not silly they make a baby." Barry was trying not to patronise his little brother and was trying to talk to him man to man.

"You do know that it's bad for girls to have babies when they are not married don't you, Markey?" Barry felt like he was skirting around the edges and wondered why he didn't come right out and ask Mark if he'd had sex with his girlfriend. "What's her name then, this beautiful soft thing that has captured your heart?"

"Her name is Susan and I'm going to marry her." At this point auntie Edie almost fainted.

"What does her family say about that then?" asked Barry, still trying to treat Markey as an adult.

"She is telling them tomorrow, anyway, we don't care, we'll run away to Gretna Green."

Barry was surprised at Mark's determination and was impressed that he even knew about Gretna Green. Voices were getting raised and Barry feared it would soon turn into a full-blown argument with no winners.

"Right let's all calm down and I will go and see this woman at the centre, maybe we could all get together and discuss things with Susan's family." To sort out the wedding?" asked Markey. Edie waved her hands in the air in a futile gesture.

"Sure champ," replied Barry. "Sure."

Barry was very surprised at the attitude of the woman, she looked exactly as he expected, Tweed suite and hair pulled back tightly in a bun fastened at the back of her head. She said she felt sorry for the world who could not see beyond their own prejudice. Just because people were different it didn't mean they didn't have feelings and should be entitled to live their lives the way they wanted to. They just needed a little help from the rest of us. But at the same time they were vulnerable young adults and had to be protected. She told Barry there was a place Loughton way that offered assisted housing. There was a warden to supervise residents and helped them to become self-sufficient. She said that there was no reason why Markey and Susan couldn't live there, the only stipulation was no children, so Susan's family would have to agree to her being sterilised. She added that it would be dangerous for a downs child to become pregnant so it would be in everyone's best interest. It was a lot to take on board, so the two families met to discuss the situation, neither side could raise a sustainable objection. Barry wasn't sure himself how it all happened but by the time they left the centre with Markey and Susan they were engaged and wedding plans had to be sorted, subject to Susan's sterilisation.

Barry arrived at work the next day informing everyone he was going to be best man at Markey's wedding. A few mouths dropped open but no one dared comment. "There's a message for you, Mr Bullock, Miss Green said she will meet you tomorrow at Lyons Corner House Tottenham Court road at eleven o'clock and one from the builders saying they will be ready to install the cloakroom furniture next week and want to know when they will be delivered."

"You can chase that up Brenda, what do I bloody pay you for?"

"There's no need to swear at me, Mr Bullock, I'll do it straight away, I was just letting you know they called." Sometimes she wondered why she stayed working for such a rude man, and then she remembered the size of her pay-packet and picked up the receiver and began to dial the plumber's merchants.

Barry walked into Lyons Corner House at eleven o'clock and glanced around the room for Grace. She was sitting at the corner table looking as beautiful as he last remembered her. He made his way towards her. "Is this seat taken?" he asked. Grace looked at Barry and smiled

"It depends who's asking," she replied. Barry leaned over and kissed Grace on the cheek.

"Tell me how are you keeping."

"Oh so and so," came her watery reply. "But you, Mr Bullock, are on the way up, just as you said you would. Opening your club at last."

"Yes indeed," replied Barry, "we will talk about that in a minute, but first tell me, why the moonlight flip? Didn't you pay the rent or something?"

Grace shrugged her shoulders, "It's complicated, you wouldn't understand."

"Try me," said Barry "I'm all ears."

"It's the old classic," began Grace. "Young impressionable girl meets older man, He was married of course."

"Of course he was," said Barry.

"That's it," said Grace.

"That can't be it, surely," said Barry and he gave a little laugh.

"Now you're making fun of me," said Grace and she stood up to leave. Barry apologised and Grace returned to her seat. The waitress came to the table bringing a pot of tea and two fancy pastries. They both sat in silence as the waitress poured the tea. When she left Grace sighed and decided to carry on with her story. "You're right of course, we had an affair, it was casual at first, but our feelings developed for one another and I found out I was carrying his child."

"So why didn't you just ride off into the sunset together and live happily ever after?" asked Barry.

"Because he was a very well-known judge and the scandal would have destroyed him, his wife would have taken him to the cleaners and we would have been left with nothing. You can't live on thin air even you know that, Barry Bullock. He rented the apartment for us to spend some time together and gave me a good allowance so I could pay my sister to bring up Emily."

"So what happened to destroy the status quo?"

Grace paused for a moment as if lost in some distant memory. "He died," she continued. "He had a heart attack; it turned out his wife had known all along and took great pleasure in telling me that my fun and games were over. The money stopped coming and as soon as the lease expired I had to leave the apartment. I went back to stay with my sister and her husband, Emily loves having me there all the time but bills have to be paid and it's not easy for a girl." Barry knew at that moment he had Grace in palm of his hand.

"Well, Grace, let me be your guardian angel because I have just the job for you."

Barry told Grace all his plans for The Blue Raven, how he wanted her expertise on interior design to make it a classy establishment. He told her that he wanted her to run the day-to-day business and oversee the girls. He would give her the power to hire and fire whoever she needed, she had, cart blanche, as they say. Grace felt a glimmer of excitement building inside her and she hadn't felt like that for a while now. Barry gave Grace the address of The Blue Raven and his office telephone number so she could liaise with Brenda. He told her that Clint would meet her outside the club tomorrow with a set of keys and it would all be left in her capable hands. He told her Clint would be at her disposal for as long as she needed him. He told her not to expect to see him for a few days as tomorrow his little brother was getting married and moving house so he would be a little busy.

Barry jumped on the number 15 bus back to the East End. He was a pleased as punch that Grace had agreed to work for him. He thought of their own, brief, affair and how torrid it had been. He had thought he was in love with Grace at the time, but looking at her again today he realised it was only sex. She had a few more lines around her eyes than he had remembered but maybe she still might be up for a few fun and games in the near future.

As the bus pulled up at his stop his cousin Irene was about to get on. "Irene where you off to?"

"To tell you the truth, Barry, I thought I'd go to the pictures just to get out of the house. Mum and Dad were arguing over our Frankie as usual.

"Have you eaten yet?" Barry asked Irene.

"No," she replied. "When I got in from work it looked like what was my dinner was on the kitchen wall."

"Why don't we grab a bite to eat and a few drinks, we can keep each other company."

"That's the best thing I've heard all day," she replied with a smile. They ate their fish and chip supper and walked down the road to the King's Head to wash it down with a beer. Irene told Barry how she was fed up with her job and could she come and work in his club. Barry said he didn't think Dot and Dick would approve. The time flew by and one drink led to another and before they knew it the bell was ringing for last orders. "I suppose we had better get you home, madam," said Barry as he held Irene's coat up for her to put on. They stepped outside the pub and there was a slight drizzle in the air. By the time they arrived at Irene's house the rain was beginning to fall quite heavy. Irene opened the front door and asked Barry if he would like a cuppa. "Better not," he said, "it's turning into a filthy night and I need to catch the bus home or if I'm lucky a cab might come along. "Why don't you stay here tonight, our Frankie won't be back tonight you could use his room." Barry felt the rain trickling down his jacket collar; he had no one waiting back at his place for him so he thought, why not.

They both had a cup of tea and visited the outside toilet. They climbed the stairs and the tread creaked. "Shhhh," said Irene, "we don't want to wake the OLDS up."

Barry opened Frank's bedroom door to the sound of his uncle Dickie snoring. "Looks like your mum has kicked your dad out of their room tonight, I guess its Shanks's pony for me then the last bus went ages ago," he whispered to Irene.

"Don't be daft," she replied. "You can share my bed like we did when we were little." Irene took Barry's hand and led him into her bedroom, quietly closing the door.

It was freezing in there and they quickly got undressed and climbed under the eiderdown. The bed was even colder and they held on to one another to keep warm. Irene was soft and smelled good. Barry could feel himself getting aroused. He tried to control himself, in God's name she was his cousin, but it had been ages since Pat had left and he hadn't had a woman in weeks. He tried to turn over but Irene put her leg between his to stop him. They had messed around when they were teenagers but things had never gone beyond petting. Now they were both grown up and knew what was going to happen. "Have you got something?" whispered Barry, he didn't want a recurrence of the Pat situation, especially with his own cousin. "No," replied Irene "You just make sure I come before you do, Barry Bullock, and then I'll let you pull out."

Dot woke up with a splitting headache, she could still hear the harsh words that she and Dickie had thrown at one another the night before going over and over in her head. If only she could keep her mouth shut and her opinions to herself, but no, she always had this compulsion to defend her boy. She knew Dickie was only thinking of what was practical. She knew that jobs on the railway were not easy to come by, and maybe if Frankie was sensible he would take a job there and have a steady income. But no, Frankie had music in his blood, just like Veronica. He taught himself to play the piano that had been grannie Maud's, just like Ronnie had, he played the mouth organ and had recently been practicing the trumpet that he had bought at the old flea market. Dickie said it was about time Frankie contributed to the running of the house and handed over some housekeeping. Frankie did earn the odd pound playing in local clubs with his friends and a bit of busking up the west end but Dickie said that was all well and good but if you wanted to eat regular you needed to pay your housekeeping regular, and so the argument went around and around. Last night things had come to a head and harsh words were exchanged. Dickie had never taken himself off to another bed in their entire married life. Dot thought perhaps she had pushed him a little too far, maybe just for once she should agree with Dickie. Part of her agreed with what he said, he was forever the practical reliable Dickie Bullock. But Little Frank had his father's restless genes and Dot knew she would continue to defend him. Maybe she was hell bent on self-punishment as she carried her guilty secret. Still what's done is done she thought as she threw off the eiderdown and dragged her weary body down the stairs and into the kitchen. The pipes clanged as she filled the kettle and the sulphur from the match made her sneeze as its fumes got up her nostrils when she lit the gas stove. She started to sneeze again and had to make a dash to the back door and the outside toilet as she almost wet herself. By the time she returned the kettle was whistling letting Dot know it was hot enough to make the pot of tea. When the tea had brewed long enough she poured a cup for herself and Irene. She would need to wake Irene up for work but decided to leave Dickie in bed as he was on the late shift. She really wasn't in the mood to continue the row of the night before, even worse they probably wouldn't speak for days It was still dark in Irene's bedroom so Dot walked over to the window to draw back the curtains.

"Cup of tea here for you, luv, wakey wakey it's time to get up." Dot turned round to put the cup of tea on the bedside table and dropped it to the floor with a large crash breaking the china in to tiny pieces when she saw Barry's head pop up from under the covers. Irene opened her eyes sleepily.

"Oh, Mum, it was pouring of rain last night so I asked Barry to stop over. He was going to sleep in Frankie's room but Dad was in there. Dot was trying to compose herself, her headache accelerated and began to pulsate, maybe it wasn't as bad as she thought. Dot had no explanation for her next action, or at least not one she could share with anyone. She walked over to the bed and pulled back the covers revealing two naked bodies. Dot began to punch and scream at Barry.

"You no good dirty bastard, you're no better than your old man," All the commotion woke Dickie up.

"What the bloody hell's going on" he said as he came into Irene's bedroom desperately trying to pull his braces over his shoulder. "Jesus Christ," was all Dickie could say at the sight before him. He grabbed Dot by the elbow and ushered her out of the room. "You two had better get dressed, we will wait downstairs for some kind of explanation but it strikes me you have both been caught red handed so to speak." Dot closed the door behind them but they could still hear her hysterical voice echoing up the stairs.

"Oh my God," said Irene, "I know it's not ideal finding your daughter and your nephew in bed together, but Mum is such a drama queen. It's not like its illegal or anything we're cousins not brother and sister."

Dot sat in the kitchen clutching her chest and finding it hard to breathe properly. Dickie was getting annoyed with her. "For God sake woman pull yourself together, it's not the end of the world, nobody's bloody died." How could Dickie possibly understand exactly what had happened; it was her secret that she could never tell a living sole. This was her punishment, what if there was a child it could turn out like Markey. If the truth came out she would never be able to hold her head up again, not only had she been unfaithful to Dickie with his own brother once but twice and neither of the children he called his own were his.

Barry dressed quickly and told Irene she could sort her parents out as he had lots to do, he kissed her on the head and thanked her for a wonderful night and maybe they could do it again sometime.

"You've got some bloody cheek, Barry Bullock," she said jokingly as she threw her slipper at him as he pulled the bedroom door to. Irene had to admit it was great uncomplicated sex and yes she would like to do it again.

Chapter 9

The blossom was on the trees, the sun was shining and it was Markey and Susan's wedding day. Susan had recovered from her surgery and the little flat was all ready for the newlyweds. Barry checked the time on his wristwatch to make sure everything was on schedule. He had to be at the house to collect Markey, Edie and Georgie and make sure they were at the church on time. Barry was taking his duties as best man very serious. Somehow he felt that this wedding was extra special and he had to make sure everything run smooth. He was sure he could feel his mother's seal of approval on the day and that she was smiling down on them. The bride was due to arrive at the church one thirty so there wouldn't be too much time for pre-wedding nerves. Barry had to admit Mark seemed to be taking it all in his stride and that it was the rest of the Bullocks that were nervous. They had hired the function room above the King's Head for a small reception and then the happy couple would go off to their new home. Barry was just finishing tying his shoes when he heard the key turn in the front door. Pat stood in the doorway with her suitcase in one hand and a rather noticeable bump around her middle. Barry just looked at Pat a little surprised, she was the last person he expected to see today. Pat opened her mouth and went to speak.

"Not now," said Barry "Your timing was always fucking shit. I'm just off to be best man at my brother's

193

wedding so whatever you've got to say for yourself can wait till I get back." And with that he picked up his car keys and left Pat standing there with her mouth wide open.

It was a beautiful day for a wedding, the sun shone and the breeze was warm. The bride and groom made a lovely couple. Susan only had a small family, her parents, grandparents a couple of aunts and uncles and half a dozen cousins Barry was pleased quite a few of the Bullock clan had made it. They never could resist a good knees up. Even Geraldine and Eric had put in an appearance. It was still a little frosty between the women but they had buried the hatchet for today at least to please Markey. Barry had hired a photographer to take the traditional pictures and once the confetti was thrown they all made their way to the King's Head. Once enough port and lemon and beer had been drunk his aunts lifted the lid of the piano and Little Frank began to play. Dot and Dick gave Barry a wide birth all day trying not to make a scene but they made sure he knew all was not forgiven. Irene had brought one of her old boyfriends to the wedding and didn't seem to be taking too much notice of Barry and for this Dot was extremely grateful.

Edie wanted to know what was going to happen to Bosco now Markey had moved out. The last thing she wanted was a dog to take care of. Barry told her to keep her hair on and Dave would take him home with him, he would come and collect him in a couple of days. Mark was very upset that Bosco couldn't live with him and Susan but unfortunately animals were off limits at the new place. Dave said he come and visit Bosco whenever he wanted and after all they were still partners at the dog track so he would still see him regular. Soon the day was over and it was time for everyone to head off home. The Bullocks patted Markey on the back and told him not to do anything they wouldn't. Barry was sure Markey knew exactly what to do as the little chat they had a few days earlier even surprised him. Goodbyes were said all round and Barry dropped Edie and Georgie back at the house. They asked him if he wanted to stop over for the night but he told them Pat had shown up, bump and all. "Oh well," said Edie, "it's too late to do anything about it now, she must be quite a few months gone if she's showing." Barry kissed Edie and Georgie goodbye and asked them to wish him luck. Edie said she didn't know who was going to need the luck more Pat or Barry.

Barry let himself into the flat. Pat was asleep on the sofa, she looked so vulnerable lying there, his eyes strayed down to her stomach. That was his child growing there inside her and suddenly he felt very protective of it. So what if this hadn't been part of the Barry Bullock's plan, it had happened and there was no way he was going to shirk his duty. Barry still didn't want to get married but he would buy Pat a ring and she could call herself anything she wanted. Pat stirred and opened her eyes, she went to speak but Barry gently pressed his finger to her lips. Pat thought that Barry would be angry with her and she was ready for a confrontation. Instead he led her to the bedroom and tucked her into bed. He kissed the top of her head and pulled the door closed behind him. Barry went to the cupboard and poured himself a large whisky; this was going to be one hell of a ride he thought.

Pat could hardly believe it when Barry gave her a set of keys and told her they were for their new home. Pat fell in love with the house immediately. It was a three-storey terrace house that had been completely refurbished. It even had an inside bathroom and toilet. Barry told her to order the furniture and anything else she needed and Brenda was at her disposal to help. Barry even told her she could borrow Grace Green if she needed her to help in any way. Pat knew that Grace and Barry had once been lovers and she hated to think of other women being intimate with Barry the same way she was. She definitely didn't want Grace stepping one foot inside her beautiful new home and tarnishing it in any way.

Time ticked on and the days seemed to speed by. The club was almost ready for its opening night, Pat and Barry were settling in to their new house and Markey and Susan were blissfully happy at their new flat. Markey was still spending time with Dave and Bosco. The dog was doing well at the track, and he had even won a few races. Barry would call in on Edie and Georgie on a regular basis to make sure they were alright and would always leave a ten-pound note under the teapot just like he had for Sadie. Barry didn't always find it easy to talk about his private life, let alone his sex life, but Edie always had a way of making you say things you would rather not. Edie was a perceptive lady and she knew when Barry was troubled. He was wearing the same look now as he had when he was a young boy.

"Well, auntie Edie, if you must know I am a little worried. You know I always use protection when I'm with a lady but still somehow Pat got pregnant." Edie gave Barry a sideways glance. "I'm not saying I have any doubts that its mine, but I don't know how we slipped up, and I don't want it to happen again not with Pat or anyone else." Barry began to feel ill at ease and stood up to leave, he couldn't really believe he was having this conversation with his aunt.

"If you are one hundred percent sure you mean what you just said I might be able to help you," said Edie. "I know of a doctor in Harley Street that can fix it that you never father a child again. It's not cheap and it's a new procedure."

Barry looked at Edie, "Let's do it then" he said without a moment's hesitation it was the answer to his payers he would never have to worry again.

Barry told Pat he had a bit of business to attend to and would be away a couple of days. Pat was almost at her due date and thought Barry was being way out of order leaving her at such a time. He told her that any problems Georgie would be on hand to help.

Barry had never had a medical procedure in his life so he was pretty ignorant of what was going to happen to him. He arrived at the Harley Street surgery with a little overnight bag in tow. An elderly nurse led him into a very posh room and told him to remove his clothing and put on the gown. Barry did as he was told, hating every moment, but he knew he just had to get through it. Ten minutes later the nurse came back and led Barry in to a small operating room and told him to lie on the couch. He could see trays of what he could only describe as barbaric torture instruments. The nurse gave Barry a small container of liquid to drink; he swigged it back in one gulp. He handed the container back to the nurse.

"I'd rather have a whisky next time," Barry was trying to make small talk to ease his nerves and feelings of awkwardness. After a few moments Barry began to relax, he guessed it must have been the stuff the nurse gave him to drink. His limbs became heavy and he felt like he was floating. The nurse lifted up the gown exposing Barry's gentiles. She shaved Barry's private parts, washed them in a sterile liquid and placed the surgical cloths around the area. The doctor came into the operating theatre covered in green operating garments. Barry looked at his face and thought he didn't seem to resemble the doctor who had done his consultation the week before but was sure that it must be. The doctor picked up a syringe from the instrument table.

"I'm just going to give you an injection Mr Bullock, just to numb the area."

For some reason Barry was expecting a needle in his arm and was a little shocked when it went straight into his testicles. The next thing Barry remembered was hearing the doctor say, "That wasn't too bad now was it? The nurses will take you to your room where you will rest, if all is well you can go home tomorrow."

Barry had a nice meal and a comfortable bed, the nurse gave him a cocktail of pills to take and he went out like a light. He had almost finished his full English breakfast when the doctor appeared. The doctor took a look at Barry's stitches and declared he was fit enough to go home. Barry had also taken a look at his testicles and they seemed to be twice their normal size. The doctor said this was perfectly normal and the swelling would go down in a few days. They made Barry a follow up appointment for two weeks' time to make sure he was healing well and they would need a sample to check his sperm count. They informed him that it would take a while for his sperm to be completely infertile so not to rely on unprotected sex for a while yet. Barry wondered if his wedding tackle would ever be the same again.

The journey in the taxi back to the east end was most uncomfortable, Barry couldn't wait to get home and swallow a few more painkillers that the nurse had given him. He had just made himself comfortable on the sofa when there was a loud knock on the front door. He swore as he painfully made his way down the hallway to open the door, if Pat's forgot her key I'll fucking kill her he thought. Barry opened the door to find Edie standing there. "Thank God you're back, Pat went into labour last night, our Georgie has been at the hospital with her the whole night, but she is having a bad time and wants you."

Edie looked at Barry and said, "No I haven't told a soul where you were not even when your cousins were on a wild goose chase all over London looking for you."

Barry couldn't drive his car because of his own medical procedure and it took them ages to find a cab and get to the hospital. When they arrived in the maternity unit they found Georgie in the waiting room, her face was as white as a sheet. "Well, what's happening?" asked Barry and Edie at the same time. Georgie was finding it hard to speak between her short sharp sobs that she could no longer hold back." The baby's here, it's a girl, Pat's in a bad way she has lost a lot of blood."

"The nurse explained that the afterbirth was in front of the baby and it broke up during delivery, Pat haemorrhaged and they are giving her a transfusion." Barry kept asking the nurse what was going on and all she said was they were doing everything that they could and that they would just have to be patient. 'Patient' was one thing Barry Bullock wasn't and he was getting seriously irritated. What seemed like an eternity a nurse appeared and said that Pat was now stable and Barry could see her for a few moments only.

Barry made his way to Pat's bed trying to walk as normally as he could under the circumstances. Pat could barely open her eyes so he gave her a quick kiss on the forehead and said he would be back to see her in the morning. Pat closed her eyes again without uttering a word; she was extremely weak and lucky to still be alive. The nurse led Barry, Edie and Georgina along the corridor to the nursery area. They were allowed to look through the window at the row of babies. Baby Bullock was nestled in a pink blanket in a crib between two boys. She looked so tiny compared to the other babies. Barry just stared at her for a while and at that moment he had never loved a living thing more in his entire life.

"Right then, girls," he said to his aunt and his sister, "it's time we were off, if I was feeling better I'd say we would go and wet the baby's head, but right now I just want to get some sleep, I'll leave it to you two to let the family know that Mary Bullock has arrived."

When Pat and Mary came home from the hospital Barry wrapped them both in cotton wool. He wouldn't let the wind blow on them, Mary was the most precious thing in his life and Pat was the person who had given him this gift and the person who for the next twenty years was to nurture his beautiful daughter. When Barry remembered how he had wanted Pat to get an abortion, he shuddered. Pat could ask for anything she wanted and Barry would get it for her. But funnily enough the only thing Pat really wanted was for Barry to love her and even marry her but neither of these was she going to get. Pat wore Barry's ring and called herself Mrs Bullock and that was what she was going to have to settle for.

The months passed quietly, Mary thrived and was growing into a beautiful little girl. She would gurgle and laugh when Barry played with her. He had endless patience playing with the child. He would spoil her rotten and Pat would moan. There was nothing too good for his girl, she was going to have the life he never had and Pat could go fuck herself as far as he was concerned. Edie and Georgina missed Markey terribly, the house was empty and had a sadness hanging over it. Georgie carried on with the clinics but Edie stayed at home most days saying her arthritis was getting a grip on her and she was weary now. It took all her energy just keeping the place tidy and doing the shopping. It's funny how old age creeps up on you when you're not looking. Barry was glad things were ticking along in a quiet way as the opening day of The Blue Raven was only a couple of weeks away and he could give it his full attention. Grace had done a marvellous job on the choice of furnishings and she had hired tiptop staff. She had sent out first night invitations to elite guests and then Barry hoped he would be inundated with top-notch clientele.

Just when they all thought things were going smoothly they received a telegram from Veronica.

ON MY WAY HOME. WILL ARRIVE AT SOUTHAMPTON 25TH MEET ME. EXPLAINE IN DUE COURSE. RONNIE.

Edie went into a flat spin imagining all sorts of disasters. Ronnie's last letter said how well the band was doing, they had lots of bookings and were making a packet. Georgina took the telegram from Edie's hand, grabbed her handbag and made her way to the telephone box on the corner of the next street. She had to let Barry know, it was already the 23rd and he was the only one who had a car to get down to Southampton and meet the ship.

Barry arranged for Clint to drive Georgina down to Southampton to collect Veronica. As far as they could make out it was just her to be picked up, why was she coming home alone when her last letter had been so positive? what had gone wrong? Georgie asked Edie to go with her to Southampton, but Edie said the journey would be too much for her, besides, it was her job to have a nice meal waiting for them when they arrived home. She would do a great big Shepherd's pie just like the old days and just in case Barry and Geraldine turned up.

Clint arrived at seven o'clock to collect Georgie. They wanted to make an early start just in case there were any hiccups on the way that would delay them. Clint put the little picnic hamper in the boot of the car and Georgina climbed into the back seat. She had no intention of sitting up front with Clint. She had never liked him much and had no intention of making small talk all the way to Southampton. Edie kissed Georgie goodbye and wished them a safe journey. Georgie waved her goodbye as the car pulled away, it was a long way to Southampton and Georgie opened her book and began to read. She was finding it difficult to concentrate and laid it back down on the seat. She stared out of the car window watching the changing scenery until the houses and shops became fields and cows. She, too, wondered what the hell was bringing Ronnie back to England so suddenly, still she had always been a bit of a drama queen so it was probably nothing much at all, just a storm in a teacup. Ronnie had been very theatrical even as a child and the slightest thing would send her into a tantrum. Georgie felt that she had always walked in Ronnie's shadow. Maybe it was because she was the eldest and had to help support her mother and somehow just got over looked. It had always been easier to give into Ronnie's tantrums and restore the peace. Maybe Georgie was too sensitive to other people's feelings. When her aunt Edie lost her first love in the war she turned to Georgie for comfort. Georgie became her rock and as time went by she found it harder and harder to break away, that's how she came to follow Edie into nursing, she felt she didn't really have a choice. Sometimes when she was working in the mother's clinic she found herself being envious of them, she longed to feel a new life kicking inside her and a loving husband to keep her warm at night. She was an attractive woman but by the time she had worked all hours God sent with Edie at the clinic, then went home to help her mother with Markey there was never any time or energy left for her own self-indulgence. Now at the ripe old age of thirty-six most would say she was over the hill. Even Markey had got married, Georgie was pleased for them but the house seemed empty now he had gone and she felt like she was grieving. Georgie was a great believer in fate and hers was never to get married, she resigned herself to dying an old spinster. She felt Edie would sometimes sense her mood and tried to encourage her to go out more. But who was she supposed to go out with, all the girls she had gone to school with were married with family's maybe it would be nice to have Veronica home again to liven up the place. Half way through the journey Clint pulled off the road beside a little café.

"Don't know about you," he said to Georgina, "but I could murder a cuppa and I'm busting for a pee." Georgina followed Clint into the café, they sat down at a table and a waitress came over to take their order of two teas and two pastries. Clint excused himself to use the toilet and Georgie glanced around the bare little café. The floor was wooden, which matched the furniture. There was a pinball machine in the corner where a couple of scruffy looking individuals were beating the hell out of it. There was a smell of cooking grease hanging in the air and steam coming from a large urn in the corner of the room. The waitress came back with their order just as Clint returned from the gents. Georgie picked at the pastry while Clint scoffed his back in seconds, he washed it down with his mug of tea. "Hurry up," he said to Georgie, "we need to make tracks, there's still a fair way to go yet." It seemed that Clint was as eager to make conversation with her as she was with him.

"I need to go to the toilet first; I'll meet you at the car. Georgie took a gulp of her tea and stood up to go to the ladies to relieve herself. When she returned Clint was sitting inside the car smoking a cigarette. She wished he wouldn't do that as the smell always made her want to heave, she wanted to tell him to put it out but thought she would create more of an atmosphere than there already was between them.

The rest of the journey seemed to take forever but finally they arrived at Southampton docks and parked the car as near to the quayside as they could. Luggage was being unloaded and people were disembarking, they scoured the sea of faces but Veronica was nowhere in sight. A man grabbed hold of Georgie's arm and began to speak to her in a foreign language, "Où est la réception, Madame?" Georgie thought it sounded French and was trying to explain she did not understand when Clint answered them perfectly, "Madam, monsieur, regardez droit devant."

"Merci Monsieur, au revoir," replied the old gentleman. Georgie wondered where Clint learned to speak French with such a beautiful accent when they were interrupted by the sound of Veronica's voice calling to them as she waved from the gangway. You could have knocked Georgina over with a feather when she saw the enormous Veronica come waddling down the gangplank.

"You can pick your chin up off the floor," came Ronnie's first words, "it's not like you've never seen a pregnant lady before, I'm famished let's get some food before I die."

Clint collected the baggage and they made their way back to the car. Georgie opened auntie Edie's picnic hamper and all three of them got stuck in. Clint was as surprised as Georgie to see Veronica's condition and hoped he was in for an interesting journey home. Picnic hamper packed away and returned to the boot they all three prepared for the drive back to the East End.

"Right then," said Veronica, "I've got to have a pee before we set off," and she began to climb out of the car. I can't seem to go more than half an hour these days without wanting the toilet."

Georgie let out a sigh; it was going to take forever to get home at that rate. With all their ablutions complete they settled down and Clint drove them slowly out of the dockside. They soon made their way to the main road and not a word was spoken.

"Well then, have I got to prise it out of you or are you going to tell me what the hell is going on?" Georgie wanted to know.

"Maybe we should wait till we get home and I can tell you and aunt Edie together."

"If you think I can wait over two hours for an explanation, madam, you're badly mistaken, now spill the beans."

Veronica took a deep breath, "I don't really know where to begin. Veronica's mind sped backwards trying to find an appropriate starting point. We were doing very well for a while; the band was getting its fair share of bookings. Solly began to start writing a bit. Yeah, it was going well. Then I discovered I was pregnant. Me and Solly argued, he said how was we going to cart a baby with us around America? He might as well chuck it all in and forget the whole thing. Well, there was this other band we had been travelling with and one of them had been giving me the eye. I never gave him any encouragement, honest I didn't, Georgie."

"So what happened next? Why did you leave?" asked Georgie.

"I was upset, I stormed out of our rooms and who should I bump straight into but Dizzy, my new admirer, he took me for a drink and before I knew it we were back at his place. Someone must have seen us and told Solly because he came round and that's where he found me in bed with Dizzy. I told him nothing had happened, but you could see he didn't believe me. We tried to patch things up but it just wasn't working, maybe it was me and my hormones, I don't know. Anyway, we moved on to the next town and played a few clubs for a couple of weeks but I was feeling really rough. I was being sick morning noon and night. Solly was so worried he took me the hospital for the poor people who can't afford medical insurance. They kept me in for a couple of days and did a few tests, and guess what? Not only am I pregnant but there are two of the little bleeders. Things didn't improve between me and Solly so when the band was practising one day I just packed my bags and left." Veronica began to cry and Georgie tried to comfort her. "I just needed my family, I was homesick and wanted to come home," she sobbed. When Veronica's tears finally subsided Georgie tried to fill her in on what had been happening at home. She told Ronnie Edie had sent letters but she never knew quite where to post them to and could only hope they caught up with her eventually. Ronnie didn't know Markey had got married and Barry was now a father. Georgie thought she had better not tell her the escapade of Dave and getting his toes chopped off as she was distressed enough. Clint had a thoroughly entertaining journey home and was almost reluctant to drop the girls off.

Aunt Edie almost fainted when she saw what Georgina had brought home. After Edie had got over the initial shock Georgina put the kettle on and the next couple of hours were spent with Veronica repeating her story.

"I'm sorry, Auntie Edie, for being such a disappointment, as soon as I can I will find somewhere to live and get out of your hair."

"You will do no such thing," replied Edie. "This is your home for as long as you need it, you and your babies."

Veronica began to cry all over again. Georgina thought Edie hadn't thought things through properly. Babies were a big disruption and Edie wasn't getting any younger, still it was good to see her smile again. Georgina walked out into the back yard to get a breath of fresh air. What with their Barry's little Mary and now Veronica's twins it was a whole new generation of Bullocks, what would the rest of the family make of it when they knew.

Chapter 10

The house certainly seem to come to life now Veronica was back. They were preparing for the arrival of the babies, which by Ronnie's calculation was about two months away, although she had never been particularly good at maths. Edie said that looking at the size of Ronnie's stomach she would say the twins were probably due any time. Edie convinced Ronnie to see her doctor friend from Harley Street. He would put them in touch with a tiptop doctor to help deliver the twins, she wanted the best for Ronnie as multiple birth deliveries could always be more difficult, she didn't want anything going wrong. Edie had known many women die in childbirth trying to deliver twins. Sometimes they lost the babies and the mother and she didn't want to take any chances with Ronnie, so she could protest all she wanted to, Edie still dragged Ronnie up to London for a consultation. Ronnie thought Edie was going a bit over the top but went along just to keep the peace. The consultant examined Ronnie's abdomen, pushing, probing and measuring for quite a while. He went over to his desk making notes and doing calculations. "Nurse, would you prepare the patient for an internal examination?" he instructed. Ronnie didn't like the sound of that and Edie was now worrying that something was wrong. Edie was asked to wait outside and the nurse sat down beside Veronica to hold her hand during the procedure. The doctor tried to reassure Ronnie that everything was alright as he wanted her to relax. It was very difficult to examine a patient who was tense. Ronnie felt like she was lying there in a humiliating position for ages, her legs held high in stirrups. She would even swear the doctor used a torch light at one point. Finally the doctor told her she could get dressed and that Edie could come back and join her. The doctor went to his bookshelf and took down a large medical journal. Edie and Ronnie sat in silence while he made some more notes and crossed referenced his records.

"Well, ladies, after careful examination this is my conclusion. One of the babies is quite a bit larger than the other, there are many reasons why this can happen, they could be sharing a placenta that is feeding one baby more than the other; it could be one placenta is failing faster than it should, but after your internal examination I do not think it is either of these. My conclusion is that you have a very rare condition known as uterus didelphys which means you have two wombs. You would most probably ovulate from each fallopian tube alternate months. I cannot be one hundred percent sure but I believe that you conceived the first baby and then the second one a month later. The doctor saw the worried expression on both their faces and did not want to alarm either one of them unduly. "This, ladies, is just speculation and nothing is certain at this point. We will keep a close eye on you and things will become clearer during and after the birth. When you go into labour it may trigger off contractions in the second womb which means the second baby will be slightly premature. As soon as you are near to your due date it is my advice that you be admitted to the Royal Free Hospital where they have facilities to cope with small babies. If you are agreeable I will make the arrangements."

Edie and Ronnie found all the information overwhelming and had difficulty in digesting what they had been told. They shook the doctor's hand and thanked him for all he had done. The girls made their way back to the underground station in virtual silence both lost in their own thoughts. They were told that they would receive a letter in a few days telling them exactly what to do and who to contact should labour begin unexpectedly. Both of them agreed only to fill Georgina in on what the doctor had said, they didn't want it all over the East End as they knew only too well how people loved to gossip and how rumours quickly spread. Ronnie didn't want to be turned into some kind of freak show. They had all spent years defending Markey, getting into fights when people said hurtful things about him. Veronica could just hear it all now, she knew how people would react calling them all dreadful things. The least people knew the better. They told the family that Ronnie was going to have her babies at the Royal Free Hospital purely because it was safe for a multiple birth and no one questioned that. The letter arrived telling them the date Ronnie would be admitted to the hospital should nothing happen before. If labour began unexpectedly they should telephone the hospital immediately letting them know they were on their way. The days were dragging by slowly and not a twinge was felt. The day arrived for Veronica to be admitted. Edie and Georgina both accompanied her, one holding the suitcase and one holding her arm. As all was calm and there was no immediate rush to get there they decided to travel by train, it was unusually packed for the time of day and they were pushed and shoved in all directions. Veronica began to complain that they should have got a taxi because now she had the most horrendous backache. The train pulled into the station and they had to fight their way to get out of the carriage. They shuffled their way towards the exit and stepped on to the escalator. By the time they arrived at the top Veronica informed Georgina and Edie that she couldn't go another step unless she had a wee. All three of the women pushed against the ever moving crowd trying to reach the ladies toilet before Ronnie disgraced herself in the ticket hall. Veronica pulled up her skirt and pulled down her knickers as fast as she could before almost bursting. Georgie began to laugh outside the toilet door, saying she didn't think it was ever going to stop. Georgie's laughter came to an abrupt halt when she heard Veronica scream from inside the cubicle.

"I'm bleeding, I'm bleeding!" she cried.

"Open the bloody door will you," said Edie, "and let me have a look." Edie expected to see a pool of blood, instead it was just a smear on the tissue paper. "For God's sake, Veronica, you've had a show not cut a bloody artery, now pull your drawers up and let's get a move on before your waters break."

By the time Veronica was settled in her hospital bed the dull backache had progressed to early labour pains. Whenever the nurse disappeared Ronnie got out of bed and began to pace the floor. Edie protested but Veronica told her to shut up in no uncertain terms.

"My mum always said pacing up and down brought the baby on quicker and she would have known she done it enough times," then she burst into tears and said she wanted her mum with her now. By the time Ronnie had dilated half way she had exhausted herself. The nurse gave her some gas and air to help her relax and ease the pain, thankfully to Edie and Georgie's relief she nodded off to sleep for a short while. They both agreed that now was a good time for something to eat and a cup of tea as it didn't look likely they would be leaving the hospital for a while. By the time they had finished their meal and were making their way back to the labour ward they could hear Ronnie's piercing screams coming down the corridor. Edie turned a little pale thinking something must be wrong. The doctor looked up from between Veronica's legs.

"It's OK, things progressed rather quickly and the baby's head is about to be born. Like I said, this is a rare and unusual condition, we don't know exactly what to expect."

"Here comes baby now, well done, Veronica you have a little girl."

The afterbirth arrived ten minutes later, luckily everything had gone smoothly and there were no complications. The second baby had a regular heart beat and seemed fine but wasn't in any hurry to make an appearance.

They tidied Ronnie up and made her comfortable. The nurse continued to check her all through the night but all was quiet. Ronnie still felt exhausted when the nurse came into the room the next morning pulling back the curtains and saying baby needed feeding. Ronnie felt a little strange feeding her daughter as she could still fell the other child kicking inside her. The nurse placed the baby in her arms and helped the baby find Ronnie's nipple and she began to suckle. Ronnie looked at the little face at her breast and decided it was like looking at Solly, how she missed him in that instant and wished he was with her now. Just at that moment the baby inside her kicked out and twin number one lost her nipple and began to cry. The nurse appeared as if by magic and took the baby from Ronnie.

"Let me give her a bottle feed so that you can get some rest, we'll try breastfeeding again later." Ronnie was pleased as the nurse disappeared with the little thing with a wisp of dark hair and translucent skin began to get louder. Lilly, thought Ronnie, she is just like a little Lilly.

Ronnie lay in the hospital bed feeling the regular little kicks inside her and wondered what this other little baby would be like. Her mind drifted back to America and the band, back to the night they first played at the same venue as Dizzy and his boys. There had been an attraction between the two them from the beginning. Ronnie tried to avoid being alone with him but there were still the stares and the looks that she found hard to ignore. When they were rehearsing as a group his hand might brush hers and she would feel the electricity between them. Both bands playing at the same venues was quite a hit and Solly suggested they tour together. Dizzy didn't have any objections so they went on the road together. It was the night that they had the best revue of the tour so far, Champagne was flowing freely in the dressing room and everyone's spirits were high. Veronica was a little quiet and Solly told her she was a kill joy. Veronica's period was two weeks late and she suspected she might be pregnant. Her breasts were sore and she felt bloated, still these were also symptoms of an impending period so she tried to push it to the back of her mind. Her visits to the ladies became more frequent and on one of these occasions as she came out of the ladies toilet Dizzy came out of the gents. He stood in front of her, blocking her path. He brushed his lips against her cheek and she melted. Dizzy turned the handle of the storeroom door behind Veronica and they both fell inside closing the door behind them. Ronnie knew this was wrong but she wanted it, somewhere in her head she thought what the hell I'm pregnant anyway, you never know it might even bring on my period if I'm wrong. It was pitch black in the store cupboard and the only sound was that of their breathing hard and laboured.

Everything seemed to happen quickly, she felt him pulling at her underwear and then his fingers moving inside her. She opened his fly but she was clumsy and he had to help her. Then he was inside her and she wasn't sure if she was feeling pain or pleasure. It was over very quickly and if it hadn't been for the warm semen she could feel between her legs she may have thought she had imagined it. Dizzy straightened himself up and left her standing alone in the darkness of the store room, he was pleased with his conquest but eager to return to the dressing room party. Veronica returned to the ladies bathroom to tidy herself up. She was nervous to return to the others in case she looked different. She checked her face in the mirror, it still looked the same but now she wore the face of guilt. She painted a smile on her lips and walked back in to join the others. Solly looked at Veronica concerned. "Are you OK, babe? You've been a long time."

"Do you think we could go now, I'm very tired and need to sleep."

"OK boys, let's break it up," said Solly, "it's getting late and don't forget we still have to work tomorrow night."

Ronnie tried her best to avoid Dizzy for the next few days but it was difficult. They worked together and played together and worst of all she wanted him to make love to her again. Not just a quick fumble but slowly and passionately. The date of her next period had almost arrived and still she hadn't bled. She would give it another week and she would go and visit a doctor, she had to know either way. It was Sunday afternoon and Solly was sleeping. They worked long hours all week, and into the small hours on a Saturday night. Solly often slept Sunday afternoons, it was his catch-up time he said.

Veronica was restless, she had too much on her mind to sleep. Maybe a walk would do her good, but who was she kidding, her walk took her right in the direction of Dizzy's trailer.

She could hear voices inside but she still knocked on the door. It was opened by Dizzy's trumpet player who also co-wrote some of the songs with him. Veronica walked up the steps of the trailer and Dizzy motioned the other guy to leave.

"Now what brings you here pretty young thing?" he asked Veronica in his soft velvet voice. Dizzy walked over to Veronica and gently stroked her arm. "Does your husband know that his wife has come out to play with Dizzy on this fine Sunday afternoon?" Veronica still didn't answer. Dizzy cupped her face in his hands and began to gently kiss her lips, then her neck and he knew she wanted him. "Well my little white swan it's time I saw what you are made of," and he tenderly removed every inch of her clothing. She lay down on his crumpled bed covers and watched him get undressed. She couldn't take her eyes off of him, his muscles were well developed and his black skin glistened in the sunlight that was shining through the trailer window. Veronica had to admit she had never imagined a man could be so well endowed in all departments. She was a woman of very little experience and only had her brothers and Solly to go by but this man was enormous and she realised she hadn't imagined the throbbing sensation that she thought she remembered from the romp in the store cupboard. Dizzy laid down beside Veronica and tenderly kissed her all over. He liked to think of himself as a bit of a stud, a ladies' man, but he truly had feelings for his little white swan, he wondered if she would leave Solly for him or was she just using him to spice up her life. He wanted her to want him so he took his time slow and easy licking and sucking her till he knew she was ready for him. He knew she was married, but he also thought she was probably inexperienced in the ways of lovemaking. He felt her hand tighten around his enlarged penis as she begin to rub him. Tenderly he pushed her onto her back and eased himself between her legs. He was as eager as she was but he was so afraid he would hurt her. African women seemed better equipped to cope with African men in that department. He felt her tense up as he pushed himself inside her. Slowly, slowly does it he thought. He felt her relax a little and knew she had accommodated him and she began to move to his rhythm. He felt her body shudder beneath him and then he let himself go. For the first time in his life Dizzy felt he was in love.

Veronica was so wrapped up in her affair with Dizzy she pushed the whole issue of the missed period to the back of her mind until she was pulled up a whole month later by early morning sickness. She told Solly she must have picked up a bug or something and would go and see a doctor. She found a doctor, who for a small fee, was willing to see her. He asked Veronica a few questions, got her to pee in a container and then asked her to lie down on the couch. He felt her stomach and informed her she was approximately three months pregnant. He said he couldn't be more specific unless she could remember the first day of her last period and unfortunately Ronnie was a little unsure. Ronnie knew she couldn't put off breaking the news to Solly any longer. He went mad, he said it was the end of life as they knew it. How could they cart a baby round from place to place and live the way they were living? He said they might as well chuck it all in and go back to England. Ronnie said he was overreacting and they should just see how things went. The few weeks that followed didn't improve. Ronnie spent most of her time feeling sick and by her fifth month Solly took her to the hospital for the poor to see if they could give her something to ease her symptoms. That's when they told them it was twins. For the following few weeks Solly hardly said a word to Veronica. He immersed himself in the band and left her to her own devices. Things came to a head one evening and they quarrelled, both of them said things that they would later come to regret and Veronica stormed out and ran straight to Dizzy's trailer. She was in a terrible state, he tried to comfort her the best he could, they just lay down on the bed and he held her in his arms until her sobs subsided and she finally drifted off to sleep. That's where Solly found them when he stormed in to the trailer the next morning. Solly and Dizzy exchanged harsh words, Dizzy tried to tell Solly that he didn't know Veronica was pregnant. Solly was in a terrible rage and punched Dizzy on the nose. Dizzy decided there was no point in returning the blows, he could have brought his opponent to his knees with a single blow but what would be the point. They tried to tell him that nothing had happened but their words fell on deaf ears. After that episode Dizzy gave Veronica a wide birth, as much as he had feelings for his little white swan he didn't want to be saddled with another man's kids. Ronnie became more and more depressed and incredibly home sick so while all the men were working she packed her suitcase and left. She knew where Solly hid some of their money in case of emergency so she helped herself and headed for home, she didn't even leave him a goodbye letter, let the bastard stew.

For the next few days Veronica concentrated on taking care of her little Lilly, she bathed her and breast fed her and tried to relax. The doctor came to see her three or four times each day. Sometimes he would bring students with him, as she was such a rare case for them it caused a great deal of interest. Veronica felt like she was becoming a bit of a celebrity. She was feeling well and longed to go home but she knew that until the second baby was delivered she would not be allowed to leave. She conditioned herself for a long stay. She lay in her bed churning over what the doctor had said to her. Two wombs, babies at different gestation periods. She was desperately trying to remember when she had slept with Dizzy but maths wasn't her strongest subject. In fact, she had probably slept with both of them during the same month so either one of them could be her unborn baby's father. She was a musician for God's sake not a mathematician. By the time Lilly was a week old Veronica began to feel the dull ache in her lower back again. This time she was afraid, she knew what she had to do. Like everything else in her life she didn't like she tried to ignore what was happening. As much as she was dreading giving birth again this time it was much easier. She thought that as this baby was premature that was the reason. The doctor did confirm that indeed the second child was early as it was covered in vernix which was the trait of an early baby but it did not have the usual transparent skin. Instead Veronica's second daughter was quite dark and rosy with tight thick black hair, which surprised everyone. By the time Veronica was discharged from the hospital and arrived home the twins had caused quite a stir by the contrast of their appearance. Rosalie's skin continued to darken, while Lilly was a milky white. As the days passed, the novelty of motherhood began to wear off. Ronnie longed to play the piano again and sing. On the other hand Auntie Edie and Auntie Georgina were like a pig in poo and couldn't have been happier. Pat would come round and baby talk would be in full swing, which was rapidly boring Veronica to death. Barry had opened The Blue Raven and it proved to be very popular. The only highlight in her life was when Barry called in at the house and told them all the current gossip. Barry knew what a good musician Veronica was so he became her saviour and asked her to work a few nights a week at the club. The twins continued to be the talk of the borough, they couldn't hide Rosalie away for ever. Ronnie tried to tell them she was a throwback from Solly's side of the family when a great, great, great ancestor had a liaison with an African seaman. She didn't think the story washed with everyone and she often saw people talking behind their hands as she walked by pushing her pram. Still, now she was working nights at The Blue Raven she left the fresh air outings to Edie and Georgie. Veronica had heard little Frank had inherited the family musical traits. She made a point of hearing him play and was very impressed at his musical abilities. They had developed while she had been away. She was surprised Barry hadn't snapped him up for the club. When Barry came round to the house she broached the subject of little Frank and herself teaming up. To her surprise Barry went straight on the defensive and shot her down in flames. Barry's feelings towards little Frank did not soften with time. The older little Frank got the more he bore an uncanny resemblance to his father and the more it made Barry's skin crawl. Veronica knew how hard little Frank was finding it to get work and she also knew how important family were to Barry and how he would always see them alright, so unless Barry was going to explain his current behaviour, she Veronica Bullock-Cohen was going to make a stand and put her foot down. If it was no to Frank then it was definitely no Ronnie, let's see how Barry liked that. Barry just swore and stormed out of the house when Ronnie confronted him, he couldn't explain the way he felt to his sister, he wasn't even sure he could explain it to himself. Now he didn't have a singer for tonight and he felt he had cut off his nose to spite his face. He headed for the King's Head; right now he needed a large whiskey to calm him down. Barry walked into the bar and who should be in there sitting at the piano and tinkling with the ivories but little Frank. Frank didn't see Barry standing at the bar so he just carried on playing his piano version of Sentimental journey. Barry had to admit the boy was good, Ronnie had tried to convince Barry that Frank was an excellent trumpet player as well and he didn't doubt it was true for one moment. Barry knew that having Ronnie and Frank playing together made perfect business sense, all he needed was Solly to join them to make the perfect hat trick. Barry gulped down his whiskey and walked over to Frank. Frank looked up surprised to see Barry standing there; he stopped playing the piano for a moment.

"Hi Uncle Barry, how you doing?" Barry chose not to answer.

"I've been talking to Veronica; she says you're between jobs at the moment."

Frank felt a little awkward, "You know how it is UNC. Not always a lot of work for an unknown musician." Barry was finding this difficult and was wondering if he would live to regret it.

"Get your arse over to the house, Ronnie tells me you will be an asset to her and The Blue Raven, so as of tonight you and Ronnie are a team."

Frank began to thank Barry, he wasn't sure what had brought on this change of heart in his uncle, normally he didn't give him the time of day and Frank was never really sure why Barry disliked him so much. Frank's mother had taught him never to look a gift horse in the mouth so he accepted the job and thanked his uncle again.

"Don't thank me yet," said Barry, "its bloody hard work, long hours and you do everything Ronnie tells you to do. If you let me down I'll make sure you never work in the music game again, is that clear?" Frank nodded. "Well don't just sit there, move your arse or you'll be late."

When Barry had stormed out Edie and Georgie came in to the front room to see what all the commotion was about. Ronnie explained to them what had happened and how she had just got herself sacked from the club. Just at that moment little Frank knocked at the door full of excitement, stumbling over his words as he was trying to get them out ten to the dozen. The three women looked at him with open mouths.

"Well there's a storm in a tea cup if ever there was," exclaimed Edie. "Looks like Barry took on board what you said after all."

Ronnie stood up all of a fluster not knowing which way to turn first. "We had better get to the club as soon as possible, before it opens, so we can get some practice in." And with that Veronica and little Frank were gone and Edie and Georgina were left holding the babies. Frank and Ronnie headed for the underground station

"Can I just ask one favour of you, Aunt Ronnie?" asked Frank.

"Go ahead, anything you want," she replied.

"Can you just call me Frank from now on?"

Ronnie turned to Frank and smiled, "OK Frank, and you just call me Ronnie."

The Blue Raven was gaining quite a reputation. The bar was always full and Veronica began to recognise the regulars. According to club gossip they were anything from judges, lawyers, police, even an MP or two, right down to your East End criminal royalty. Everyone knew about the rooms upstairs that were hired out for private parties and the other rooms where some of the hostesses would give one to one massages. Ronnie was good at closing her eyes to things she didn't want to acknowledge, especially when Pat would say how hard Barry was working and some nights didn't even manage to get home. How could she tell Pat that she knew Barry had been seen going to his office, which had full overnight facilities, with Grace Green? Ronnie had heard the rumours that they had once been lovers; she knew that they were not in a serious relationship any more, but she also knew Barry took his pleasure with her whenever the mood took him.

Ronnie arrived at the club long before opening as usual. She liked to take her time getting ready and she enjoyed the quiet of the place before the hustle and bustle of the evening began. She also liked to escape from the house before bath time arrived for the twins. The twins was what everyone called them because it was too complicated to keep going over the story of her two wombs and she kept her thoughts about two daddies to herself. When the girls were older and could understand she would try to explain things to them, although she barely understood it all herself. The doorman informed Ronnie she had a visitor waiting inside for her. He told her that they weren't going to let him in but he said he was her husband and had come a long way to see her. Ronnie stopped in her tracks, the colour draining from her cheeks and her body began to shake. What the bloody hell was Solly doing here? Ronnie tried to compose herself and walked into the bar. The barman nodded to the far corner of the room and Ronnie made her way there feeling breathless, not knowing why, now, after all these months, Solly had decided to show his face. Ronnie slipped into the cubicle opposite Solly and he looked her straight in the eye. "What's a nice girl like you doing in a place like this?" Ronnie chose to ignore his remark.

"What you doing here? What do you want?"

"I tried to put you out of mind, but the way you just left without a word. There are things I need to know. You may have been a bitch and cheated on me but there are still the babies to consider, I'm not a complete bastard leaving you to support the kids on your own." The silence hung in the air for a few moments. "Well," said Solly. "Are you going to let me know what you had or what."

"Girls," replied Ronnie. "Two little girls, Lilly and Rosalie."

"Can I see them?" he asked. Ronnie wondered if it would be better if Solly didn't ever see the girls. Maybe it would be better for all concerned if he wiped them from his life, he could go back to the States and carry on with his career, but she knew he wasn't the type of man to abandon his family lightly.

"Maybe you could come and visit tomorrow," replied Ronnie, still wondering if it was such a good idea.

"Where are you staying or have I got to guess that as well?"

Ronnie still had grave reservation and thought it would be a better idea to say no to Solly and exclude him from the girls' lives altogether but she knew him better than that, she knew he was not the type to let go easily.

"We're staying at Mum's old place with Edie and Georgina, they look after the girls while I'm working, come round tomorrow about two o'clock, the girls should be awake from their afternoon nap by then."

Just as they had concluded their conversation Frank arrived for work. Solly stood up to leave, "Tomorrow then." he said and left without another word. Frank went to open his mouth but Ronnie stopped him by raising her hand.

"Don't ask Frank, just don't ask."

Solly arrived at the house at one thirty, eager to meet his daughters. Ronnie explained that they were still sleeping and anyway she had a few things she wanted to tell him first. She told him about her two wombs and how the doctor had told she had conceived the girls at different times. She expected Solly to say something, maybe ask her questions, but he remained silent. She told him for now it was easier to say they were twins rather than to go into lengthy explanations with all and sundry. Edie popped her head round the front room door and announced that the girls were awake and should she bring them in. They were getting a handful now as they were crawling and had begun to pull themselves up on the furniture. It wouldn't be long before they were walking. Lilly was still a pale looking child with silky black hair that was just beginning to reach her shoulders, Rosalie on the other hand had much tighter curls and an olive coloured complexion. Edie popped the girls on the floor so that they could crawl over to their mother and then she closed the door behind her. Right at that moment she would have liked to be a fly on the wall.

The street door opened and Georgina struggled in carrying two bags of shopping.

"Is he here yet," she asked as she pulled off her headscarf.

"Shhhhhhhhhhh," said Edie, "I'm trying to listen."

Georgina carried on walking down the passage to the kitchen dragging the shopping bags along the floor. Georgina was getting cross with Edie.

"Will you come and bloody help me, let's get the dinner prepared before the shit hit's the fan and all hell breaks loose."

But there was no shouting and no fireworks. Twenty minutes later they heard the front door bang and Solly was gone. Ronnie came into the kitchen with a twin on each hip.

"Well," said Georgina. "Don't keep us in suspense, what did he say?"

"He thought that the girls were gorgeous, he came back to England to see if we could start again. He asked me to think it over and he would come back at the weekend to see what I had decided."

"What did he say about the girls being different colours."

"Oh," replied Ronnie in a distant voice "He didn't seem to notice."

"Is she stark raving made or what?" shrieked Edie, Georgina just shrugged her shoulders and sat the twins in their high chairs ready for tea.

Ronnie thought it over and decided to say yes to Solly, so within the week he had moved into the house and to Barry's utmost delight joined the band at The Blue Raven. Now complete with a saxophone player it was the hottest band in town.

Chapter 11

Barry bought Pat a television set and she was the talk of the street. Edie said it would never catch on and replace the wireless. Just to prove her wrong the following day he had a set delivered to the house. Georgie was ecstatic and said the twins seemed to enjoy watching the moving pictures as well as the test card. Pat enjoyed being the talk of the town and she began to invite groups of women round to the house for coffee mornings, as she put it, just to show off her new furniture and posh fabrics. Well you could have knocked Barry over with a feather the morning he popped home for some clean clothes to leave at the club, because there sitting in his living room was none other than Maggie Murphy. Motherhood suited her as she had blossomed and grown even more beautiful than he remembered her. He winced as he recalled the night in the King's Head when he had propositioned her and her posh boyfriend had ridiculed him in front of his friends and family. He had told his cousin to organise a spanking for him and the next thing he knew the bastard was dead. He would have liked to have been the shoulder she had cried on, but before anyone knew what was going on Maggie had married that prat Bob White. Barry couldn't get Maggie out of his head and a few days later he saw her again this time struggling along the pavement with some shopping bags; he pulled his car slowly alongside her and wound down his window. Barry gave her his charming smile.

"Don't suppose you remember me, Maggie, but I wondered if I could be your knight in shining armour and give you a lift home with that lot."

Maggie knew exactly who he was; he was the handsome, over confident Barry Bullock. Maggie pretended to ignore Barry and carried on walking. He drove his car very slowly to mirror her steps. Maggie felt flustered, she knew Barry Bullock's reputation, but she felt flattered that he should be giving her attention.

"My mother told me never to accept lifts from strangers," she said wondering at his persistence. Finally, her arms gave way and the carrier bag began to split. Barry pulled the car to a halt and went to her assistance to rescue the shopping. Maggie seemed reluctant to get into the car. Barry wasn't sure what she thought he was going to do to her in broad daylight but he just drove her home as he said he would. Maggie got out of the car and thanked him, after all it was just a lift, an act of kindness but she couldn't help the little flutter she felt in her chest. She continued to go to Pat's coffee mornings. She enjoyed talking to the other mothers, but most of all she was hoping to get a glimpse of Barry. She knew all about Barry's business affairs and the club he had opened because Pat found it hard to resist bragging about how well off they were. Pat's life seemed very glamorous compared to her own but what Pat failed to tell her friends was all the hours she spent alone and all the time Barry was never at home. Pat was sure he only came home occasionally to see Mary. If it hadn't been for Mary she would have lost Barry long ago.

It was Sunday afternoon Bob was sleeping off his lunch time pint and digesting his enormous roast dinner, Karen was taking a nap as well. Maggie and her mum had just finished the washing up and her mum was settling down in the armchair to carry on knitting the cardigan she was making for Karen. Maggie felt stifled and she told her mum she was going for a walk. She got as far as the park and sat down on a bench to watch the world go by. She found people-watching fascinating and used to make up little stories in her head about their lives. She almost jumped out of her skin when Barry Bullock came and sat down beside her.

They made small talk for a while then he asked her, "What's a good-looking girl like you wasting away in a dreary dump like this?"

"In case you hadn't noticed," replied Maggie. "It's not jam packed with opportunities around this particular dump." Maggie tried not to sound sarcastic.

"You could come and work for me," said Barry.

Maggie laughed out loud "As what exactly."

"I'm serious," said Barry, "you could come and be a hostess at my club."

Maggie looked at Barry suspiciously, "I've heard about hostesses and anyway I'm not that kind of girl." Barry tried to look shocked at what Maggie had said to him, he tried to reassure Maggie that it was all above board and there would be no funny business, He was trying hard not to laugh, he knew if she caught him he wouldn't stand a chance.

"All you have to do is look good and have a drink and a chat with whoever needs a bit of company." Barry put his hand to his heart. "Like I said I promise no funny business, and I pay good wages." He felt her falter, now was his opportunity to go in for the kill. "Why not give it a try, scout's honour I will take care of you.

Maggie loved the buzz she felt when she was around Barry, "I suppose it can't do any harm."

"That's settled then," said Barry and before Maggie could change her mind he pressed some money in her hand and told her to go to Madison's Dress shop in Eastham and get herself a decent outfit. She wasn't to get any shit from the market. He told her he would send a car to pick her up and if she had any trouble with the family send them round to his place and he would soon sort them out.

Maggie was so excited, what had been a boring Sunday afternoon had suddenly become very exciting.

Maggie had a lot of opposition from Bob and her mum. They said Barry Bullock was bad news and she should stay well clear of him and his lot. For the first time in ages Maggie felt alive and she was not going to let them spoil it, no, she was determined to go to work for Barry. As promised, a car arrived to pick her up and take her to The Blue Raven. Barry was there to meet her and he introduced her to a very nice lady called Grace Green who was in charge of all the escorts. Maggie could not believe how casual all the girls appeared, taking their duties in their stride. Maggie felt a bundle of nerves and way out of her depth. Grace explained to Maggie what was expected of her. Whenever she was bought a drink her escort would be charged for what he ordered but under no circumstances was Maggie to drink alcohol, so she would be given a tonic water or soda. Any confidentialities that might be whispered in her ear would never be repeated outside of the club. If a gentleman asked for any personal service she was to refer back to Grace to make the arrangements. Maggie look alarmed at this last statement.

"It's not a compulsory requirement, it's just that some of the girls are happy to earn a little extra cash, that's why you refer it to me." Maggie let out a sigh of relief and thought right at that moment she could do with a large gin and tonic.

After a few shifts at the club Maggie began to settle down and enjoy herself. Then things changed,

Maggie began to spend more time in Barry's private rooms, she loved being with him, he made her feel alive. Barry always sent the car to pick Maggie up and when she arrived Barry would get the bouncer to take her straight to his private rooms and they would have dinner and a bottle of wine together, he even took her to a little hotel in the country where they spent the most amazing evening. Maggie wasn't quite sure how they became lovers but Barry was magnetic and she was having the time of her life. She never knew that sex could be so good. She hoped that when she got home Bob and mum couldn't see straight through her, if they noticed any change neither one said a word.

Then Barry began to change, he seemed moody and his lovemaking was rough and aggressive. Maggie thought that she had upset him in some way but she was afraid to confront him. She hoped it would soon pass and things would return to how they were. Maggie's hopes were in vain, she found it hard to recall the last night that she went to The Blue Raven. Her mind was clouded, she remembered going straight upstairs to Barry's private rooms; his mood was very odd. There was another girl there, she was sure that Barry called her Lorna. Barry ordered Lorna to pour them all a drink and he stood beside Maggie until she had drained her glass. Maggie's recollection of what happened next is somewhat hazy. She felt like she was in slow motion, dreamlike but awake. She vaguely seemed to recall that all three of them were naked, she thought that Barry was kissing and fondling her but then she could see him at the end of the bed rubbing himself and it was Lorna who was pleasuring her. Maggie remembered being in a taxicab and feeling very sick. She wasn't sure if she had opened her own front door or Bob had opened it as he was standing right in front of her in the hallway. She could see his arms in the air and thought he was going to strike her. Instead he grabbed her shoulders, pushing her hard against the wall, pushing himself into her groin. Maggie could feel the dampness of her underwear against her skin and Bob pulling her panties down. Surely this must be a dream, Bob had never behaved like this before, he was no saint but he had never been brutal or rough towards her, ever. Maggie opened her mouth to try and protest but no sound came out. She could feel Bob pounding inside her, she was in pain, her limbs were like lead and she was powerless to stop it.

Maggie slowly opened her eyes and she could see daylight through a gap in the curtains. It was morning and she couldn't remember how she had got to bed. She tried to sit up and winced with pain. She felt bruised and dirty, God she needed to bathe. Maggie stood in front of the mirror and could see some bruising beginning to show. She was supposed to be at The Blue Raven that evening. Barry had told her they would be entertaining some special guests in the Nightingale Suite. After what had just happened to her she felt afraid. All the trust she had once had for Barry had now gone. He could be capable of anything; he was no longer the man she thought he was. She couldn't go back, not now, not ever. As soon as she was dressed she would speak to Mum, get Mum to go down to the telephone box and call the club. She was never going back there again. Fuck Barry

Bullock, she thought, but deep down she knew she was going to miss him. Maggie missed her period and put it down to stress and the trauma of what had happened. Her and Bob wasn't speaking properly, he was behaving very sheepishly, Bob tried buying Maggie flowers and chocolates but she said it was going to take a lot more than that to allow him back in their bedroom. As far as she was concerned Bob could stay permanently in Karen's room. Mum kept a low profile and didn't ask any questions, she was just happy Maggie was no longer going to The Blue Raven, that was enough for her. By the time Maggie missed her second period she was being sick. She went to the doctor as a matter of routine, but she really didn't need him to tell her she was pregnant. Mum was excited when Maggie broke the news, Bob didn't say a word, he just put his coat on and said he was going out. He did a lot of that lately, Maggie wondered if he was seeing someone else but she couldn't care less, as long as he brought home his wages and he slept in Karen's room the arrangements suited her. In fact, they got on better as friends, just like when they were kids. Maggie did think that Barry should know she was having his baby. Maggie didn't expect him to leave Pat and Mary for her but she wanted to tell him, especially if it turned out to be a boy, it would be like rubbing salt into the wound. Maggie wrote Barry a brief note, telling him she was having his baby, she didn't want anything from him but if he wanted to speak to her she usually took Karen to the park in the afternoons when the weather was good. After a couple of weeks of Barry not showing up Maggie gave up, fuck you Barry Bullock was all she could think.

Barry received Maggie's letter, he read it and burnt it. The woman's delusional, he thought, whoever the kid's father was it wasn't him, Edie had seen to that with the vasectomy. He had enjoyed his fling with Maggie but all good things come to an end and after all there were plenty more fish in the sea.

Chapter 12

6th February 1952

The whole nation woke up to the news that King George V1 had died in his sleep at Sandringham, he was only fifty-two years old. His eldest daughter Elizabeth who had taken his place on an international tour was in Kenya when she was told the news that her father had died. Elizabeth and Phillip flew home; Elizabeth was twenty-five years old, a wife and mother of two young children when she came to the throne. It was a sad day and the whole country mourned with the monarchy. Time passes and a veil was drawn over the Kings death. The whole country was getting excited as the day drew nearer for the coronation of the new queen. It was a new beginning, the royals were popular and the country was rebuilding itself after the war, and deep in the thick of it, becoming quite a legitimate businessman was none other than Mr Barry Bullock. He even managed to lay his hands on some bunting and flags for coronation day. He was going to sell it cheap around the local streets but suddenly he had a bout of conscience and gave it away as his contribution to coronation day street parties. The year of 1953 had started very wet; in fact there had been many floods. On 31st January there had been bad storms along the east coast of England, by Sunday morning the sea defences on Canvey Island gave way and fifty-nine people lost their lives. Many died in their sleep, or were wrenched from their roof tops washed away by the raging current that had been driven down from the North Sea. Coronation day was no better; it was a typical English summer day, pouring with rain.

Edie, Georgie and the twins were sitting in the little kitchen eating their breakfast when they heard a loud knock on the front door. "Who the bloody hell can that be this time in the morning" grumbled Edie as she slowly lifted her arthritic bones from the chair to go an answer the front door. It was Pat and Mary full of excitement about the coronation. "Can't you two sleep or what?" she continued as they all made their way back to the kitchen. "Me and Mary have decided to go up London to watch the coronation and wondered if you lot wanted to come with us."

"You must be mad," said Edie. "You'll never get anywhere near Westminster Abbey, it says on the television people have been camping out their all night just to get near enough for a glimpse of the royal carriage, what bloody chance have you got?" The twins were getting excited and wanted to go.

"Come on, Edie, don't be a spoil sport," said Pat.

Edie turned to Georgina "You take the twins and go with Pat if you want, my old bones aren't up to it, anyway Markey and Susan are coming this afternoon for the street party, and I'll stay here and wait for them to arrive."

Georgina and the twins quickly got ready and the five of them headed off towards the tube station. They had kissed Edie goodbye and promised to be back in time for the party. The trains were packed as every other bugger had the same idea. They were packed in like sardines all the way to Westminster and relieved when they stepped off the train and were outside the station in the fresh air. Why they thought it would be less packed there God only knows, every step was a shuffle and they couldn't get anywhere near the front of the barriers. They could hear the crowd begin to roar and knew that the royal coach must be approaching. The three girls managed to climb up on to a wall and caught a glimpse of the top of royal coach as it passed by. Georgina and Pat could only see the back of other people's heads but they had to admit the atmosphere was fantastic. The noise died down and people began to move around knowing it would be a long wait before they saw the Royal party return to the palace. They all declared they were starving and went to look for a hot dog van to grab a bite to eat before they made their way home. The girls wanted to stay at Westminster to watch the coach as it made its way back to Buckingham Palace but Georgina reminded them all that Edie would skin them alive if they weren't back by two o'clock when the street party was due to start. The underground was a little emptier as the majority of people were staying in London and making the day of it. They even managed to get a seat this time. The girls were swinging round the bars of the train and making quite a noise. Pat pulled a bag of sweets from her bag and Mary and Rosalie sat down next to her to eat them. Lilly was tired so she sat next to Georgina opposite the others and laid her head on her lap. The train slowed down as it approached a red signal, the tunnel was pitch black but the driver was used to this and his eyes adjusted to the surroundings. The driver sat in his cab waiting for the signal to turn to green; he thought that only the week before this stretch of the line had been flooded. He checked his wristwatch, Ah one thirty, half an hour or so and he would have finished his shift and be making his way home. He had been working

237

extra hours for weeks now and was looking forward to the afternoon off to spend time with his family and join in the coronation celebrations. The door of the driver's carriage opened and the guard came inside.

"What's the hold up this time?" he asked.

"That signal's taking a bloody long time to change."

They exchanged a few pleasantries and the signal changed to amber, "Better get back inside the carriages, thank God we're nearly finished, my plates of meat are throbbing, I swear it's all this damp weather." The guard walked back throughout the carriages, he smiled at the two little girls eating their jelly babies.

"Would you like one, mister?" asked the dark looking one. The guard sat down on the empty seat next to the little girl and accepted a sweet. Out of nowhere there began a loud crashing noise as the road above collapsed into the tunnel engulfing the train in concrete. In the street above there was chaos. The front of a shop had given way and fallen into the large crater where the road had once been. All around people were screaming and crying in shock. The emergency services were quick to respond, they dealt with the casualties in the street but the fire brigade said it was too unsafe to go underground and the medical staff would have to wait until the special lifting equipment arrived to haul the large concrete slabs up safely. The underground officials turned off the electricity and rescue teams made their way along the tunnels to assess the damage and help people back along the tracks where possible.

Edie was furious when Pat, Georgina and the girls were not back when the street party began, they had promised her. Markey and Susan, who were like children themselves, were disappointed. Solly and Veronica were cross and worried all in one and were finding it difficult to play the music they had promised to provide. Georgina had promised to be back for the party. Edie blamed Pat, she was no better than their Barry, always wanting her own way. You wait till they get home she thought, I'm gonna give them a right ear bashing. It wasn't until someone had caught the six o'clock news on the television and said there had been a few words at the end, after the coronation coverage, that a road had collapsed into an underground railway tunnel and there were no trains running.

"Well that's it then," said Edie. "I suppose they're trying to make their way back by bus, that's why it's taking them so long, the traffic must be bloody murder."

The emergency services had rigged up some generated powered lighting as they knew it was going to be a long and difficult job and for safety's sake the power had been turned off until it could be inspected and made safe in the daylight. There were people trapped and there were many serious and life threatening injuries, even fatalities. Many people were led to safety along the tunnel and they thanked God that the train had not been packed like it had been earlier in the day. It looked like the worst of damage was at the front of the train. The driver's compartment and the first carriage had taken the brunt of it. It was getting late and still Pat, Georgie and the girls hadn't returned home. The street parties were coming to an end and people were tidying up. Edie, Solly and Veronica were now beside themselves with worry. No one had heard from Barry and guessed he was still at the club and wasn't even aware that Pat and Mary were missing. Solly said he would walk down to the phone box and ring Barry at The Blue Raven. Barry must have wondered why he and Ronnie hadn't turned up for work, he wondered how Frank was managing alone.

Barry was spitting feathers that Solly and Veronica hadn't arrived for work. "You don't expect your own fucking family to let you down" he cussed. The telephone in his office rang and he picked up the receiver. It was Grace on the other end of the line

"Barry it's your brother in law Solly on the line, he sounds in a bit of a state."

"OK put him through, and this had better be good or they're fucking sacked. Solly was talking ten to the dozen and Barry was finding it difficult to make head or tale of what he was talking about. "Slow down, Solly, what do you mean the girls are missing, I thought they were at your street party."

"Yes, I have heard there has been some kind of underground accident. Listen, mate, calm down and I'll get down there and try and find out some information, you just get Markey and Susan back home to their place and I'll be with you as soon as I know anything," and with that Barry put down the receiver, he yelled at the top of his voice for Clint to get the car and they were soon speeding their way to the scene of the accident.

It was pitch black inside the train, the lighting had gone out and the only glimmer came from the torch the guard was shining backwards and forwards. He shone his torch at the two girls and the woman "Are you OK?" he asked.

"I think so," came the woman's reply. Pat pulled Mary and Rosalie as close to her as she could to try and stop them from shaking and being afraid. The guard managed to take off his coat and wrapped the children up to keep them warm. They could hear cries of help from further down the carriage. The guard tried to move down the train but it was difficult not being able to see where he was going. Pat called out to Georgina but there was no reply, she called to Lilly but still there was no answer.

As the hours passed by the calls for help went silent. The guard tried to reassure Pat that help would be with them soon but Pat thought that they were all going to die and she pulled Mary closer to her. God, she had survived the blitz only to be buried alive on the underground. Pat tried to keep the girls awake, she thought that if they fell asleep they would surely die so she began to sing to them making them join in.

"Old McDonald had a farm ei, ei, oh and on that farm he had a cow ei, ei oh," and so she went on until she felt exhausted herself. Pat thought she must have lost consciousness for a while herself, she opened her eyes and could see the light from a torch shinning from the other end of the carriage.

"Hello, hello" came a voice "Can anyone hear me in there?"

Thank God thought Pat. "Over here, please help us," she cried. As the men came closer with their large lamps Pat could make out the large piece of concrete in front of her almost touching them. The firemen seemed to move bits of rubble and make a gap for them to crawl through, it was a slow process to make it safe.

"Can you pass the children through to us?" they asked.

Pat tried to lift Mary but her arm hurt. Mary was crying, but with reassurance the firemen managed to persuade her to ease herself towards them. The guard continued to help with the girls and then he assisted Pat through the gap. There were ambulances waiting to take them to the hospital when they arrived at the surface. Pat saw Barry's face pushing through the crowd. She had never seen Barry look so shaken, he was white as a sheet. He climbed into the ambulance with Mary and Pat before the paramedic had chance to stop him and say no.

"Maybe you should go in the other ambulance with Rosalie she must be terrified," said Pat.

"Don't fucking tell me what to do, I'm staying here with Mary," said Barry. "Anyway, the guard is with her, she'll be OK."

The emergency services continued all through the night moving the debris and recovering the bodies. Every firefighter was affected when they brought people out in black body bags, but the worst was when it was the body of a child. They finally made it to the driver's compartment, the concrete had broken the glass on the carriage window and it had almost cut the driver in half. His family were upset that he hadn't made it to the street party, but his wife had assumed he had stayed on to do an extra shift. It was his little girl's birthday in a few days and she wanted a doll's pram and she knew he wouldn't want to disappoint her.

The whole Bullock family were in shock. Mary and Rosalie had escape with just a few cuts and bruises, thank God. Pat had a fractured arm but was otherwise unscathed. But none of them could take in the fact that Georgie and Lilly were dead. Once the bodies had been formally identified there were funeral arrangements to be made. Solly said that in the Jewish faith the body had to be buried in twenty-four hours. Veronica was hysterical and didn't want Lilly taken to the Jewish cemetery with a load of strangers. Every Bullock put in their two pennies' worth of opinion and it turned into a right old bull and cow. Pat blamed herself saying if she hadn't got

Georgie and the girls to go with her and Mary to see the queen's coronation they would still be alive. Edie agreed with what Pat had said and blamed her for Georgina and Lilly's death. Edie made it very clear Pat wasn't welcome at the house. For once Barry was at a loss because there was no way on this earth he could make things right. He couldn't bear to see his sister so distraught and in the depths of despair. Veronica wailed how could Lilly be laid to rest with Solly's family when she didn't even know them. She wanted her to be with Georgina and her mother. Barry felt that he would have to have a word with Solly.

"Listen, mate," began Barry, "for the sake of your wife's sanity can't you let her have her way on this, our own mother was Jewish but she is still buried in the catholic cemetery with the other Bullocks." Barry tried a few more words of persuasion but Solly refused to answer him one way or the other. Barry grew tired of a one-way conversation and knew his words were falling on deaf ears so he decided to walk away, after all he still had a club to run and he was now short of a band leader and a singer.

Barry arrived at the club to find Grace in his office sitting in his chair. She had a pen in one hand and the telephone receiver in the other. She looked up as Barry came into the room.

"I'm so sorry, Barry," she said with tears welling up in her eyes. Barry was surprised that she knew what had happened. "Clint came in earlier and filled me in, what a terrible shock for you all, do they know what caused the accident yet?"

"No," replied Barry. "The papers say it could have been a gas explosion or even an unexploded bomb, another bloke said it looked like the foundations had collapsed on the building above due to all the rain we've had, it's bound to be a bloody cover up cause the railways will want the line opened up as quick as possible."

"Anyway, we need to sort out tonight's music."

"It's all in hand," said Grace "that was Solly on the telephone, he said he had to get out of the house for a while so he would be here in about an hour, he said he was leaving Edie and Veronica to see Father O'Malley to make the funeral arrangements at the church and that you were right he had to let Veronica make her peace or they might as well all bloody top themselves.

"What about a singer?" asked Barry as he was beginning to enjoy the neck and back massage Grace was giving him.

"It was obviously short notice but I did manage to find a male and female singing duo for tonight, the agency said they come highly recommended, I think he said they were from Nigeria or somewhere like that."

Barry pulled Grace round in front of him and began to kiss her full on the lips. Grace had felt the tense muscles in Barry's shoulders and knew that if he didn't unwind a little and relax he would become very unpredictable, so for the sake of them all she would do her best to take his mind of things. Grace could feel him responding to her, she bent down between his legs and unzipped his trousers. She wondered if this would be enough for him and take his mind off all that had happened, her mind drifted back to when they had first become lovers and she had been the more dominant of the two of them. Suddenly Barry stood up and brought her back to the present. He led Grace into the other room which was his overnight quarters. He slowly removed her clothes and then his own. For a while he just lay naked beside Grace holding her very close and very still. Grace thought that she could feel damp patches on Barry's cheeks and knew they were silent tears, but would never dare question him. Then he slowly made love to her, kissing and caressing her. Sometimes Barry's lovemaking could be a little rough, but when he entered her this time he was tender and gentle like she was made of china. Barry waited for Grace to climax and then he relieved himself. They both lay there for a while after it was over, neither one speaking, neither of them needing to, they both knew what the other was thinking. This time it was Grace whose tears made the pillow damp crying for things that might have been.

The funeral was arranged for the following week and as usual crates of beer, bottles of gin and plates of food began to arrive at the house. Pat took a homemade trifle round to the house, but Edie told her they had enough food and to take it home, they wouldn't need it. Pat was in floods of tears by the time she got home, she knew everyone was blaming her for what happened and they made it blatantly obvious she wasn't welcome. When Barry came home she told him what had happened, thinking he would defend her.

"It might be better all-round if you stay away, it's going to be a hard enough day as it is, I don't want any trouble."

Well at least she knew where she stood, even Barry was shutting her out, did he blame her as well?

The day of the funeral arrived Edie was in a shocking state. She and Georgina had been so close she said it was like burying her own daughter and poor little Lilly, she hadn't had any life at all. The doctor had given Veronica a mild sedative to help her through the day.

Solly didn't really drink but Barry had brought a bottle of brandy and told him to have one. The two hearses arrived and the flowers were placed around the coffins, the Bullocks followed behind in a sombre silence. The only sound that could be heard was the muffled sound of sobs. No one asked where Pat was and why she wasn't there, no one cared, after all she wasn't even really a Bullock. She was still Pat Fuller and always would be and they cursed the day she crossed their threshold. The coffins were carried into the church by members of the Bullock family, father O'Malley conducted the service. Cousin Tilley sang a wonderful version of amazing grace and read the eulogy. Barry, who never missed an opportunity, wondered if she might like to sing in the club sometime, he would have a word with her later on at the wake. The service came to an end and the congregation followed the coffins to the graveside. Dot and Dickie were supporting Edie by the elbows as she was near to collapse, what with grief and her arthritis she was very unstable. The immediate family threw handfuls of dirt into the open graves, all except Veronica who threw a pink rose for Georgina and a white rose for her beautiful Lilly.

The family returned to the house for the wake, it was bursting at the seams with Bullocks. No one had any funny stories to tell like they normally did about the deceased's life. The mood was very sombre, they ate the food and drank the drink in virtual silence. The whole affair was very bleak and under an enormous cloud. Veronica was unwell and had to be put to bed, the family began to break up unusually early for a Bullock wake. They all offered their condolences and shook Solly and Edie by the hand as they left. Barry sat talking most of the time to Irene, he kept getting steely looks from his aunt Dot. Little Frank had done them all proud by playing the organ in the church. Solly wanted to play his saxophone when they were walking the coffins out of the church but he broke down and couldn't do it. The weeks that followed were hard for all the family. Nothing was ever going to be the same again. They just all had to learn how to stay alive before they could learn to live again.

Life is a funny thing and when something is taken away then something often happens to balance the scales. Within the year Veronica gave birth to a beautiful baby boy who they called Aaron and the following year twin boys arrived, Elijah and Jacob. These twins had nothing to do with Veronica's two wombs this time as they were identical and the only person who could tell them apart was Ronnie herself. Edie said they were breeding like rabbits and she was getting to old to look after babies. Veronica gave up working at the club and put all her concentration into motherhood and Rosalie adored helping her. They say that time heals but to anyone who has ever lost a child they know that just isn't true. They talked about Lilly all the time saying "Lilly would have liked this or that," Rosalie would show the boys a picture of when she and Lilly were small and tell them all the games they used to play and places they would visit, but she never ever mentioned Coronation Day. Veronica was sure she couldn't remember them doing all the things Rosalie said but if it helped her to come to terms with the loss of her sister what harm could it do to make up a story or two.

Barry didn't take Pat to the house anymore; he kept the two worlds apart. Pat was quite happy playing lady of the house and taking care of Mary. He always made sure she had plenty of money in her pocket. Pat never asked about the Bullocks and they never asked about her. The only one who asked the odd thing was Geraldine and Barry thought that was probably only out of politeness. Geraldine wasn't particularly close to the Bullock family now either, Eric was on the way up in the world and mixing with politicians. Geraldine found the family a bit of embarrassment. Things had never been the same since her mother had died and they had quarrelled over who was going to look after their Markey. Barry on the other hand was a businessman, he owned his own club and was a property developer and she had heard his name mentioned in a few high and unexpected places. When Geraldine and Eric were entertaining their fellow MPs and important people in politics Barry would usually join the gathering. Barry was a good conversationalist and kept the occasions interesting. He liked to go alone and only took Pat if the occasion required you went as a couple. Pat absolutely loved going to Geraldine and Eric's functions, it gave her more to brag about when she met the ladies that lunched.

Dave hadn't become the invalid everyone thought he might. He and Markey became part of the dog track scene. They had to retire Boscoe because of a leg injury he had got when he was a puppy which was a shame as he showed a lot of potential. Dave had a soft spot for him and kept him as his own pet. But they now had three greyhounds on the circuit and were making a reasonable living. Even Susan was becoming a convert and joined them down the track from time to time. Uncle Dickie retired from the railway and him and Dot bought a caravan down on Canvey Island and spent most of the summer there. Dot still gave Barry the cold shoulder whenever they met and she absolutely hated the fact that Frank played in the band at the club. Irene used to question her mother as to why she had such a hatred for Barry. Dot just said he was a bad lot and had a great deal of his father's traits in him. Then she would change the subject and that was the end of that. In fact Dot was over the moon when a talent scout had been in the club and offered Frank the chance to play with a group of young lads in Liverpool. Dot did worry that it would mean Frank living away from home and fending for himself and of course she would miss him very much, but this was a sacrifice she was willing to make to get him as far away from Barry as she could. Irene had different memories of her uncle Frank and thought he was a nice man. She remembered he came to the house a lot, usually when her father was out. She remembered he used to buy her sweets and tell her to go and play outside in the yard. She did have one terrible memory of her mother and her uncle Frank that she had never managed to get out of her mind. She remembered having a bad dream and waking up. She called out for her mother but she didn't come. Irene went downstairs and saw her mother and uncle Frank being very close together and bumping up and down against the kitchen sink. She had stood at the kitchen door for a while watching the pair of them, not knowing what to do and being afraid to speak. When her mother saw her she became very cross and told her to go back to bed immediately and she would bring her a glass of milk. Irene went rushing back upstairs to her bedroom and buried her head in her pillow. It troubled Irene very much and she wanted to talk to someone about what she had seen, she knew she couldn't tell her father because in her young mind she knew he would be angry. Still, her uncle Frank died shortly afterwards and then her little brother came along so she put it to the back of her mind thinking whatever it was would never happen again now Uncle Frank was gone. She may have forgotten it altogether if her mother hadn't gone and named her little brother Frank.

Barry was still thinking about Tilley's singing voice and was still waiting for an opportunity to speak to her about coming to sing at the club for him. He felt that she could be moulded into a future lead singer now that Veronica had retired to devote herself to motherhood.

Barry offered Tilley a spot of singing in the club but she was all loved up with a spotty faced youth from the meat market she had met in the King's Head. Tilley said she wanted a proper life, husband, kids and a nice home. Barry thought she was mad, opting for a boring humdrum existence, anyone could knock out kids but not everyone could sing, still you just couldn't help some people.

The African duo that were singing in the club at the moment were proving very popular with the members. Solly was enjoying the mixture of Jazz and blues and had started writing his own material again. So with Solly in charge of music and Grace running almost everything else Barry had the time to spend on the other side of business. He still liked to spend time at the club and sometimes worked from there on his other business interests. The property development side of things was growing in leaps and bounds. He had quite a growing workforce now, foreman, tradesmen and labourers. He had been expanding and buying land on the outskirts of London. He was building houses left right and centre. He had a few projects now in Eastham, Barking and Dagenham. Life couldn't have been sweeter. Pat was busy joining ladies' groups and Mary was growing into a beautiful young lady. Where Barry was concerned Mary couldn't do a thing wrong. When she brought her school reports home and all the teachers said she was below average Barry would always blame the teacher never Mary. To Barry there was no one more beautiful or more clever than his princess. With his connections he would find her a wealthy husband so she would never have to do a day's work in her life. Most of Mary's friends had Saturday jobs in local hairdressers or chemist shops. When Mary told her parents she would like to do the same all Barry said was, "You're not working all day in some poxy shop for a pittance," and he would press twenty pounds into Mary's hand and tell her to go shopping if she was bored. Mary knew how to take full advantage of her father, she knew how to wrap him around her little finger and get everything she wanted, including the boy she wanted to marry.

Chapter 13

Mary had been unwell and Barry promised her he would be home for tea to see her. He had stopped off at the newsagents and bought her a large box of chocolates and a copy of her favourite girl's magazine for her to read. Barry opened the door to the living room and Mary was lying on the sofa wrapped in a blanket. He walked over to her and kissed her on the forehead.

"How's my princess?" he asked in a concerned voice. Mary just gave him a weak smile.

"Mum's in the kitchen, she wants a quiet word when you come in."

She listened to her father walk down the hall and the kitchen door close behind him. She knew there was going to be an almighty scene when her mother dropped the bombshell. Pat carried on chopping the vegetables on the chopping board; she was in two minds whether to hide all the knives before she broke the news, given that Barry had a temper on him.

"What's all the mystery then?" asked Barry.

"Do you want a cup of tea?" asked Pat, trying to put off the moment.

"Fuck the tea," replied Barry. "What's going on?"

Pat gripped the edge of the sink and took a deep breath, "Our Mary's got herself into a spot of bother.

"If she's been shoplifting again with those so-called friends of hers I swear I'll tan her arse." Mary had got into a bit of trouble shoplifting when she was out with her friends Karen, Tina and Jan. Barry had to grease a few palms to have any record of her involvement conveniently erased.

"No, it's not that," said Pat and she could feel herself beginning to shake. "Mary's gone and got herself pregnant." For a minute Barry thought he had misheard. When the realisation of what Pat had just said sank in he slammed his fist down hard on the kitchen table.

"The stupid little mare, a slag just like her mother." Barry stormed out of the kitchen and flew down the hallway to the living room. When Mary saw the look on her father's face for the first time in her life she was afraid. "Did he fucking force you? I'll cut his fucking bollocks off and feed them to the crows." Mary began to cry and Barry, as usual softened and cradled her in his arms.

"Nobody forced me, Daddy," sobbed Mary. "Me and Tony are in love and we want to get married, I told him to come round about eight o'clock tonight to speak to you."

"SPEAK TO ME, I'll knock the fucking shit out of the little bastard for laying a finger on my little girl. When did this happen then?" demanded Barry.

Mary was still snivelling. "It was the night you and Mum went away with aunt Geraldine and uncle Eric, I had a few mates round for a party and me and Tony ended up in bed."

"In my own fucking house," said Barry in dismay. "If that's not rubbing salt in the wound I don't know what is." Barry walked over to the sideboard and poured himself a large whisky to try and calm himself down. All the dreams he had for Mary were wiped out all because she couldn't keep her knickers on, just like her mother. It was Pat's fault for not keeping a tighter rein on her. He had left her to take care of the one precious thing in his life and she couldn't even manage to do that properly. No, it wasn't Mary's fault, she was too young to know the evil ways of men. Pat should have been there to protect her, now he had another bloody mess to sort out. Mary was afraid when her father got this angry, maybe she should tell Tony not to come round tonight, maybe give her father a chance to calm down.

Mary kept thinking about the night her parents went away and how she had arranged the party. She had wanted to steal Tony McCarthy from her friend Karen for ages but they seemed to becoming more of an item than ever. Everyone had been drinking and people seemed to be pairing off and disappearing to quiet secluded places. She watched Tony and Karen go upstairs and she followed them. Mary stood outside the bedroom door listening, desperately trying to think of a way to stop what was about to happen. Suddenly the bedroom door flew open and Karen came stumbling out, Mary didn't think Karen even noticed her as she was trying to dress herself and get down the stairs in a hurry. Mary walked into the bedroom to see Tony McCarthy lying stark bollock naked on the bed. Mary slipped out of her clothes and climbed under the covers. Tony leaned across Mary and then suddenly he stopped moving, Mary wondered if he had passed out from the drink. Mary had never seen a naked man before and almost had the urge to turn tail and run away herself. She kissed his mouth, trying to wake him up, she ran her hands up and down his chest and she heard him groan. Mary almost died of fright when she looked down and saw that his penis was changing direction and growing to twice its size. Mary thought that maybe this had been a bad idea and that she had better get dressed and go back down stairs herself, just at that moment the bedroom door opened and Tony's elder brother Charlie was standing there. "Well, well what have we here?" Charlie walked over to the bed and gave Tony a prod but he was out for the count. He walked around to the other side of the bed where Mary was lying. Mary pulled the cover tighter over herself to hide her nakedness. Charlie began to laugh. "Come now, don't go all coy on me." Charlie kissed Mary on the mouth and she was pleasantly surprised at how soft it felt. He began to suck at her tiny pert nipples and she responded to his touch. Charlie had, had his fair share of women and knew how to please them, he knew Mary was probably a virgin so he took it nice and slow, until in his words, she was gagging for it. He normally went out well prepared for the ladies but he had used his last durex a few nights before and hadn't had chance to replenish the goods. Still he would just give her a little dip then he would pull out, no harm done. She would lose her cherry and he would have had a virgin. Something he hadn't had in a long time. He swore to God he was going to pull out but she actually acted as if she was enjoying it for a first timer. She wrapped her legs around him and her tightness seemed to imprison him and never once did she say NO! Charlie was cross with himself for his lack of control and swore as he came inside her.

After it was over Charlie got dressed, Mary didn't move from the bed, neither did she say anything. Charlie kissed her on the forehead and thanked her for a wonderful evening. Through all of it Tony never stirred or moved a muscle. Mary lay there in the dark for a while wondering how she had allowed what had just happened to happen. Yes, she was OK about losing her virginity but she had wanted it to be with Tony, not his brother Charlie. Mary could hear a commotion coming from outside in the street. The neighbours were making a fuss about the noise and threatened to call the old bill. Everyone left quickly and Mary spent hours cleaning up the mess. When her parents came home the next day all the old busy bodies couldn't wait to let them know what had happened.

Mary kept going over and over in her mind the events of the party night. She concluded that sex was quite a nice experience and she was keen to repeat the activity. She was glad she hadn't paid too much attention to her friend Tina who had shared her own sexual experiences with the girls telling them it wasn't all it was cracked up to be. Tina had told them how the boy from school who was two years their senior at the time had taken her back to his house one lunchtime. He was afraid someone may come home unexpected so he took her out into the back yard and in the outside toilet. Tina said she wasn't sure what was going to happen as it was the first time she had been with a boy. The girls were eager to hear all the details. Tina said they did a bit of kissing for a while and then he put his hand inside her bra. She said it was neither pleasant nor unpleasant, all she could remember was that his hands were cold. Tina had never been the centre of attention like this before and was determined to hang things out and make the most of it.

"Is that it then?" asked Jan, who was beginning to lose interest.

"No it wasn't, I was beginning to think we had better make our way back to school when he lifted up my skirt and put his hand inside my knickers, it made me jump and I pushed him away. Then he took hold of my hand

and put it down his trousers, well that gave me a bit of a shock, I'd seen my brothers' in the bath a few times but never had their bits been like what was in my hand."

"Oh my God," said the girls in unison.

"The next minute my hand was all full of gooey stuff and not at all pleasant, I wanted to go in his kitchen to wash my hands in the sink but at that moment we heard someone inside the house."

"So what did you do?" asked Karen.

"He made me put my hands down the toilet and he flushed the chain to wash them, we just got out the back gate before his mum came into the yard to see who was there."

"Is that it then?" Mary had asked. "I thought you wasn't a virgin anymore."

"I'm not, but I wasn't going to let that prick grope me again, no, I lost my cherry to Micky Pritchard."

"The day he arrived at our school caused a bit of a stir, every girl fancied him."

"I never did," said Karen. "I only have eyes for Tony." Mary thought Tina was exaggerating and not everyone fancied Mick the dick. Tony McCarthy was much better looking out of the two of them. Mary would have given her high teeth for a date with Tony. She wanted Tony for herself and was constantly trying to gain his attention and lure him away from Karen.

"Anyway," continued Tina. "After my experience in the toilet I thought I knew it all and I let Micky think I knew all about sex, one day he asked me to go round to his place while his parents were at work. We knew that no one would be back for hours so we both stripped naked, I was a bit embarrassed in my birthday suit so I got under the covers a little lively and watched him carry on undressing. Luckily, I wasn't shocked at the size of a naked man ready for action, I have got to admit, though, I was shaking. He thought I wasn't a virgin and I knew what I was doing but I was a bit worried about him sticking that large thing inside me. I couldn't tell him I had never done it before as I would have looked stupid. He told me not to worry as his father always had a drawer full of Durex because his mother was a nymphomaniac. He fiddled about a bit pushing his fingers inside me, it felt a little uncomfortable at first but the more he did it the better it became. Then he put the durex on and climbed on top of me. All the while he was moving up and down I felt pleased I wasn't a virgin any more but I can't say it was particularly pleasant. I had heard my mum talking to my aunt about how sex was more pleasurable for men than women so I wasn't too worried and thought it would probably get better with practice. After it was all over and we got up to get dressed and saw there was a patch of blood on the bed sheet. We tried to scrub it off but it wouldn't budge. We had a few afternoons in his bedroom when we should have been at school, I can't say that it improved much for me but I was pleased that he got the pleasure. I thought we would probably be together forever and get married one day. Then right out of the blue he went off with that Barbara Jones in 5b because she had the most enormous tits, the bastard," and they all laughed.

Chapter 14

The clock struck eight o'clock and there was a hard knock on the door. "I'll go," said Pat. Pat opened the front door and almost felt sorry for the poor wretch that stood in front of her. He looked as white as a sheet and she hoped he wasn't about to faint, or worse still be sick on her lounge carpet.

Tony was expecting Barry Bullock to at least castrate him before he left the house. His brother Charlie had worked for him for a while now and going by the stories he told the family Barry Bullock was a mean bastard who took no prisoners. Tony had broken the news of Mary's pregnancy to his family before he left the house that evening. His mother cried and his father told him he should have learned how to keep his dick in his trousers. Tony wouldn't have minded taking all the flack if only he could have remembered having sex with Mary. All he could remember was being in the bedroom with Karen, and then in his brother's car going home. He remembered winding down the car window and vomiting down the passenger door, and he remembered the almighty hangover that he had the next day. The whole family said he had to do the right thing and marry the girl. Charlie said if he didn't they would probably all be murdered in their beds or found lying in the foundations of one of his new property developments. As Tony walked into the room Mary stood up to stand beside him, she slipped her hand in his and gave it a little squeeze. Tony could see the vein pulsating in Mr Bullock's neck and wondered if he would leave the house in one piece.

"So you're Tony McCarthy," said Barry. Tony could feel the bile rising in his throat and found it hard to resist the urge to run away.

"Yes, Sir," was all he could manage as a response.

"By rights I should give you a bloody good hiding for what you have done to my girl."

"Yes, Sir," said Tony again.

"You're both very young and have no idea how hard it is bringing up a kid, nonetheless, Mary tells me you want to get married so I suppose we have a wedding to organise, you had better go home and tell your parents what has happened."

"Yes, Sir," seemed to be the only words Tony could manage." I told them before I left just now."

"Well you tell them I will be in touch tomorrow and make sure that brother of yours is there as well, and if any one breathes a word about the baby I will skin them alive." I know how people round here love a bit of gossip and I am not having me or mine talked about and slagged off. Do I make myself clear?"

"Yes, Sir," replied Tony again.

"Well go on then," growled Barry. "Get the fuck out of my sight."

Tony turned around and left the house wondering how his legs were going to carry him home.

When Tony left the house Mary walked over to her father and sat on his knee like she did when she was a little girl and wanted him to do something for her. When she was a little girl it would be to ask him to buy her a doll's house or a doll's pram. Now she was asking for the biggest present of all.

Barry could never refuse Mary anything. "Well then princess, it looks like you and your mum will be going shopping after Christmas for some wedding outfits. Your mum's sister's kids can be bridesmaids and we will have a mid-January wedding. Pat started to protest saying that it wasn't nearly enough time to arrange everything.

"I'll go and sort out the church and you do whatever it takes for the reception, I'm not having Mary showing as she walks up the aisle so you had better get a move on."

When Barry pulled up in his black limousine near the church he could see a funeral taking place. He recognised Maggie Murphy standing by the entrance with that Harry Taylor holding her arm. Barry still dabbled in some of the old ways and had a small money lending business on the side. Maggie's husband, Bob White, had started going down the dog track, it was about the time they first started to run Bosco. White began to get a liking for gambling and had borrowed a fair bit from Barry's firm. He was having difficulty with making the repayments. He said he was on short time at the docks and money was tight. Things were getting out of hand and the interest was mounting up. He told Clint to go round and put a bit of pressure on him but still they didn't get their money back. He told Clint that he needed to be given a stronger warning and Clint said to leave it to him. Next thing Barry heard was that there had been a fire at Maggie's block of flats and her husband and boy had been killed. Barry couldn't have cared less about old White, as far as he was concerned he was a dirty little shirt lifter. Christ, he had caught him at it himself when he had left some papers down at the dockside office and went back to get them unexpectedly. He had actually felt sick when he saw him with his trousers around his ankles bent over his office boy, Tom Hall, the brother of one of Mary's friends. Still all was not lost, Barry moved Tom from the dockside office to The Blue Raven to service the needs of some of his customers who like things a bit different from normal. Barry sat in the car watching Maggie until she was out of sight. They had been good together for a while and he was deeply sorry that her boy had been killed. Still you couldn't turn back the clock, what's done is done and right now he had other things to think about. After his business was concluded with the priest he climbed back into his limousine, "Right now take me to that slag Tony McCarthy's place and let's get them inbreds sorted out," he told the driver of his car and off they went.

The McCarthy house was in need of a paint and the furniture was shabby. How the hell could his Mary get mixed up with this piss pot poor lot? She could have had her pick of the best. She could have married into money with his connections, what a fucking mess. If he had his way he would have talked to Edie and see if there was a way they could get rid of it discreetly and safely or if not send Mary away to have it and put it up for adoption. Sure, she would be upset for a while, but there would be other babies and her life wouldn't be ruined saddled to a loser. Barry decided that as soon as the wedding was over he would bring this Tony off the building sites and train him up to take care of the development side of the business. If he proved himself and was any good then it would free himself up a bit to concentrate on Geraldine and Eric. Barry had been thinking more about politics lately and was beginning to fancy himself as a local counsellor or even a member of parliament.

Barry threw a rolled-up wad of money on to the table.

"That's for you lot to buy some decent clothes for the wedding, I don't want you showing me up." Mrs McCarthy burst into tears again. Barry had, had enough of all this for one day and decided to go home to make sure Pat had managed to do all her arrangements. There might not be much time but he wanted this wedding to be the best the East End had ever seen and he didn't care how much it cost.

The wedding day arrived and it was chaos at Barry's place. Pat's sister's kids were running riot all over the house and Mary had her head down the toilet with morning sickness which seemed to last until lunch time. Barry said he had to get out for a while and decided to go and see if Edie and the others were alright. He needed a bit of peace and quiet otherwise he felt like he was going to punch someone. He had given Charlie McCarthy his orders on getting his brother and the rest of the McCarthy lot to the church, God help him if he cocked it up. Barry let himself in the front door of Edie's house, he had never given up his key, it was his way of holding on to his mother. He felt that while he could come and go as he pleased a little bit of her was still with him. Barry could hear the noise of children's laughter coming from the kitchen. The old tin bath was in the middle of the room and Veronica's boys were covered in soap suds. Veronica was on her knees scrubbing the kids clean and looking extremely flushed. Solly was looking very dapper in his wedding suite that Barry had hired for him. Barry felt a bit bad that he hadn't let Rosalie be bridesmaid, he had made sure she had a beautiful dress to wear, in fact he had kitted the whole bloody lot of them out. None of the family ever talked about Rosalie having a little bit of tar brush in her but it was blatantly obvious. Barry just didn't want her in the main photographs it was a simple as that. Barry was the first to defend his family and would kill anyone who bad mouthed them. He was feeling even worse now he was sitting in their little kitchen, watching the excitement on her face as she came and showed Barry her outfit. Right at that moment he wished he hadn't cared about other people's opinion but it was too late to change things now.

"Anyway, what you doing here?" asked Edie "I thought you would have been busy at your place, being father of the bride and all that."

"It's bloody chaos there I had to get away before I exploded." Edie rolled her eyes to the ceiling.

"I'd better make you a cup of tea then," she said as she pulled herself out of the armchair. When Barry first told Edie and Veronica about the wedding they both refused to go. They still held a grudge against Pat over Georgie and Lilly's death. Barry wasn't used to begging anything from anyone but he desperately wanted all his family to be there, it was important to him so he made as many promises as it took and assured them they would not have to be anywhere near Pat if they didn't want to. Reluctantly the women gave in and agreed to go but Edie still couldn't talk about it without a venomous vibe.

"How's Mary holding up?" she continued as she took the top off the kettle and began to fill it with water from tap.

"It's hectic enough having a wedding without having to cope with morning sickness. Barry had told the close family about Mary being in the family way. There was no point in denying it because if you arranged a wedding in a hurry it was a plain as the nose on your face that there was a baby on the way, but God help anyone else who said a word. Barry gratefully drank his tea, Solly placed a brandy in front of Barry.

"Here, get that inside you it might help you feel better."

Barry drank it down in one gulp, "Thanks, mate, I suppose I had better get a move on, I've just got time for a quick shit, shave and a shower," and with that Barry left.

Edie lowered herself back into the armchair. "I could do without this wedding today, my arthritis is playing me up something shocking.

"We all could," agreed Ronnie, "but the kids are looking forward to it now so we will just have to like it and lump it.

"I think our Barry's in a bit of a state Mary getting herself pregnant and having a shotgun wedding, he had high hopes for the lady Mary, still like mother like daughter," said Edie and they all nodded in agreement.

When Barry got back to his house it was still pandemonium, he went straight to the bathroom and locked himself in and began to shave. There was a banging on the bathroom door.

"Dad, quick, open the door and let me in, I'm going to be sick again," cried Mary from the landing.

"For fuck's sake, can't you use the kitchen sink?"

"No, Dad, I can't. Mum's in there with the kids making them a sandwich." Barry swore again as he nicked himself with the razor. He opened the door and Mary came flying in just making it to the pan before she vomited again.

"It will be a bloody miracle if we even make it to the church at this rate. Hurry up," he said to Mary as he tried to finish shaving.

Finally, the cars pulled up outside the house and Pat and her nieces drove off to the church. Thank God for the quiet thought Barry as he finished tying his shoelaces, just time for a quick snifter before we go he thought. Barry turned round to see Mary standing in the doorway. He wasn't a man given to displays of emotion but he felt a lump rise in his throat. She looked amazing, her skin had a radiant glow and her dress was amazing. He couldn't believe he was giving his beautiful baby girl away; still it was only for a week because after the honeymoon, which incidentally he had paid for as well, they were all moving out to Barking. Barry had reserved two houses on his new development in Barking for personal use. It was just by the Barking Park and would be perfect for pushing the new baby Bullock in its pram. Pat was excited about the move and the cherry on the cake was Mary, and oh yeah, Tony, were going to live right next door. Barry still found it hard to think of him, let alone mention his name without spitting venom. The bridal car pulled up outside the church the customary ten minutes late, all the guests were already inside the church and it was just the bridesmaids waiting inside the doorway to get into position. Barry held out his hand to assist Mary out of the car and they walked side by side down the pathway.

"Thanks for everything, Dad," said Mary and she kissed Barry on the cheek. Barry smiled at her.

"That's OK princess, that's what your old man's for."

The wedding march began and they slowly made their way down the aisle.

"Who giveth this woman to this man," came the vicar's fatal words.

"I do," said Barry reluctantly as he gave Mary's hand to the McCarthy boy and stepped back in to the pew and sat down. Pat put her hand in his and gave it a squeeze. He found it hard to respond kindly to Pat as he still held her responsible for the predicament they were in and how this was all her fault. He had left her to look after his precious daughter and she had failed him. Now Mary was gone, even though it would be only next door, would things ever be the same again.

The vows were exchanged and the register was signed. They took a few photographs outside the church but it was getting cold and everyone was eager to get to the reception for a sherry. The meal was eaten and the wine glasses were kept topped up. Barry did the usual father of the bride speech, saying all the things that were expected of him. Welcoming Tony to the family, talking about Mary as a little girl and when the champagne glasses were charged he made a toast to the bride and groom's future happiness.

Barry spent the next hour circulating amongst the guests. Everyone was congratulating him on such a fantastic do and how much they were enjoying themselves. The disc jockey announced the first dance was about to take place and he watched Mary and her new husband take to the dance floor. Barry was getting fed up with the whole charade now and he stepped outside in the cold night air for a cigarette. He wondered if anyone would notice if he disappeared and went to the club, just at that moment he heard a noise coming from the basement area. Barry moved closer to the railing to see who it was. It was that bloody Charlie McCarthy down there with one of Pat's nieces.

"What the fuck are you doing down there, McCarthy?" bellowed Barry.

"Just my duty as the best man to the chief bridesmaid boss."

Barry turned and walked away, he couldn't wait for the day to end. Pat was standing at the doorway now waving to Barry to come back inside.

"Come on," she yelled. "You have got to dance with the mother of the groom."

You must be fucking joking he thought, and he turned his back on Pat and lit up another cigarette. Barry thought the day would never end. Even after they had waved the bride and groom goodbye and they had left for their honeymoon the bloody guests lingered on. Barry stayed at the Blue Raven all the time Mary was on honeymoon. He left Pat to move house alone. Barry had supplied her with enough helpers so he didn't have one shred of guilt. Pat on the other hand wished he had been there to share in the excitement. Why she thought Barry would change his ways after all these years she never knew. Maybe it was time she changed hers instead, after all what's good for the goose is good for the gander. So at the end of moving day the big burley removal man got more in the way of a tip than he had bargained for.

Tony McCarty turned out to be a lot brighter than his brother. He cottoned on quick and was proving to be more of an asset than Barry could ever have hoped for. He would never have admitted it to anyone but he was actually beginning to like the boy. He was just what the business needed. Someone who came across as squeaky clean, he scrubbed up well and was the right person to negotiate with the council bods. Sometimes Barry would send him out with his brother Charlie and Clint to collect the insurance money from the publicans. Barry knew that Tony hated this, but the boy had to know how to handle the shit stuff as well, you can't be wrapped in cotton wool all the time. Barry would make this week's collection the last one he went on, he had learnt enough for now. The baby was due soon and Mary would probably want him at home a bit more.

Clint, Charlie and Tony spent the morning collecting the protection money from the pubs; it was another scorching hot day so they decided to stop off at the Prospect of Whitby for a pie and a pint before they made the last collection and headed back to the club with the takings. Charlie was digging Tony out about how tired he was looking lately.

"Wait till the kid arrives, how you gonna survive the broken night's sleep when you look like a sack of shit now?"

Tony didn't bother answering. Charlie's mouth continued to move on up to top gear ribbing Tony on the pleasures and the pain of married life.

"For a single bloke you've got a lot to say about marriage, why don't you leave Tony alone and get on with your pint," said Clint.

Charlie was irritated by Clint's remark. "Why don't you mind your own bloody business, anyway, you can talk, I've heard you been running around the borough with girls young enough to be your daughters."

Clint jumped up knocking his chair over, he stood there for a few moments just staring at Charlie. Silence fell over the bar. "Come on let's go, we're drawing attention to ourselves and the boss would go bloody ape shit. The three men climbed back into the car and drove to the final pick up, not one of them uttering another word.

Clint took up his position as look out on the door and the McCarthys went inside to collect the money. There was a young girl behind the bar helping herself to a bag of crisps and a lemonade. She had false eyelashes and a low-cut blouse, her firm breasts were spilling out. She had backcombed her hair into a fashionable bouffant. Tony guessed that she was about fifteen or so, but she looked older. Charlie began to chat her up. This made Tony feel uncomfortable and motioned his head for Charlie to get a move on and get out of there. The next thing they knew Clint came flying through the bar doors and onto the floor. There must have been about four big blokes that came hurling in after him. Charlie and Tony didn't stand a chance and got the hiding of their lives. The landlord of the pub was in shock at the scene before his eyes. First of all he thought he was the target and someone was trying to rob his till. The three injured men looked in a pretty bad way so he had no choice but to dial 999. It wasn't until later that evening he discovered it was his own sons who had attacked the men. They said the first one they clumped had been interfering with their sister, Sandra, he was old enough to be her father and should have known better. They had tried to warn him off a couple of weeks earlier but the prick hadn't taken any notice. They hadn't wanted to worry their father as he had enough on his plate running the pub, so they decided to take matters into their own hands. If only his sons had spoken to him first he would have sorted it in a different way. Now they had given Barry Bullock's men a good hiding he knew revenge would be top of the list. Barry Bullock had a reputation for being a hard bastard, they would probably all end up wearing a cement overcoat.

Barry was spitting feathers when he got a call from Charlie telling him what had happened. The car was still parked outside the pub. It had a suitcase full of money in the boot and needed to be collected. Barry told Kosey, one of his minders to find his brother Bobo and go and pick up the car, there were a lot of undesirable types around the East End and he didn't want anyone nicking the motor. His first priority at the moment was to go to the London Hospital and get Tony and Charlie, maybe there would be some news on Clint's condition. Barry found Charlie and Tony in the accident and emergency department. They both looked a mess but were fit enough to be discharged. Clint on the other hand was in a bad way and had been taken to theatre. He had pressure on his brain and they had to operate to relieve it. He would pay the landlord of the pub a visit at a later date to find out exactly what had happened. Pat had telephoned him a couple of hours earlier saying Mary had gone into labour so they had better get a move on down to the maternity hospital. Tony thought Mary's timing was impeccable. All he wanted to do was to go home to bed and nurse his broken ribs and his bruises. The thought of spending hours in yet another hospital filled him with dismay. Tony and Barry arrived at Barking hospital and made their way to the maternity unit. Pat was sitting in the waiting room with and anxious look on her face and chewing her nails to the quick.

"Well," said Barry "what's happening then?"

"The nurse said it could be hours yet, what with it being the first baby and all that," replied Pat.

"For God's sake, can't she get a move on we can't sit here all bloody night," grumbled Barry. He walked up to the nurse's station and informed her who he was. Barry seemed to think the mere mention of his name would make people jump through hoops for him. The name didn't mean a thing to the nurse, all she was interested in was who was the husband.

"Listen, love, we've been sitting in that waiting room for an hour now and haven't seen a bloody soul, if you don't go and find out what's going on I'll go my fucking self."

"Mr Bullock, if you do not refrain from using such language I will have to call security and have you removed. Barry glared at the nurse, who did she fucking think she was talking to. Tony could see the night going from bad to worse and thought he had better intervene and talk to the nurse himself before Barry got them all arrested. The nurse said it might be a good idea if Mr McCarthy sat with his wife for a while as it was going to be a long night. Tony followed the nurse to Mary's room and Barry was hot on his heels.

"Mr Bullock," said the nurse "it's strictly husbands only." Barry ignored the nurse and walked over to Mary kissing her on the forehead.

"Hello, Princess, how are you?"

"Oh, Dad, it really hurts, make them give me something."

"Oi, you over here," he yelled at the nurse. "Get my daughter something for the pain, I don't pay my fucking taxes for nothing you know." Tony thought it was part of his job to help Barry find every tax loophole there was and exploit it, but now wasn't the right moment to remind him.

"Would you kindly keep you voice down, there are other ladies in here trying to have their babies and would appreciate a bit of peace. It's too early for pain killers, it will just make mother and baby sleepy. Now, Mrs McCarthy, let's use the gas and air like I showed you before."

Barry thought all this giving birth lark was too much for him. "Listen, Princess, I'll have to go, I've got some business to attend to. I need to find out who put your old man and his brother in hospital and deal with it. He didn't bother mentioning Clint as Mary probably wouldn't even remember who he was.

Barry left the hospital, glad to be outside in the air. He had never liked that overwhelming smell of disinfectant that hung heavy in the air in those places, hopefully by the time he returned Mary would have had the baby and he wouldn't have to hang around in there again for too long. Barry went back to the club to get Kosey and Bobo. The boys had come to England with their parents from Africa after the war. Their father had worked on the buses but the boys had turned their noses up at doing that kind of job for a living. They were both over six feet tall and had muscles like melons and were perfect for the job of bouncer. They had two younger brothers who did some driving for Barry, helping Clint with distributions, as he liked to put it. Barry didn't want to visit the landlord on his own and leave himself open to a spanking, but if he had been expecting trouble he needn't have worried. The pub was empty when they arrived and the landlord was sitting behind the bar nursing a large drink. The landlord thought there wasn't any point trying to pull the wool of Barry's eyes and pretend he didn't know what had happened and who was responsible for the attack. He would come clean and try to salvage something. Maybe Mr Bullock would allow them to keep their knee caps if he grovelled enough. Barry wasn't unsympathetic when the situation was fully disclosed. The landlord's daughter may have only been fifteen years old, but by God she looked older and Barry said if they didn't want any more trouble they had better get her to tone down her appearance. Barry said the landlord should have come directly to him if he had any concerns with the behaviour of any of his employees and he would have put a stop to it immediately. The landlord assured Barry that he had no idea what was going on until all this kicked off. Barry always said that Clint would come unstuck one day with his attraction to young girls. He had tried to tell him but would he listen, no, now he was in the hospital with what was probably a fractured skull. Barry tried to explain to the landlord that he was now in an awkward position. Word had already travelled over half the manor and people would be waiting to see what he did in retaliation. Barry decided he had other more important things to deal with at the moment and told the landlord that for now he wouldn't do anything.

"Just let's say you owe me a favour, and rest assured I won't forget."

Barry arrived back at the hospital just in time to hear the nurse announce Mary had given birth to a baby girl. Tony and Pat stood up but Barry barged past them and made his way to Mary's room.

"Excuse me sir," said the nurse. "It's husbands only."

Is that right thought Barry, who the fuck did she think she was talking to? No one was going to stop him seeing his precious Mary and his first-born grandchild.

As with everything Barry took over, he made decisions and never dreamed of asking anyone else what they wanted. He was as proud as punch with his new granddaughter and told the girls to get cracking on arranging the best ever christening. It certainly was a lavish affair, it was like a mini wedding reception. First of all the Bullocks moaned that it was a long way to go to Barking and they probably wouldn't be able to make it. Barry was really annoyed, why did they have to make a big song and dance about everything. Barry did what he always did and came up with the perfect solution. He hired a double decker bus, he had it covered in pink ribbons and transported the entire Bullock clan down to Barking. Everyone said what a beautiful baby Carol Ann was and what a fantastic day they were having.

His Uncle Vinney surprised them all by saying he had received a letter from their Terry. It was a bolt out of the blue because they hadn't heard a word in over ten years. Not since he had absconded from the army and Barry had arranged for him to go to Ireland, but instead he had ended up as a stowaway on a ship bound for America. He told them he had spent the first couple of years travelling from town to town picking up casual work wherever he could. Then he met Esme and things changed. He became fond of her and she was head over heels in love with him. Her parents were well off and tried everything to break them up. They described Terry as a low life dirty hippy who would never amount to much and be unable to support their daughter. A hardware store in the town was broken into and fingers started to point in his direction. He didn't want any dealings with the law so he told Esme he would have to skip town. She insisted on going with him so they packed up a few belongings and left. They bummed around for a bit and survived best they could. Esme was getting near her time to have the baby, and as luck would have it they came across a commune. The people that lived there took pity on them and they had been their ever since. He told them it was a great place, everyone mucked in and worked and lived off the land. The kids had plenty of space to run around and they thought they would be there till the end of their days. Then some church going do-gooders decided to poke their oar in. They said the children were at risk because their parents didn't have proper morals. The police came snooping around, everything would have died a death if they hadn't discovered the marijuana plants. They tried to tell the cops that they were for medicinal purposes. It helped relieve the pain of arthritis. They refused to listen so they were all carted off to the police station and fingerprints were taken. They weren't so bothered that Terry turned out to be a deserter from the British Army, they were more concerned that he was in the states illegally. Next thing they knew they were all deported. They did say Esme could stay in America with the kids as they were born there and they were American citizens, but she said Terry was her family and the father of her children so they all had to stick together. They all spent a few weeks in detention at the military barracks and then they shipped them out to a place called Basildon New Town. Terry says it's a bit of a tight squeeze in this three-bedroom house, what with Esme and the six kids; luckily the new baby isn't due for another five months. They are causing a bit of a problem for the local council as they are already overcrowded and they haven't got any bigger houses. The locals don't seem to like us and keep calling us gypsies, the kids are upset and hate going to the school as they feel bullied. Hawk and Jay are in constant trouble with the head teacher for defending their younger brother and sisters. Would love some of you to come and visit us and catch up on old times, but understand its miles away out in the sticks. The whole Bullock clan talked about nothing but cousin Terry and his story all day. Barry was a bit annoyed and thought his aunt and uncle should have waited until a better time to tell everyone their news. This was supposed to be Carol Ann's christening and it had somehow become overshadowed. Terry's sister Lorraine said as Barry built houses he should get their Terry moved back to civilisation, after all he was family. Barry's uncle Ted said he couldn't see why everyone should bend over backwards for Terry Bullock; after all they hadn't heard hide nor hare of him in a decade. Voices were getting louder and Barry could see tempers getting raised. If anyone started a punch up to today he would kill the bloody lot of them.

Chapter 15

Barry hated to admit it but Tony McCarthy had shaped up quite well. Although he could have castrated him for getting his precious Mary pregnant, there was something about him that made you like him. He was a quick learner and could handle the administrative side of Barry's business impeccably. Barry hadn't suddenly become all sentimental it was just that it suited him to have someone like Tony to front his business and get the work in. But, as usual just when things are ticking over smoothly something happens to upset the apple cart. Barry was working at the club, catching up on some paper work with Grace when Pat telephoned. She was a little hysterical that Carol Ann was running a high temperature and they had called an ambulance, she said Tony and Charlie had been fighting and Tony had packed a bag and stormed out. Carol Ann had a viral infection and was out of the hospital after a few days but as for the rest of the carnage that had erupted that was another matter. Mary told her parents that Tony wasn't Carol Ann's father; she confessed that Charlie had got her pregnant the night of the ill-fated party. Barry didn't know which one of the McCarty brothers he wanted to throttle the most and for once he wanted to give Mary a bloody good slap.

Barry knew that there was no way Tony would come back to work for him now and he was left truly in the lurch. Mary had moved Charlie into her house and the three of them were playing happy families. Barry was concerned that all the upheaval would have a bad effect on Carol Ann but as Christmas was just around the corner all the excitement was taking the edge off things. Mary and Charlie had decided to buy Carol Ann a puppy as a surprise Christmas present. Pat and Carol Ann were going to have a trip to Hamley's toy store while Mary and Charlie collected the puppy. Pat and Carol Ann bought something from every department and by the time they paid for all the toys they had more parcels than they had bargained for. "There's no way we are going to get his lot home, why don't we get a Taxi to Granddad's club and we can go home in his big car with him," said Pat. Carol Ann thought this was very exciting and she clapped her hands as they bundled into the Taxi. When they arrived at The Blue Raven Bobo was standing at the main entrance. He helped carry all the parcels upstairs to Barry's private room and said he would let the boss know they were there. Pat was exhausted; she kicked off her shoes and rubbed her aching feet. What I need, she thought, is a large scotch. She poured herself a drink and Carol Ann some lemonade. "Come on princess," Pat said to Mary. "Let Nana switch the television on for you to watch while we wait for Granddad. Carol Ann watched the television and Pat sat down at Barry's desk cradling her glass of whisky. She opened the drawers and began to rummage through Barry's private things. Pat wasn't sure what she thought she was going to find. The papers just looked like a lot of work documents. Then right at the bottom of the drawer she found a few old photographs, they seemed to be of a lot of people Pat didn't recognise, all except one face. It looked like a young Maggie Murphy and Barry had his arm wrapped around her. She knew Barry had a soft spot for and she wished that he looked at her the way he was looking at Maggie Murphy in the photograph. Pat could hear Carol

Anne laughing at the television program, she put the photograph back in the drawer and poured herself another drink. Pat sat down next to Carol Ann and put her arm around her little granddaughter, Carol Ann continued laughing at the program and Pat drifted off to sleep.

Clint didn't think he had deserved the beating he got; it wasn't as if Sandra hadn't been willing. In fact, she had stalked him. Whenever he went to her father's pub she would be all over him. He knew she was young but didn't think she was jail bait. The doctors told him he was lucky to be alive, maybe he would have been better dead. The terrible headaches that he continuously suffered from got him down. The humiliation of no longer being able to work and having to accept Barry's handouts. Maybe he would be able to convince Barry he had recovered and he was the old Clint again. Barry would give him his old job back and it would be just like old times.

Clint waited in the alleyway opposite The Blue Raven, hidden in the shadows, waiting for the right moment to go inside and confront Barry. Clint could feel one of his headaches coming on so he decided it was now or never as he made his way towards the entrance. Bobo was on the door, he saw Clint coming towards him, he already had orders from Mr Bullock not to let him in. Bobo moved in front of the door to bar Clint's access.

"I've come to see Barry, is he in?" asked Clint, his eyes beginning to squint as the light above the club door began to flash on and off."

"Sorry, Mr Clint, Mr Barry is in a meeting, I'll tell him you called" Clint didn't like the patronising way Bobo spoke to him, once upon a time he would have been able to take Bobo on and win the fight but not anymore. Clint's head began to throb, he turned and walked away, maybe the lavatory out the back still had a dodgy lock and he would be able to get into the club through there.

"Bollocks" he said as he tried the door, it wouldn't budge. Just at that moment the back door to the bar opened and the barman brought out a couple of black bin bags and threw them into the wheelie bin. The door was still on the jar so Clint took the opportunity to slide quietly inside unnoticed. Clint let himself into the storeroom and sat on the floor, contemplating what he was going to say to Barry. Who did he think he was kidding? Barry was never going to give him back his old job, he would just get someone to throw him out of the club and humiliate him all over again. Clint took his cigarette lighter out of his pocket and turned it over and over in his hand. There was a bottle of Brandy staring right at him from the shelf close by, he opened the bottle and took a large gulp, maybe that would settle his head. He emptied the rest of the contents of the bottle on to the floor. Now Clint had forgotten all about asking Barry for his job back, all he could think of was revenge. Clint pulled his heavy bulk up off the floor, he ignited his lighter and threw it down. The brandy-soaked floor burst into flames instantaneously, Clint moved quicker than he should have and lost his footing, a pile of boxes fell on top of him rendering him unconscious.

The alcohol and paper towels in the storeroom soon fuelled the fire, the alarm was raised and the occupants of the club spilled out onto the pavement. Barry managed to get outside safely. He was coughing and spluttering trying to shift the smoke that had entered his lungs. He saw Bobo helping Grace and one of the girls escape the burning building. Barry yelled to Bobo, "What the fucks going on?"

Bobo was also coughing and finding it difficult to talk. "Mr Barry, Sir, Miss Carol Ann and your wife are upstairs." Barry was shocked.

"What the fuck are they doing here, get back inside and get them out."

Bobo wasn't sure if he was more afraid of Barry Bullock or the flames. Luckily for Bobo the fire brigade arrived just in the nick of time. There were bottles exploding everywhere which was making the rescue of Pat and Carol Ann extremely dangerous. Barry stood by watching what was happening but unable to help. He had a sudden flash in his mind of how Maggie Murphy must have felt the night her flat burned and her son and husband died and he mouthed a silent sorry Maggie, forgive me. What seemed like an eternity, he saw the fireman passing out the limp body of a child. He could barely bring himself to ask the question, his throat was a dry as a bone.

"Is she …" Barry couldn't finish the sentence.

"It's OK, Sir, she is still breathing, now stand by and let the doctors do their job. He saw the firemen passing Pat's body out of the window and he didn't even stop to ask after her. He jumped in the back of the ambulance and it sped off towards the hospital with lights flashing and bells ringing. God, he thought to himself, it's like the night of the train disaster all over again.

Barry sat in the hospital corridor with his head in his hands waiting for the doctors to report back to him on Carol Ann's condition. Barry was far from a religious man, but right now, he was praying and trying to make a trade off with God. The doors at the end of the corridor flew open and Mary and Charlie came hurling towards him.

"Dad, Dad," sobbed Mary. "I want my baby, where is she?"

The doctor came out of Carole Ann's room and for one moment he thought that Mary was going to faint. The doctor looked directly at Mary.

"Are you the child's mother?" Mary nodded. "We have put your daughter on a ventilator, her lungs are very delicate but she is a little fighter.

"Thank God she's alive, can I see her?" asked Mary.

"Just for a while," replied the doctor. "What she needs now is rest." Mary thanked the doctor She hesitated before she went into Carol Ann's room and turned to ask the doctor another question. "What about my mum? I have to let her know Carol Ann is OK."

"The other female was your mother? I'm very sorry miss, there was nothing we could do she was dead on arrival. Mary could hardly take in what the doctor had said and Charlie rushed to her aid to support her as she sank into the nearest chair. The doctor turned to Barry, "Are you next of kin, Sir?"

"Yes," replied Barry. "I am or was her husband.

"Please accept my condolences, when you are up to it the sister will need to go over a few formalities with you." Barry wondered what Mary would say when she found out that he and Pat had never actually got married.

Mary refused to leave Carol Ann's bedside and she sat beside her until the sun came up. Charlie spent the night slumped in a chair in the waiting room. He woke up just in time to see the sun rise; his joints were stiff and he needed a wash. He shook Mary by the shoulder

"Carol Ann is sleeping peacefully now, let's go home and have a bath. We need to gets a few bits together for when she wakes up."

"You go, I've got something I need to do first."

Charlie shrugged his shoulders. "Suit yourself, I need something to eat and a shave."

Mary didn't even look up as he left, tears were rolling down her cheeks. She was crying with relief that her baby was going to be alright and crying because she would never see her mother again. Her father had left the hospital hours ago; he said he had business to attend to. All her life her father had business to attend to. Yes, he had bought her wonderful gifts. She always had the best toys but what she wanted most of all was a father like the other children had. A father that would come to parents evening and the school play. He always promised to be there but always let her down. He would come home with a grand gesture of a gift and say, "Sorry, princess, it was business." Her mother had been her rock and now she was gone.

Mary stood outside the hospital building breathing in the early morning air. She hailed the first taxi that came along and asked him to take her to the Blue Raven. Mary couldn't believe her eyes; the club had literally burned to the ground.

"Don't go too near there, lady, it's not safe," came a voice from behind her. Mary didn't like the look of the shifty looking man and tried to ignore him but he was persistent. "Do you know the owner by any chance" he continued. The man was beginning to irritate Mary and she wanted to tell him to fuck off.

"What's it to you?" she asked. The man pulled a card out of his pocket and handed it to her. I might have known, she thought, a bloody journalist. "Why are you sniffing around?" was all Mary said to him. Mary sensed he was still fishing for information but he wasn't going to tell her too much as he was just as suspicious as she was.

"Well, lady, let's face it, when the club that is owned by the famous Barry Bullock burns down, there's bound to be a story in it somewhere. He paused for a moment as if trying to weigh up who she was, then he continued, "Especially when a charred body was pulled out of the store room."

"Do they police know who it was?" she asked, trying to sound matter of fact.

"Not yet, there wasn't much left of him from what I heard, they will probably have to rely on dental records to identify the poor bastard, still it will all come out in the wash so they say." The journalist knew he wasn't going to get any information out of Mary so he left. "Don't forget, lady, if you know anything just give me a call, I pay good money for reliable information."

Mary was going to throw the journalist's card in the gutter but decided to put it in her pocket. You never know when you might need the services of a low life little prick. Mary smiled to herself, maybe she was more like her father than she thought. The old club was gone, lying in ashes, but she, Mary Bullock, like the phoenix, could rise up. She had lots of new ideas, it was time for her father to let go of things a little and pass them onto the next generation, after all, if she had been a boy it would have happened. She would show her father she could be better than any man.

Barry sat in the dockside office going over the events of the day. He thanked God that Carol Ann had been spared. He tried to put the thought of arranging Pat's funeral out of his mind. Maybe Brenda would sort that out for him. It saddened him to think of the club. It was insured so there were no worries on that score, but he was tired of the club now. It had been his dream but now that dream was over. Maybe he could pass it on to Mary; he would speak to her tomorrow. It was time for pastures new; he would telephone Geraldine and tell her he was available and ready to join her world of politics. She could pull a few strings and call in a few favours. Barry Bullock member of parliament for Stepney, that would suit him down to the ground and who knows, maybe one day PRIME MINISTER!

We close our eyes and close our ears

To try and chase away our fears

We only see what we want to see

But cannot stop what will be will be

If we could do it all again

Would it just turn out the same?